PIECES OF HATE

WONKY INN BOOK 15

JEANNIE WYCHERLEY

Pieces of Hate
Wonky Inn Book 15
By

JEANNIE WYCHERLEY

Sign up for Jeannie's newsletter:
www.subscribepage.com/JeannieWycherleyWonky

Pieces of Hate was edited by Christine L Baker
Cover design by JC Clarke of The Graphics Shed.
Formatting by Tammy
Proofreading by Johnny Bon Bon

Please note: This book is set in England in the United Kingdom. It uses British English spellings and idioms.

CHAPTER ONE

"What are you up to, darling girl?"

I tipped my head back. Silvan, clad only in a pair of black James Bond-style swimming trunks, his pale skin speckled with tiny silvery bubbles of water, smiled down at me. No sooner did I meet his eye than he shook his long black hair and showered me in cold drops.

I shrieked. "Do you mind? You're making my post-cards wet!"

Laughing, he threw himself onto the lounger beside me. We were moonbathing beneath the most beautiful waxing moon, the sea lapping gently against the sandy shoreline only a few metres away.

Sssshhhh! it said. *Sssshhhh*!

And so I shushed.

There was something so relaxing about listening to the waves here on our island paradise, that numerous times over the past few days I had nodded off and lost all track of time.

After the exhausting events of a few months earlier, Silvan had been as good as his word and arranged flights to this remote resort far from my wonky inn. We were marooned on a small holiday island called Naarangi, somewhere in the Indian Ocean where nothing bad could get to us and, for three glorious weeks, I wouldn't have to serve breakfast to cranky witches and wizards from six in the morning every day, or pick up stray undercrackers hidden beneath the guests' beds, or intervene every time Monsieur Emietter started attacking Finbarr's pixies with a meat cleaver whenever they came to raid the larder, or listen to Gwyn wax lyrical about how napkins had been folded 'just so' in her day, or try to entice Ned and Zephaniah back inside to work behind the bar even though my semi-dead father, Erik, had them fielding for his cricket team—guests versus ghosts—on my lawn, or try to keep Colonel Peters awake on reception, or share my bed with a pernickety, vocal, overly self-assured owl!

You see? How thoroughly exhausting!

But by Jove, I missed them all!

What I didn't miss were the endless hours I had to spend in the office, typing numbers into spreadsheets and working out prices, profit and loss and how much VAT and tax I needed to pay. National Insurance contributions? Holy moly! Nope. I didn't miss that one teeny weeny bit.

"How was the water?" I asked, dabbing at the postcard I'd been in the middle of writing. It had splodged. I was too chilled to stay cross with my fiancé though. After all, hadn't he brought me all the way out here to marry me?

To marry me!

Finally! We were committed! We had set the date!

Well, we *kind* of had a date. 'Sometime next week' was the plan. We hadn't settled on a venue yet, but as long as we were in the same place at the same time, things would work out. I didn't have a dress, but I was sure I'd find something in one of the beautiful little open-fronted boutiques on the seafront. Something floaty and figure-skimming would do. Failing that, I'd wear my bikini and a sarong. Why not? Nobody else was here to see us. It would just be Silvan, me, an official and a couple of passing witnesses. Job done. Then we could get on with the serious business of relaxing.

"Wet," he said in answer to my question and began towelling his hair. "Salty."

"Cold?" I asked.

"A little cool perhaps, but you soon get used to it. You should go in!"

"I will do in a bit. I just want to finish writing my postcards. If I don't get them in the post by tomorrow, we'll arrive home before they do."

"You could save on stamps and just take them home and hand deliver them," Silvan suggested.

"Ha ha." I signed my name—*and Silvan's!*—with a flourish. How strange that felt. Writing a postcard from *us* rather than only me. "I'm short of a couple of cards. I need to buy some more tomorrow."

Silvan picked up the pile I'd written so far. "How many have you got here? There's loads. Who are you sending them to?"

"Well, Charity, obviously. Look." I fished one out of his hand to show him three women wearing beautifully bright saris and smoking cigars. "She'll love this. And this one." I reached for another depicting a market scene with lots of fruit and vegetables, all of which would be unrecognisable back home in Whittlecombe. "This one's for Rhona and Stan."

He picked out another market stall scene. This had peculiar-shaped objects hanging from hooks. They may or may not have been bits of animal; I didn't care to find out. "Who's this for?"

"Millicent, of course." I flipped over the one I was writing, covered in exotic flowers. "This is for your grandmother. And I have a historical scene depicting Dakti Bhoin when there were no cars or tuk-tuks, only donkeys and elephants, that I'll send to Gwyn."

"Very nice. They'll all appreciate—"

"I have this one for Florence." I reversed a black and white card depicting some British maharaja and his maharani on the lawn outside an enormous house built in the colonial style. They were surrounded by their loyal servants, each wearing impressive headgear. I wasn't sure what Florence would think of it, or even if she would approve of the whole imperial aspect thus depicted, but she might appreciate the historical significance.

"Lovely—"

"I still have to write cards for Freddie, Gertie and Marissa, my mum, my dad, Mouse, Venus, Fleashee and Fleahee, Marc and Kat, and Ross. Ooh!" A sudden thought occurred to me. "Do you think I should send one to Perdita Pugh?"

Silvan smiled. I could tell he was indulging me. "If you want."

"What about Penelope Quigwell?"

"A step too far," he said. "Besides, too many more and you'll bankrupt us." He reached for my hands, extracting the cheap biro and the postcards, placing everything down on the table between us. Enclosing my fingers between his, he rubbed them, his thumbs tracing the scarring on my palms, a legacy from my last adventure. When I instinctively recoiled—I hated the feeling of the ridges on my skin—he took each hand separately and kissed each one. "Beautiful warrior woman," he said, his dark eyes shining. "Postcard writing addict. Stalker of forests. Purveyor of mischief. Befriender of the weird. Have I told you how much I love you?"

I giggled. "Not for the past hour or so."

"Then I am a negligent fool, because love you I do."

"You're a *romantic* fool, I'll give you that." I grinned.

He kissed my knuckles and allowed me control of my hands once more. "Would you like another of those Shirkey Temple drinks?" He nodded at my empty glass.

It was our joke. I didn't like to drink too much, so had a growing fondness for the bar's Shirley Temple cocktail, which mixed ginger ale, a little orange juice and a little lime juice with a splash of grenadine, the whole thing garnished with a maraschino cherry. Luscious! The thing was, the bartender, whose first language was not English, had misspelt Shirley Temple on the drinks menu board behind the bar. So Shirkey Temple it was.

"I'd love one," I enthused.

"Okay." Silvan pulled his shirt on. "I'll order that and then I'm going to borrow one of the hotel's bicycles and head into the village."

I sat up, puzzled. "In the middle of the night?"

"I want to see a man about a ..." He clamped a hand to his mouth. "Oops. It's a surprise."

"Oh yes?" I narrowed my eyes.

"Trust me!" Silvan said, eyes sparkling. "Don't wait up. I may be a little late back."

"Alright," I agreed. I could finish writing my postcards in peace, have one more quick dip, then meander back to our lodge for a shower and bed. "Just don't be too late."

"I won't."

"And be careful on the bike. You've seen how pockmarked these roads are!" Basically mud and dust and donkey poop, without the slightest hint of tarmac! Drive through a rut at high speed and you'd catapult yourself to Goa.

"I will!"

"And—"

"Alfie!" Silvan laughed. "I'm a big boy." He leaned down and kissed me lightly on the lips. He tasted of salt. "I'll get the waiter to bring your drink over. See you later."

"Bye." I smiled. "Love you."

I watched him walk away, over to the beach bar, lit with candles and coloured faery lights. He spoke to Sebestao behind the bar and indicated me on the lounger. I waved. They both waved back.

Then he strolled up the beach towards the resort's main building, the location for both the reception and the cycles. I lost him in the shadows.

Feeling fuzzy with love, I returned to the job in hand, writing a postcard to my mum.

Dear Mum

Having a wonderful time here. There are so many chickens running around loose. They dart out in front of our bicycles when we ride into the village. People keep them as both pets and food. They're much skinnier than the ones at home. I think you'd love it here! You could feed them up.

But please don't come out and join us, I thought.

All our love,

Alf and Silvan

I glanced up, senses snaking through the night, searching, searching, looking to connect with Silvan ... and there he was, a slight breeze blowing through his damp hair as he cycled towards the village. He was fine.

We were on our honeymoon, even though we hadn't actually tied the knot yet. We were happy, healthy and having fun.

What could possibly go wrong?

CHAPTER TWO

The utter luxury of being on holiday!

I collapsed onto the bed around the time I would normally be getting up to oversee breakfast, and fell into a coma brought on by doing absolutely nothing at all. Awaking just before eleven, I contemplated another couple of hours, but when I rolled over to snuggle into Silvan's back, I found his side of the bed cold and empty.

"Hmm." I plumped his pillow, which didn't need plumping, and stretched out so that I was taking up as much of the bed as possible. This wasn't easy because the bed in our lodge was a super-super king-size. The thing was the size of a small town. The management must have had their bedsheets specially made because in my career as East Devon's premier innkeeper—*ahem* —I had never come across sheets that would fit a bed as big as this.

Imagining that Silvan was merely visiting the bathroom, I closed my eyes and easily lapsed into another doze. After five minutes, maybe more, it occurred to me that I couldn't hear water running.

I opened my eyes and blinked. The Midnight Flower Luxury Lodge Resort catered specifically for the paranormal—just as my wonky inn did—and so they had blackout blinds, heavy curtains and air conditioning to suit a variety of tastes. Even so, I could tell the sun was high outside because the bright light filtered in through tiny chinks in the room's armoury.

"Silvan?" I called, but there was no answer.

Sitting up, I yawned and reached for the bottle of water I kept by the bed. It was feasible that Silvan had left me sleeping and nipped out for breakfast. He could be a bear with a sore head if he didn't eat at regular intervals. He'd feed his face with fruit and yoghurt and toast, drink a gallon of coffee and be back in no time, already thinking about lunch.

Rather than hang around for him, I decided to get up and get going myself. After a quick shower to sluice off the night, I piled my hair on top of my head in a great red pineapple and slathered factor 100 suntan lotion all over every part of my body before donning a black t-shirt and cargo shorts. I slid my celebrity-style sunglasses over my nose, threw on my sunhat—replete with an impressive eight-inch brim and a pretty, rainbow-coloured silk scarf tied round the stove—then picked up the postcards I had finished writing during the early hours, along with the murder mystery novel I'd started reading the day before, and flip-flopped my way over to the resort's main building.

The resort was a beautiful wooden enclave full of lodges placed higgledy-piggledy in such a way that everyone had a view of the sea from their patio area, but the hedges, trees and flower bushes had been organised so that each lodge was perfectly private.

The common areas—the bars, restaurant, spa and yoga—were all roofed using cane and coconut palms, but otherwise open to the elements. Further privacy, where needed—if you were having a massage, for example—could be afforded by lowering the soft blinds that flapped gently in the sea breeze. I supposed there was so little rain here, apart from during the monsoon, they didn't need to worry about building walls.

Not something I could try at Whittle Inn. My guests would have been blown away during the storms, frozen during the winter and soaked, just at the moment they least expected it, by cloudburst at the height of the British summer.

"Good morning, Miss Dee-moon," the deputy manager sang as I approached. He was a sweet and slender young man, probably in his mid-twenties, with a wide and ready smile. His English was far better than my Konkani.

"Morning, Joki!" I beamed back at him. "Would you mind sending these for me?"

"Not at all, madam!" He checked the cards for stamps. "You have been busy!"

"I don't want my friends to think I've forgotten them," I told him.

"Madam, you have only been here three days." Joki wobbled his head in that wonderfully ambivalent way the people of India have. "They are probably glad to see the back of you."

Surprised, I gaped at Joki, then guffawed. "You cheeky blighter. Did Silvan tell you to say that?"

"I can't reveal my sources, madam." He grinned.

"Hmm." I raised an eyebrow. "He'll get you into trouble."

"Are you having breakfast, madam?" Joki asked.

I peered through the reception area into the dining room. "Is Silvan in there?"

"I haven't seen him go through."

I nodded. Perhaps Joki had been busy. I for one could appreciate how busy reception could be at times. "I'll go and have a look." I smiled and left him to it.

The restaurant was about half full. With no sign of Silvan, I opted for a table with a good view of the beach. The sun shimmered on the tops of the waves, sending sparkles cascading onto the sand. For a moment I enjoyed a fantasy of lying there, a beached mermaid, resplendent in my shell necklaces and barnacle earrings, a mitre in my right hand. Not sure what I'd use that for—maybe to skewer fish for the barbeque? But then I thought about my risk of sunburn, how knotty my hair becomes when it's been submerged in seawater, and the likelihood of having my extremities nibbled by crabs, and decided that would not be a good look.

Nah. I'd grab a dip in the pool later instead and do a mix of doggy paddle and breaststroke with my head high above the waterline in an attempt to keep my hair dry. Until some whiny, snot-nosed brat decided to dive-bomb into the pool and shower me all over and ruin my solitude.

My thoughts kept me company for some time. I wasn't fully awake, and in any case far too relaxed to be concerned about much. The waiter came to take my order, returning promptly with a pot of tea—of course—orange juice and a full English. A bit of a busman's holiday, to be sure, but it pays to keep abreast of the competition.

Not that Whittle Inn was in competition with this incredible resort halfway across the world.

Just as well, because we'd have lost.

"Have you seen Silvan this morning?" I asked my waiter, and he smiled his sunny smile, while at the same time managing to appear sad and regretful. Quite a feat.

"No Silvan, ma'am," he told me. "Would you like extra toast?"

Extra toast? "Yes, please!" The way to a girl's heart is surely through hot buttered toast.

Although only if there is no cake on offer.

With one sleepy eye on the beach and the other on the parakeets singing their hearts out in the trees, I polished off my breakfast when it arrived and ordered more tea to go with my toast before diving back into my novel. Time passed. Plates were cleared. More tea was brought. Eventually, when I came back to reality, well over an hour had been lost and there was still no sign of Silvan.

I finally vacated my table. If I'd stayed any longer they would have been serving me lunch, and knowing me I wouldn't have minded. I could hang out by the pool, maybe start on the Shirkey Temples.

But as I strolled through reception, Joki called me over. "Madam?"

"Alright?" I asked.

"Everything is wonderful, madam."

"Good."

"I made a few enquiries, madam. The night receptionist tells me Mister Silvan borrowed a bicycle last night," he told me, gesturing at the bicycle shed, where three or four were lined up awaiting guests.

"That's right."

"It hasn't been returned, madam."

I stared at the bicycles stupidly, as though by doing so, Silvan's would magickly reappear.

"Perhaps he got a tuk-tuk back," I suggested, my heart sinking because I knew he hadn't.

"Or perhaps he stayed in the village, madam."

That would be it. He'd said he was meeting someone in a bar. He was a social being who liked a drop of whisky. If he'd overdone it, the chances were he'd have found a group of palm trees and gone to sleep underneath them. Silvan could sleep anywhere.

Even outside, cuddled up with camels.

"The night receptionist has gone to bed now, but I can wake him and ask him, madam," Joki told me, striving to be helpful.

"Oh, don't worry," I replied. I knew exactly what it was like to be disturbed in the middle of much-needed sleep after working your socks off for hours and hours. I never found it particularly amusing when one of my guests had mislaid something—a key, their purse, a familiar—and one of my ghosts had to wake me. Invariably the missing item would be located straightaway. Usually before I'd even made it as far as their rooms.

"It's fine!" I shook my head. "I might head into the village myself and buy some more postcards."

And find my errant fiancé.

And then I'd kick his perfect butt.

"Very well, madam. Would you like to borrow a bicycle? We have a nice pink one right here."

Goodness gracious, no! Do I look like someone who likes pink? "I think I'll walk ..."

"A tuk-tuk, madam?" Joki appeared concerned by the idea I might actually want the exercise.

"I'll be fine, thank you." I smiled and hurried away, back to our lodge where I brushed my teeth, threw my purse, my mobile, ChapStick, suntan lotion and wand into a hippie cotton over-the-body beach bag I'd bought on my last holiday a few years before, changed into my walking sandals and threw on a multi-coloured coverall shirt. Before I left, I scrawled a message on a piece of hotel stationery.

Gone into village. Call me. A xXx.

Passing back through reception, Joki indicated the bicycles once more. "It's a very hot day, madam!"

I couldn't see how riding a bike, something I was not that accustomed to doing, would keep me any cooler than walking. "I'll hire a tuk-tuk on the way back," I told him and waved goodbye.

Setting out, I took my time, adjusting my floppy sunhat to keep the worst of the sunlight from my shoulders and face. That great golden orb beat down from directly above me, but it was a dry heat, in some ways easier to bear than the short-lasting but muggy heat-waves so typical of the British summer. The air was fragranced with cattle and donkey poop, frangipani flowers on the trees, herbs and spices from the tiny shack-like houses I passed, and the warm, clean tang of salt being driven in from the ocean. It was exotic, something so deliciously distinguishable from the scent of the lanes around Whittlecombe that I found myself taking deep breaths, inhaling the different aromas and trying to commit them to memory.

Dashing the dastardly flies away as I strolled, I had to keep a careful eye on where I was going. The potholes were worse than the ones in Devon, although I'd never have dreamt that could be possible. At least we had tarmac, mostly, because here, I imagined that during monsoon, the rain turned the roads to mud, which would then be churned up by heavy Tata lorries, taxis, tuk-tuks and four-wheel drives. When the sun eventually came out again, it would dry the land rock-hard. Hence the dust.

The village of Dakti Bhoin sat on the south-eastern side of the island, slightly north of the Midnight Flower resort. As Indian villages go—not that I'd seen many of them, only a few from the Ambassador car that had transported us from Goa International Airport to the ferry terminal—it wasn't a bad size. It served three or four nearby resorts similar to the one Silvan had booked us into, and so there was a range of restaurants and gift shops, along with a generous smattering of the small lock-up shops and stalls that the locals preferred. On my visit the previous day, I'd seen the market in full swing too, and the incredible array of fresh produce had blown my mind. I wouldn't have known what to do with almost half of the fish and vegetables on display. The stalls were out again today, but given that half the day had already passed, some of the fish and meat stalls had packed up, meaning things were generally quieter.

I wandered along the main road—or what passed for the main road, and in this regard at least, it was exactly like Whittlecombe, with not enough room to manoeuvre a tractor—to where the little shops were grouped. A couple of these had doors and windows and displays and—luxury of luxuries—air conditioning, but for the most part, they were simple wooden stalls with palm leaf roofs and makeshift shelving. Strangely, they were served with electricity, so they all had fridges and offered a variety of canned and bottled drinks.

Close to the beach were a number of licensed premises. One or two of these were little more than sheds with a dozen mucky plastic chairs arranged in the dust outside and decorated with tatty, faded coloured ribbon and faery lights. I couldn't see Silvan hanging out in one of these. He wasn't fussy, but he adored traditional pubs. I imagined he would prefer to visit one of the others, along the shoreline and closer to the harbour, that at least had some semblance of home.

But then ... didn't that rather depend on who he'd been meeting and why? I cursed myself for not finding out more.

Standing there in the middle of the road, I debated whether to visit one of the bars or not. All of them were open, and holidaymakers dressed in swimwear and little else were coming and going. But which one should I try? How stupid would I sound, enquiring whether anyone had seen my husband-to-be?

Hello, I'm Alf, and I'm a controlling girlfriend. My boyfriend didn't come home last night, and now I'm relentlessly tracking him down so I can give him a flea in his ear.

Oh dear.

But what if he was lying in a ditch somewhere? *What if he's been attacked*? What if ...

What if he was dead?

A tuk-tuk drove up behind me and blasted its horn. To be fair, a tuk-tuk's horn has all the ferocity of a clown car's horn, but even so, it startled me. I shrieked and panicked, tried to go one way and walked straight into the path of another tuk-tuk. Tried to go the other way and found myself making nose-to-nose contact with the biggest white cow I had ever seen.

"By all that's green." I patted it on the head, and then, after looking all ways—left, right, left again, behind me, back in front of me and left again for good measure—retreated, hurriedly, to what passed as a pavement. I say 'what passed as a pavement' because there were long lengths of concrete standings in place to create the *edge* of a pavement, but that's as far as the pavement building had gone. It had never been filled in. The rest of the pavement was simply more of the dirt road, and you had to step over the standings to cross.

An older Indian gentleman with grey in his long hair, and slightly grizzly white whiskers, peered out at me from beneath the palm-tree roof of his diminutive shop shack. Alongside the ubiquitous fridge, chock full of fizzy pop, he had a small window out on the world, from which he appeared to be dispensing lotto tickets, long plastic strips of individually wrapped sweets and colourful bags of Lays crisps. However, the shack itself was a decent size, so perhaps he had plenty of stock behind his makeshift walls.

"You appear in need of a drink, madam. We have water. You want water?"

"No—" I began to say, but then noticed the black bicycle leaning against the wall to the side of his window. I removed my sunglasses and made a beeline for it, studying it carefully, stroking the cross frame as though that would confirm my suspicions.

"You like the bicycle?" the man asked. "Or are you trying to make it purr?"

"It belongs to the Midnight Flower Luxury Lodge Resort," I said.

The man grinned. "Maybe. Twenty dollars to you."

"Not maybe, definitely." I pointed out the metal tag welded onto the frame. *Property of the Midnight Flower Luxury Lodge Resort, Dakti Bhoin.*

He held up a bottle of water. "You look thirsty. Two dollars."

I narrowed my eyes at him. "Where did you get it?"

He shrugged again, busying himself with tidying up the stock on his counter. *Infuriating*!

"I'm looking for the man who was riding this bike," I told him. "Do you have any idea where I could find him?"

The Indian gentleman regarded me with something akin to scepticism. "Why would you want to?"

"Why would I want to find him? Because we're

getting married!" I said. "It would help if he was actually present when we do."

"Aaah!" The Indian gentleman's face lit up and he beamed at me. "You must be the famous Alfie! Welcome! Welcome!"

Famous Alfie? "Erm ..."

"Yes, yes, I met Mister Silvan last night. He told me all about you!"

"He did?" *Excellent!* We were getting somewhere. "So where can I find him now?"

"Ah. It's a small problem. A very small problem." He demonstrated how small by pressing the tips of his finger and thumb together. Impressively small. That was a relief. "We can take care of it. I will help you."

I wafted at my face, becoming increasingly sticky. What was this chap talking about? "Help me with what? What problem?" I asked. "Where is he?"

"There was a little trouble in the bar last night. A man taken to hospital."

"Hospital!" That wasn't a little trouble! "Is Silvan in the hospital? Where is it? How do I get there?"

The man smiled broadly. "Peace, madam, peace. He's not in the hospital."

"Oh!" *Phew*. I fanned my hot face with my hand.

"He's in the police station."

"He *what*?" *Hello*!

"Mister Silvan was arrested early this morning. You'll find him in the police station."

Chapter Three

The police station was a surprisingly familiar-seeming building; it was located behind an enormous expanse of green lawn, beautifully cultivated like the bushes encircling it, and currently being watered by a state-of-the-art sprinkler system. There were official signs stuck into the turf, displaying the same instructions in several languages, fortunately including English. *Keep to the pavement. Absolutely no admittance to the grass.*

That would refer to everybody with the notable exception of the big white cow. For some reason, the authorities had failed to translate the sign into cow. She had somehow safely made it across the road and was now happily munching away on a month's worth of breakfast, lunch and dinner. I supposed it saved on paying someone to mow the municipal lawn.

However, I for one accepted the strict instructions and took the long way round, joining a line of locals doing pretty much the same thing. I fanned myself with my sunhat as I pootled along, noticing that all these gentlemen in their loose shirts and trousers, and the women in their glorious saris, hardly ever broke into a sweat. That had to be because they took their time doing *everything*.

But that's not Alf's way! *I* was in a hurry, and the sweat was positively pouring out of me. All I wanted to do was get back to the Midnight Flower resort, throw myself into the pool and order a jug of Shirkey Temple. Blast Silvan! My emotions see-sawed between irritation, fury and fear. What had he managed to get himself into now? Why couldn't he behave like a proper adult for five minutes?

The doors of the police station were standing open, with guards posted at each. When I tried to barge in through the first door, the guard blew his whistle and pointed at a sign mounted on a wooden plinth. "Exit only, madam," he told me and waved his arm to the next door where, a line of people was waiting.

"There's a queue," I told him indignantly, not quite able to believe my eyes. I could not, for the life of me, imagine having to queue in a British police station. Well, not in a village at any rate.

If that village still had its police station.

Which Whittlecombe didn't.

"Please," the guard told me, ushering me along because I was holding up the people behind me.

Huffing a little, partly in disbelief and partly with

the heat, I did as he asked and joined the queue of people waiting to go through the entrance. When nobody immediately moved, I craned my neck to see around them. It turned out we were in a line that curved out of immediate view.

"It'll clear in a sec," I muttered to myself, wishing I had something to fan my hot face with besides my increasingly battered sunhat, and maybe a bottle of water.

Phoopf!

I finally made it through the door about two minutes later but, to my absolute horror, realised that the curving queue was actually a snake that went back on itself—rather like the game many of us once played on our phones—and coiled around several rows of chairs. In fact, weren't the locals essentially playing an over-subscribed game of musical chairs? The person sitting in chair number one, in the row immediately facing what must have been the reception area, was next to be seen. The person sitting in chair sixty, in the fifth row and closest to me, was at the back of the queue.

At the back of the queue, that is ... with the obvious exception of those of us who had yet to get to the chairs. As I watched, the woman in chair one was called forward and the man next to her jumped into her seat. Immediately, everyone shuffled up one chair so the person in front of me could sit in chair sixty.

What in the goddess's name is this? I wondered,

looking around for someone who could direct me to a police officer. But the only officers I could see were the ones behind the ten glass reception kiosks.

"Ma'am?" A gentleman waiting patiently behind me indicated that chair sixty was now free.

I gave the chair a once-over then glanced back at him. Perhaps I'd got it wrong and this wasn't a police station. "Is this a post office?" I asked the man. I had vague memories of visiting post offices when I was very little, and there would be queues and queues of people in them. I seemed to recall that you joined one of the multiple lines and watched the other queues shrink faster than your own. Then they'd brought in the queuing system with the rope barricades. Well, here in India they had taken it to a logical conclusion, and now you could sit while you queued, even though, when the queues were moving quickly, your backside would barely touch the seat.

"No, ma'am." He wobbled his head softly. "This is the police station, ma'am. Please take a seat."

"Can I sit at the side?" I asked. There were more chairs there, with not so many people waiting, and the ones who were sitting there remained where they were without joining in any of the party games.

"Not if you want to queue, ma'am," he explained. "This is the queue. That is not the queue."

"Why is it so busy?" I asked, doing as he instructed, then quickly shifted into chair fifty-nine.

"Many people have many problems, ma'am. They

come here to tell the police of their troubles." He talked loudly, and others around us smiled, or nodded or wobbled their agreement. One or two began to converse with him in their own language. They spoke over each other and shouted to make themselves heard. He dismissed them. "They bring their families, ma'am."

As I shuffled up six seats to the middle of row five, I realised what he meant. A whole group of people: a young man, an older man, an older woman, three children and a baby had rushed to the empty kiosk at reception and were now haranguing—or so it appeared to me—the poor uniformed woman behind the counter.

"Like a day out?" I asked, immediately shuffling up another three seats, impressed by how quickly I was moving. At this rate, it wouldn't take as long as I'd feared.

The woman behind the counter had begun to give as good as she was getting. She raised her voice and spoke quickly, eyes narrowed, elegant fingers gesturing towards the exit.

"Some people even bring a picnic, ma'am."

I laughed at that, but it soon became apparent that this wasn't an exaggeration. By the time I made it into the third row, I could smell the rich, spicy scent of fried vegetable pakoras. Peeking behind me, I watched a young family sharing out their spoils. I tried not to dribble.

Catching my look, the husband grinned and said

something to his wife, who then leaned over to offer me one.

"Oh, I shouldn't," I said, instantly feeling awkward. I'd been warned about eating the local food and heard some real horror stories of what could result. On the other hand, it would be rude to turn down an offer of such generous hospitality.

"We insist," the husband told me. "What we have, we share." When I reluctantly took one of the crispy vegetable battered pieces, one of his small daughters offered a bowl of what might have been a satay sauce, so I dunked the pakora in as I'd seen the children doing and took a bite.

Wow!

The heat hit of the spice was instant, nearly ripping a hole through the top of my mouth and into my nose. I choked back a cough and a wheeze, my eyes watering. Around me, people dissolved into giggles and there was more excited chatter. I could only imagine what they were saying about me. What a loser!

I sputtered, wishing again for a bottle of water. After I'd finally swallowed the mouthful, the man's wife gently nudged my hand and made me eat the remaining half of my pakora. Without the devil's chutney, or sambal, or whatever it had been, the pakora was a delight. So fresh. So tasty. My tastebuds performed a little tango all by themselves.

I decided there and then that I needed to

encourage Florence to attend an Indian cooking course. No use sending Monsieur Emietter. He'd refuse point blank to go. In fact, maybe I'd accompany her. Not to learn to cook, I'd spare the instructors that. No. I'd just be chief taster.

"Ooh!" I moaned. "So good." The woman beamed at me and offered me another. I felt bad, eating their lunch when I hadn't long had breakfast, but eat another I did. And a third.

All the while, we performed the bum shuffle, moving along the seats relatively speedily thanks to the number of kiosks available and the size of the family groupings waiting. I'll say this for India. They utilise plenty of workers rather than cutting back on everything to the point where you have to rely on machines for everything that real humans used to do. Where are the cashiers and ticket offices?

I found that, out of the sun, with the enormous wooden fans cranking away above my head, the waiting area was relatively cool, but the sheer number of people and the noise made me a little anxious. The locals chatted away, and it stood to reason that some of what they were discussing concerned me. I seemed to be the focal point for a great deal of interest. Men, women and children stared at me in a kind of horrified fascination. One or two women even reached out a cheeky finger and twirled one of my curls in wonder.

"Red," one woman ventured to tell me. "Fire!"

I smiled. It was all harmless enough. I was as fascinated by them and the way they could move and fold their bodies, and the shine of their silky dark hair in comparison to my frizz, as they were by my larger, curvy frame and wild hair.

Finally it was my turn in seat number one. I perched on the edge, gaze pivoting from kiosk to kiosk, wondering who would finish first. Hooray! Kiosk three! I sprinted across the tiled floor, fearful the female officer behind the counter would slam down a blind before I could speak to her.

"Can I help you, ma'am?" she asked.

"Hi! Hi!" I fumbled for words. What was I asking? "You ... erm ... I believe you have my fiancé here?"

"Fiancé, ma'am?" She frowned. I decided she probably didn't know the word.

"My, erm, boyfriend." When she didn't look any the wiser, I tried, "Husband? Do you have my husband here?"

"What is his name, ma'am?" the officer asked.

"Silvan? Horace T Silvanus."

"I will check for you, ma'am."

Before I could say another word, she flipped a board over the window—*Closed,* it said—and ambled away. I pondered whether I should stay where I was or ... no. There was no point in trying to get a seat. One look at the mad shuffle-waltz behind me reminded me that that would be a stupid thing to do. I leaned against the counter and waited.

And waited.

It felt like an interminable time, but eventually I saw her returning with a single piece of paper in her hand. She flipped the board back up and shoved the note through the gap below the glass. "He is being held here, ma'am."

I raised my eyebrows, expecting her to say more, perhaps fill in some blanks, but she had already dismissed my existence and was gazing in the direction of chair number one.

"May I see him?" I asked.

She glanced back at me, surprised I was still there. "He's in a cell, ma'am."

"I need to talk to him," I told her. "We're on holiday."

"Yes, ma'am." The head wobble. This one seemed to indicate I was an absolute idiot. Of course I was on holiday.

"What's he being charged with?" I asked. Was fighting in a bar a major misdemeanour in India?

She didn't immediately answer.

"Do I need to get him a lawyer?" I asked, my voice a little shrill. "What about the British Embassy? Should I contact them?"

"We are finding him a lawyer, ma'am."

"Well, can I see him?"

"Please take a seat."

"And then I can see him?"

"Yes." The woman nodded and pointed towards the chairs at the edge of the room. "Please, ma'am."

Sighing, I sloped over to the nearest free chair and threw myself into it, praying to the goddess that I wouldn't have to wait long.

The heat of the afternoon, the hum of the fans above my head, the chitter-chatter of people, the warm pakoras in my belly lulled me into a doze. I awoke with a start to hear someone calling to me.

"Ma'am? Ma'am? We're closing now."

I sat up with a jerk, swiping at a line of drool. "Wha—?"

"We're closing now, ma'am."

Staring around in confusion, I realised that the place had all but emptied. How long had I been asleep? "Closing?" I asked. "Why? What time is it?"

"Nearly four pm, ma'am."

"That's early!" I protested, jumping to my feet. I'd been asleep for over an hour?

"We close at four and we reopen at eight," the officer explained. "You can come back then."

"Eight pm tonight?" I clarified.

"Yes, ma'am." She indicated the door.

"But if I come back, I'll have to join that wretched queue again!"

"Yes, ma'am."

I held up the piece of paper I'd been given previously. "I was told I could see my fian—my husband! I need to see him!"

"Did you take a number, ma'am?" the officer asked. Poor thing, she was only around five foot tall and slender framed. I wouldn't have liked to be her, facing up to a red-headed, red-faced giant by comparison.

"What number?" But even as the words spilled out of my mouth, I spotted a little red plastic machine that emitted numbered tickets. "Nobody told me to take a number!" I pulled a face. "Why do I need a number, anyway?"

"You take a number. When it's your turn, you go to see the prisoner."

The prisoner? *Dang and blast, Silvan.* "Haven't they let him go yet?" I asked, and my lower lip began to tremble. Maybe it was the heat. Maybe it was the situation. Suddenly I felt tired and alone and vulnerable. "Horace Silvanus?"

"No, ma'am. He's still here." Her expression was kind.

I dropped my shoulders, sighed and reached for a ticket. If nothing else, I would be first in the queue when I came back at eight.

"Number sixty-seven?" a male, almost robotic voice called.

Were they still taking people through? I scanned the room. I was the only person left in the side chairs.

There were half a dozen people sitting in the bottom-shuffle chairs.

"Number sixty-seven?"

I glanced at the triangular green ticket in my hand. Sixty-seven.

"Here!" I shouted. "Here!"

CHAPTER FOUR

Visiting Silvan in a cell in an Indian police station was a much different experience from anyone visiting me while I'd been in Witchity Grubbs. There was no visiting room here; you simply walked down the corridor—accompanied by a guard carrying a heavy truncheon—until you came to the cell of the person you were visiting. Then you merely spoke through the bars while the guard loitered close by.

I heard his whistle before I saw him. Silvan was reclining on some kind of iron bunk when I found him, in much the same pose he used when lounging on a sunbed by the pool. One knee up, hands behind his head.

I stood outside the cell and glared at him. He didn't immediately jump up, only smiled, his eyes shining. How very dare he! If I'd been able to get close enough to him, I might have strangled him.

"What are you doing here?" I hissed, aware that I'd already attracted a fair amount of attention simply by being a tourist and walking along the corridor in my mega-brimmed sunhat and silk coverall combo.

"Ah." Silvan reluctantly straightened up and dragged himself away from his hard bunk. "Therein lies a tale."

"Well, you'd better spill the beans quickly," I told him. "The police station closes at four and they'll be chucking me out."

"In a nutshell, there was a fight." He shrugged.

"Where?" I asked.

"At The Monkey Nuts bar on the beach. It's one of the better ones there. Has some decent whisky. I was meeting a man about a boat."

To say I was confused was an understatement. "A boat? What sort of boat? Were you buying one?"

"Hiring it. A big boat."

"Why were you meeting a man about a boat at that time of night?" I couldn't get my head around it.

"It was supposed to be a surprise." Silvan clasped one of the bars, and immediately the guard rapped the iron with his truncheon.

I jumped.

Silvan let go of the bars and glared at the guard. Turning back to me, he said, "I thought it would be romantic if we tied the knot on a boat."

"Oh." I considered this. It did seem like a nice idea, not one I'd thought about. I'd have preferred to be consulted first, though. "So, how did you end up in a fight?"

"*I* didn't," Silvan told me. "I needed to visit the little boys' room, and while I was in there I heard a commotion outside. Men cursing each other, a few raised voices. Then it suddenly escalated. Lots of shouting. When I came out of the bathroom, there was this great burly bearded chap lurching around the bar, clutching his side."

"Who was he?" I asked.

"I have no idea, my love. I'd never seen him before." Silvan arched an eyebrow. "He was injured—that was obvious given the amount of blood. I went to help him, and he suddenly drew this cutlass from his belt. Obviously I disarmed him. He collapsed and I tried to help him ... but the next second there were all these police officers throwing me on the ground, and they hauled me away."

"But you explained what had happened? Some of them speak really good English—"

"Of course." Silvan's smile was soft. "But they claim to have taken a statement from someone who alleges they witnessed me stab him."

I reeled away from him. "We have to get you a lawyer."

"That's taken care of," Silvan told me.

"What about your friend?"

"Friend?"

"The man you were going to hire the boat from?"

"Huh." For the first time, Silvan's expression darkened. "Not a friend. He did a runner."

Our eyes met through the bars. Silvan pursed his lips and nodded. "He'd already disappeared by the time the police arrived."

"Do you think it was him?" I asked. "Is he the murderer?"

Silvan shrugged. "Maybe so. I can't be one hundred per cent certain, of course, because I didn't see what happened. But I recognised his as one of the raised voices."

"The police can track him down, then," I said, ever hopeful. "You tell them it was him, and they'll go and search for him."

"I did tell them, but he's on a boat and they're in tuk-tuks, Alfie. Short of getting the Indian Navy involved—" he said, wagging a finger at me, "and don't even think about doing that! I *know* you—they're not going to find him. They'll take the easy way out and charge me."

I stamped my foot and glowered at the guard. "This is ridiculous!"

"I had the cutlass—"

"Circumstantial!"

"They have a witness—"

"Who's telling them a bunch of porky pies! You don't have a motive!"

"I'm not sure that will wash." Silvan smiled reassuringly. "I have a lawyer. We can leave things to him, but—"

I pricked up my ears. "But?"

"Perhaps you could have a go at tracking down the chap I met? It would be helpful to find him and see what he says."

"Using my witchy wiles?" I asked.

"Exactly."

I took a deep breath. "What's his name?"

"Stanmore Duke. Known as 'Salty Dog' to his friends."

"I'm surprised he has any," I muttered. "Rightio."

"His boat is called *Seawolf*."

"Okay." I didn't have the foggiest notion of how to start looking for a boat in the Indian Ocean, but the sooner I made a start, the sooner I'd be able to ensure Silvan's release.

"That's my beloved." Silvan smiled.

"You could always just walk out of here," I told him. There was nothing here that would prevent either of us from using our magick.

"Sure I could. But what would be the point?" he asked gently. "We came here to get married. That's what I intend us to do. If we're on the run, we can't."

"No," I admitted. "Good point."

"It's an *excellent* point."

"Can't the victim exonerate you?" I asked. "I mean, even if they had to operate on his wound, they could talk to him when he came out of surgery. He'd be able to tell them it wasn't you—"

Something dark passed over Silvan's face. He

pressed his lips together and gave a tiny shake of his head.

I stared at him, trying to comprehend. "What are you saying ...? Why? Oh my ... he's not ...?"

"Yeah." Silvan sighed. "I'm afraid so. He didn't make it. He died a few hours ago. This is why I need you to go out there and find old Salty Dog for me, Alf." He nodded at the guard. "They're holding me on a murder charge."

CHAPTER FIVE

I traipsed out of the police station, back into the heat, and scarcely noticed. Winding my way back around the lawn—and the sprinklers—I could only think about Silvan having to spend the rest of his life behind bars. And not only that, he'd rot in a fly-ridden Asian jail while I worked my backside off at home trying to raise money for his legal bills and my flights over here to visit him.

Part of me was furious! Marry him? I'd rather see him in a boggy marsh alongside Jed! But part of me was scared to death. We could be separated. Forever. For something he hadn't even done!

Not that it would come to that. If he did end up going to trial and being found guilty, then we would have to break him out. He couldn't stay there. The problem was that as an international fugitive, that might well mean he'd never be able to work again, doing whatever it was he did, which was top secret but was something to do with bringing bad witches and wizards and other paranormal beings to justice.

I have to be positive, I told myself. *I have to find Sandy Dog. No. Seadog? Who was it? Salty Dog.*

Someone would know how to find him. But who?

I reached the pavement in front of the police station and paused there, staring up and down the road. This was the main street. Tuk-tuks puttered past me, swerving around Tata trucks with their musical horns. There were dusty buses, people clinging onto the outer railings, motorbikes and mopeds, old cars, new cars, enormous air-conditioned four-by-fours. All of them slowed down and gave way to pedestrians—none of whom seemed remotely concerned about being knocked flying—and of course, the ever-present sacred cows that roamed the streets at will.

Who, among all these strangers, could help me?

Numb to my core, I tried to get my bearings. Which way had I come? The guy at the stall had given me directions and I'd blindly followed them, but now when I had to reverse them, I wasn't sure I could. Except ...

Except, when I lifted my head and inhaled, I could smell the ocean. It made sense that, by following my nose, I'd end up in more familiar territory.

And so I did, ignoring the tuk-tuks that pulled up alongside me, touting for business. There would be time to cadge lifts later. For now, I wasn't far from the bars. In just a few minutes I found myself back on the rough track with its makeshift roundabout and the ramshackle stalls that lined the lanes. The white cow had been tethered to a pole in the middle of a patch of rough, dry grass. Perhaps she belonged to somebody after all. She munched away on whatever she could find, her tail sweeping backwards and forwards and dislodging the flies that alighted on her flanks.

The little shop I'd paused at earlier was closed, the fridge secured with a padlock. I realised that I'd been hoping to find that man again. Someone vaguely familiar. Suddenly, I felt alone in the world. Absurd. My mobile was in my bag. This wasn't the nineteenth century. I could be in touch with the folks at home within seconds.

Nonetheless, exhausted by an afternoon of inactivity and emotional distress, I sank onto the kerb beside the cow and stared down the lane towards the beach and the little bars. That's where I needed to start my search.

"You look troubled, my friend."

I glanced up, shielding my eyes against the falling sun, to see the man from the shop standing to the side of me. My heart gave a little leap. A friendly face. Kind of. Someone familiar, at any rate.

"Mister Silvan is in big trouble, yes?" the man asked.

I slowly dragged myself up to standing. "Possibly." I rubbed at my face. "You didn't tell me someone had died."

He pressed his hands together in front of his chest, fingers pointing towards the sky. "I wasn't aware of that."

"They're blaming Silvan," I said. "They have a witness, apparently. A man who claims Silvan did it."

Tipping his head to one side, the Indian man asked, "And what does Madam Alfie think she's going to do about it?"

I pointed in the direction of the bars. "I'm going over there, to The Monkey's Nuts, to ask some questions."

"Monkey Nuts." Roy corrected me, shaking his head. "I would not recommend that."

We stood facing each other. I wondered whether he could be trusted. Did he imagine I was some deranged white woman who didn't know one end of a bar from another? A tuk-tuk meandered past us and blew a cloud of diesely exhaust in my face. I batted it away and coughed.

"Nevertheless," I countered. "I have to do something."

"Come," he said, and without a backward glance, crossed the road, weaving nimbly between oncoming traffic.

For a second there, I almost didn't follow, but his casual confidence convinced me and, after checking in all directions, I scampered after him. He disappeared to the side of his shack, and horrified, for one moment, I faltered. This was India! I couldn't simply trail a strange man round the back of his bike shed of a home!

And then I decided ... *whatever*! I'd literally do anything! Silvan was in deep doo-doo and I needed all the help I could get. Skirting a gross pile of trash, most of it plastic bottles and discarded food cartons, I carefully watched my step and navigated around to the rear. There was a porch of some kind here, the floor covered in wooden boards and the roof extending out over the top to create a cooler, shaded area. Plants had been hung from struts, and several parakeets in cages—the doors wide open—sang happy little tunes.

"Take a seat," he instructed me, and I did as he said. He disappeared inside his humble house and I took a moment to study my surroundings. This space was swept clean, with old but clean cushions on the chairs and floor cushions scattered at my feet. From my seat I had a panorama down to the ocean and the harbour off to the right, although the views weren't uninterrupted given the location of the bars, restaurants and little shops along the seafront.

There were other tiny dwellings littered about, palm trees and water barrels providing privacy, and a smattering of goats and chickens behind wire fences.

The whiskery gentleman returned a few moments later with a bottle of water and a clean, cold cloth. "For you."

"Thank you." I used the cloth to wash my hands and face, wiping away the dust of the roads and the dried perspiration. This was standard etiquette in India. I was thinking of adopting it back in Whittle Inn. "You didn't tell me your name," I said, cracking the seal on the bottle of water.

"You can call me Roy."

"Roy." I made the universal toasting gesture in thanks to him and his kindness. "How did you and Silvan get chatting?"

"He recognised me as a brother." Roy's brown eyes sparkled.

I narrowed mine in response. "You're a witch?"

"I am, sister."

Ha. If I'd been less het up about Silvan's disappearance, perhaps I would have paid more attention to my gut instincts. Of course he was. I could feel it now. His magick. Light and yet exotic. More shamanic than mine could ever be.

He and Silvan would be kindred spirits in that regard. Where I was a ghost whisperer, Silvan had an affinity with the dead and forgotten. He could conjure spirits from deep in the netherworld if need be. It was something I'd seen him attempt when we'd been pursuing Mr Wylie. Fortunately, to my way of thinking, I hadn't seen him use this skill since.

Roy dropped into the seat opposite me, and I noticed how strong his wiry frame was. He had the physique of someone who practised a great deal of yoga, in my experience.

"So he just happened upon you, recognised you for who you are, and ...?"

Roy laughed. "A chance encounter. He stopped to buy a bottle of water yesterday afternoon, and we began to talk. He told me he was visiting, spoke of you and how you are betrothed, and said he was looking for a special way to do that."

"Did he ask you to marry us?" It was within the realms of possibility that Roy could.

"No, alas. Perhaps it would have been better if he had." Roy smiled. "He said he wanted to hire a boat, and I directed him to The Monkey Nuts because I assumed he didn't mean a fishing boat." Roy waved a hand in the direction of the sea. "There are often skippers in the bars there. They have boats for charter. I suggested he come back much later, because they tend to hang out after midnight. I was closing up as he came by again."

"That's why he left it so late." I nodded. "Did you have anyone specific in mind?"

"No, sister. These sailors come and go. If I'd had a specific recommendation, I'd have sent Silvan directly to him."

"So you don't know anyone called—" *Oh, what was it again?* "Stanmore Duke?"

I could tell by Roy's face that the name meant absolutely nothing to him. "Salty Dog?" I tried instead.

His brow creased. "Come to think of it, that does ring a bell. If it's the one I'm thinking of, I believe he is

American. Or Canadian. North America, certainly. Perhaps British, come to think of it."

Make your mind up. "His boat is called *Seawolf*," I remembered.

"Yes. That's right. I know the boat."

"You know the boat but not the man?"

"Do you want some more water?" Roy stood and disappeared inside again. When he returned, he had two bottles. He handed me one and opened the other for himself. "It's a nice boat. Not too big, like some of the expensive yachts that occasionally moor here. I walk round the harbour most afternoons. I like to look at the boats. I always have, since I was a young boy."

"You've lived here in Dakti Bhoin all this time?" I asked.

"Off and on. Mostly on. I spent some years in London. Studied at the School of Oriental and Asian Studies."

That would explain why his English was so good.

"But you came back here?"

"I can't think of anywhere else I would rather be." His simple smile said everything. I understood exactly. That's how I felt about Whittlecombe. It meant everything to me. I would never forsake it now.

He tilted his head back, staring at the sky. The sun was a big orange ball, dropping quickly towards the horizon, just above the roofs of the shacks that spoiled his sea view, less than a hundred metres away. Night fell quickly, and early, in India, I'd realised. Eventually he sighed. "I ought to open the shop," he told me. "The evening crowd will be out and about soon."

"Oh, yes! I'm sorry I've kept you." I pushed my chair back, startling the parakeets, who fluttered around in alarm. *Oops*. Anxiety began to gnaw at my innards. Chatting with Roy had temporarily eased that, but now I'd be on my own again.

"What is your plan, sister?" Roy was enquiring.

"I'm going to The Monkey Nuts," I told him, standing, "to ask some questions. Thanks so much for your time." I jiggled my half-full bottle while retreating. "And all the water."

He followed me as I made my way back around the side and out to the front of the shack, and I assumed he was simply seeing me out.

"It's this way," he told me, and fell in step beside me.

"What are you doing?" I asked.

"I can't let you go in there alone," he replied.

"But you have a shop to open!" The thought of robbing him of his much-needed, and probably meagre, income filled me with guilt.

"What will a few minutes matter?"

"I don't need a bodyguard," I told him, in case he was in any doubt. "I can take care of myself."

"I don't doubt that, sister. I don't doubt it at all. But —" He turned and offered me an endorsing head wobble. "A translator will never go amiss."

CHAPTER SIX

From the outside, The Monkey Nuts had the appearance of a well-loved tourist bar. The abundant faery lights, tea lights burning in jam jars, wooden tables and benches, decking and umbrellas and signs for all the most popular global soft drinks. There were blackboards with lists of the cocktails served—no Shirkey Temples here, I noticed—as well as food options such as popular vegetarian Indian dishes, particularly thali. I noted that the sign for the toilets directed people outside and around the back.

The place was probably half full, with most of the tourists opting to sit outside where they could enjoy the view of the small harbour area to the left and the beach to the right as the sun sank lower and lower, while the locals, or sailors and boat crews, remained inside.

They'd seen it all before.

Life was continuing very much as normal, I realised, comparing it with what would undoubtedly have happened in the UK if someone had been murdered. The place would have been cordoned off for days, possibly weeks. The bar would have been closed and might never reopen if the magistrates withdrew its licence.

But here in India, such things—homicidal things—appeared to be a fact of life. Had I not already known that a man had been killed here in the early hours of this very morning, I'd never have been able to tell this evening, that much was certain.

I marched up to the bar. A dozen pairs of eyes watched me do so, but the bartender didn't appear to notice. He carried right on cleaning his tumblers in water that looked highly suspect to me. I reminded myself not to buy a drink.

"Ahem." I cleared my throat. "Excuse me?"

Reluctantly, the bartender glanced over. He was a young man, early to mid-twenties, petite and slim, and handsome with dark eyes and hair. He had the faintest trace of a moustache.

"Were you working last night?" I asked.

The bartender set down the glass he'd been rinsing on the counter. "You want cocktail?" he asked. "What cocktail you want?"

"No, I don't want—"

Roy held his hands up. "Peace, sister," he said. "No use getting hot under the collar. Leave it to me." He pressed his palms together and bowed his head towards the bartender. "Brother," he intoned, then started speaking in his own language. I watched the conversation unfold, unable to understand a word of it. The words flew fast, lyrical in an alien way. If I hadn't been quite so invested in Silvan's predicament, I might have listened with more wonder and appreciation. As it was, I tapped my finger on the bar, watching head wobbles and gesticulations and the looks directed my way.

Eventually, Roy and the bartender must have come to some arrangement, because the latter called out to the kitchen and an older man in long trousers and a pale blue, short-sleeved shirt joined him. There followed another lightning-fast exchange before the older man snapped at the bartender and Roy stepped back, nodding in satisfaction.

"Let's sit outside," Roy told me. "Lazar here will join us."

We made our way outside once more. The leanest slither of the sun burned a bright fluorescent orange just above the sea, the sky around it coloured blue and violet and yellow and pink. On any other occasion, I would have thought this stunning beyond words. Magickal even.

I chose a table away from everyone else. Holiday-makers laughing, drinking and eating and having the time of their lives. That had been me, only twenty-four hours previously. Funny how life turns on a sixpence.

The bartender followed us out with three clay beakers of steaming liquid. Roy handed me one as he took a seat beside me. "Chai," he said.

"Oof! It's hot!" Hot enough to burn the tips of my fingers. I hurriedly set it down on the table.

"Very refreshing," he told me, and took a swig.

I curled a lip, thinking of the water I'd seen the bartender rinsing his glasses in a few minutes earlier. "Thanks."

"Perfectly safe, sister," Roy said, as though he could read my mind. "They use bottled water, and it's boiled. To keep the tourists safe." He quickly repeated what he'd told me to the bartender, who smiled widely.

"Yes. Yes," he agreed. "Safe." He pointed at my beaker. "Drink. Refresh."

I took a sip. It was sweet and yet somehow peppery. I didn't immediately dislike it by any means, and I needed the sugar rush.

"Good! Good!" The bartender grinned.

"This is Lazar." Roy formally introduced us. "He was working last night until the early hours."

"Hello, Lazar," I said. "I'm Alf."

"Alf," he repeated, his face serious.

"Can you tell me what happened last night?"

"Fight," Lazar told me. "Man dead."

"Yeah." I turned to Roy, who was sipping his chai. "I know that much."

"Let me." He waved his beaker at the young bartender and began shooting words at him. Lazar pouted, then stared at me askance. He wobbled his head, offered a few one-word answers, then smiled. Once Roy had finished speaking, Lazar took his turn.

He spoke quickly and with emotion, pointing out a few places to Roy. I waited, striving to be patient, until at last Roy turned to me.

"Lazar tells me that Silvan came here sometime towards midnight. That would be after he spoke to me as I was closing up. He met with a man—"

"Salty Dog?" I asked.

Roy repeated what I had said, and Lazar nodded slowly, although reluctantly.

"That's the name the man goes by," Roy confirmed. "Silvan came in first and asked for Salty Dog, and they sat inside at a table in the corner."

"Were they drinking?" I asked, wondering if things had become heated.

"Cobra," Lazar said, imitating drinking from a bottle.

I'd seen the signs for Cobra beer all over the place, so I imagined it was a popular brand.

"Silvan and Salty Dog were having a discussion—"

I opened my mouth to ask a question, but Roy held up a hand. "Lazar wasn't listening, and I don't think his English would be good enough to follow along with the conversation anyway, but I think we can assume Silvan was enquiring about hiring a boat."

Asking about a boat didn't sound like something that would get out of hand. "So what happened?"

"A group of sailors came in. They were a bit, how do you say, loud—"

"Rowdy?" I suggested, *like a family of vampires rowdy?*

"Yes," Roy agreed. "At sea for a while. Glad to be back on the old terra firma."

I examined Lazar's expression, searching for any clue. "Then what? Were these rowdy sailors causing trouble?"

Roy and Lazar conferred again—more rapid-fire questions and answers—until Roy was satisfied. He turned back to me. "No. Just rowdy."

That was it? All that conversation and that was all Roy could come up with? "No disagreements?" I prompted. "Spilled drinks? Vengeful husbands? Insulting of mothers?"

Roy regarded me the way someone might study an alien life form, but I'd been a bartender long enough to know full well that the feeblest slight could spark a conflict. "Lazar says it all calmed down again."

That couldn't be the case. If everything had been calm, then a man would never have been stabbed, would he? "What was Silvan doing all this time?" I asked.

Roy checked with Lazar. "Just drinking. Several drinks."

"And there were others here?" I asked.

Again, the quickfire questions and answers.

"The sailors. Some Dutch tourists and some Germans. A couple of Americans," Roy told me.

Had the police questioned the tourists? The event

would have been traumatic for them. "So explain to me how it all kicked off?" I said.

"Lazar went out the back to get some more bottles, and he heard shouting. English people shouting—"

"Right—"

"He came back to see Silvan standing over the man with a knife in his hand." Roy nodded at Lazar. Lazar held his hand loosely curled in front of his chest, palm towards himself.

"That's how Silvan was holding this *knife*?" I asked, knowing it hadn't been a knife at all. This wasn't the way someone who had just used a knife—or a cutlass, for that matter—held their weapon. Not that I was an expert on such things.

"There was no magick involved?" I asked Roy.

Roy asked Lazar the question, and now the young bartender stared at me in horror and began gabbling.

"I take it that's a no," I said. Lazar, and many of the people in the bar, were mundanes. Yes, the Midnight Flower Luxury Lodge Resort was a wonderful escape for the paranormal, but most of the rest of Dakti Bhoin was given over to ordinary humans. Bless their souls.

"I don't think he would recognise it, Alf," Roy told me. "These people are Catholics. They're very superstitious."

"Alright. But he's saying he didn't see Silvan stab or otherwise harm the victim?"

"He didn't see anything, just heard the commotion," Roy confirmed.

"What about other witnesses?" I asked. "The other sailors? Tourists?"

"They went away," Roy said.

Great.

It was a shame I couldn't get on the blower to George. He'd have sorted this whole mess out in no time. However, I didn't think Silvan would appreciate me inviting my old flame to what was supposed to be our honeymoon. "Is there anyone else I could talk to? The Monkey Nuts' owner?"

Lazar shook his head, his eyes betraying panic. He spoke animatedly, his voice becoming increasingly high-pitched. Roy held up a placating hand. "It's all good, brother," he cooed and, turning to me, said, "Lazar is worried you're trying to get him fired."

I smacked my hand to my heart. "Oh, I'm sorry!" I told the young bartender. "Of course that's not what I'm trying to do. I just want to help my fiancé."

"Don't worry, don't worry. Everything is fine and dandy." Roy dismissed my concerns.

Right on cue, The Monkey Nuts' owner marched out of the bar and called to Lazar. The young man hurriedly stood up and collected the clay beakers.

"I think our time is up," Roy said. "I need to open my shop too."

"Of course." I forced a smile at Lazar. "Thank you," I said, pressing my hands together in front of my chest and offering him the head bob that appeared to denote respect and thanks and a million other things. He returned my gesture, albeit a little uncertainly.

"What will you do?" Roy asked.

"Go back to the resort, I suppose," I replied. I couldn't help feeling glum. So far, I hadn't been able to help Silvan at all.

"I can rent you a bicycle, if you like?" Roy suggested.

For a moment I almost took him up on that, but then recalled that this would be the very bicycle that Silvan had ridden down on the previous evening. The one that belonged to my resort. I pressed my lips together and shook my head.

"Incorrigible," I told him. "Absolutely shameless!"

CHAPTER SEVEN

In the end I did ride the bicycle back to the resort, but I steadfastly refused to pay for the pleasure of doing so. I say pleasure, but believe me, I'd rather have stuck pokers in my eyes. The track back to the resort was difficult to navigate anyway, and the lack of light anywhere meant that you couldn't see the potholes until you had already dropped into one. Throughout the course of the journey, I jarred my back, knocked my teeth together and bit my tongue. I also feasted on several flies, but at least they provided good protein after a day of limited food options.

Abandoning the bicycle at reception, I waved at the night receptionist and limped like an old woman back to our lodge. Once there, I threw off my clothes and sloped into the shower, turning the water up high —but on a cool setting—allowing it to pummel my head.

I needed to eat, sleep and realign my priorities. Finding Salty Dog was the first of those. Presumably he had gone back to his boat. Why hadn't I thought to look in the harbour? I decided to make that my main concern in the morning.

Then there was the question of who the victim was. Had he been with the sailors that Lazar had complained were rowdy? If I could track down those sailors, perhaps I'd find out more about the victim. Knowing who he was might give me a motive. Knowing the motive might point to the killer ...

If the police couldn't do this work, then I would need to. With a little bit of evidence, I could go to the British Embassy, wherever that was, and ask for help. I didn't know for sure whether they offered such a service, but surely they could advise?

Yawning, I wrapped myself in a towel and dripped through to the cool bedroom. The air conditioning was going flat out, and I found it somewhat soothing after such a stressful day. Plucking up the room service menu, I considered supper options. Thali? Mmm. Too spicy. I probably wouldn't sleep. Something easier on the stomach would be better ...

Retreating to the big bed, freshly made up by some hardworking housekeeper, I stretched out and considered my options. Burger? Might repeat on me. An omelette? That would be nice and light. Perhaps a few French fries and some ketchup, or ...

I lay back.

Grilled chicken would be tasty ... maybe with a salad. And a glass of mango smoothie.

Make that a jug ...

Or ...

The phone next to the bed began to shriek. I shot upright, the room service menu slipping onto the floor. Light was stealing through a gap in the curtains. Disconcerted, it took me a moment to react. The phone wailed on. Daylight? I'd fallen asleep?

I reached across and grabbed the receiver. "Hello?" I said, my voice hoarse.

"Ma'am? Alfhild Daemonne, ma'am?" A polite young woman's voice.

"Yes. Hello?"

"Ma'am. It's Sergeant Prabhu from the Dakti Bhoin police station."

Uh-oh. "Is everything alright?" I asked, swinging my legs over the side of the bed, ready to make a dash for my shoes, although given that my only covering was a towel, I might need to get dressed first.

"This is a courtesy call, ma'am. To let you know that Mister Silvanus will be in court this morning at ten o'clock."

"In court?"

"Yes, ma'am."

"Already?" This couldn't be happening.

"Yes, ma'am, already. The court will hear him and he will be arraigned for trial."

Oh. Arraigned. They weren't hearing the case per se, just deciding whether to hold him for trial, I supposed. Except, the way that Sergeant Prabhu had phrased it, it did rather sound as though they were preparing him *for* trial. Talk about locking him up and throwing away the key.

"If he's arraigned, what does that mean?"

"He'll be taken to the jailhouse on the mainland, ma'am, and held there until his trial."

Remanded into custody. "May I see him?" I asked.

"Ma'am, the courthouse is open to the public. You can come there by ten o'clock and you will see him."

"But can I *speak* to him? Will I be allowed to do so?"

"No, ma'am. Only from a distance, ma'am."

Fab. Nevertheless, I would have to attend.

"I'll be there," I said. "Thanks for letting me know."

"No problem, ma'am. Have a nice day." The phone went dead.

"Have a nice day!" I repeated, jumping off the bed. "Have a nice day! Ha!" *What time is it*? Just after eight. I'd need another shower and to do something with my hair. Lots of conditioner.

I chased around, making myself hot. What clothes should I wear? Something smartish? I'd mainly brought summer outfits with me—meaning loose black t-shirts and baggy shorts, swimsuits and flip flops. The shirt I'd been wearing the previous day was the only non-black item I possessed. I picked it up from the bathroom floor and tentatively sniffed it.

No. Best not.

I had my robes though. I'd been wearing them on the plane when we left Heathrow. As long as I hadn't dropped any of the airline's woefully bland food down them, perhaps they would do. But, then again, given the heat outside they would be entirely the wrong thing to wear. Too thick.

There was *one* dress.

I'd bought it because my ghostly housekeeper Florence had loved it, and I'd worn it for her book launch. Unfortunately, subsequent events had seen it being mistreated, and Florence had spent a good few hours making it wearable again. I pulled it out of the wardrobe where it hung and inspected it. It was a pretty maxi-length dress, with a pale mauve background and a pattern of small flowers in pink, purple, yellow and green, but not my usual apparel. I haven't the foggiest idea why I'd brought it with me. I think because dear Florence had spent so long fixing it, and she'd done so out of love for me, her employer—after a fashion—but most importantly, her friend. If I wore this, surely I'd feel her support reaching out to me across thousands of miles.

Examining the dress more carefully I could barely see the repairs, so neatly worked in were they, in matching thread and Florence's impeccable stitches. I slumped on the bed again, suddenly missing all my friends rather badly. Florence. Charity. Even—

"Really, darling! Hadn't you better get a move on?"

I nearly jumped out of my skin. "Grandmama?"

"Who else?" She apparated into the room wearing an Edwardian tweed travelling outfit in heavy Scottish wool, beige and dark brown with a hint of red, and a cream blouse fastened at the neck with a chunky brooch that may or may not have been solid gold but, given the way it sparkled, definitely enclosed a ruby.

Hmmm. Is that part of my inheritance? Because if it is, I've never seen it anywhere.

"What are you doing here?"

"I thought I'd pay you a visit." She spun around, examining the facilities. "Very nice."

"All the way to India?" *How had she even travelled here?*

"Yes. It's one of my most favourite places on the planet," she told me. "Are you going to have a shower because you look like you need one. What is going on with your hair, my dear? You can't possibly go to court like that."

"How did you know?" I asked, laying the dress aside and trying—but failing—to run a hand through my hair. I'd fallen asleep with it wet, so it had dried without having had a comb pulled through it or copious amounts of products added. Big mistake. Huge! Gwyn was right. I would need to redo it.

As if I had time!

"I know all, darling," she crowed. "I know all. I see all."

"Super," I mumbled and stomped, naked, through to the bathroom for a speedy shower. I doused my hair quickly—no need to shampoo it again—then worked through some conditioner and a comb until my curls were detangled. I wouldn't need to use a hairdryer—not that I ever did. Oh, the frizz!—because the heat outside would diffuse it far better than any blower. I really appreciated that about the Indian climate.

Gwyn joined me in the bathroom as I worked some curl cream into my locks. "What's he done this time?"

"He hasn't done anything," I told her. "He's been accused of murder, but he didn't do it. No doubt this kangaroo court will make everything much more difficult than it needs to be though."

"Really, Alfhild. Have some respect. India is a wonderful country, and they learned a great deal from the British. Their legal system is based on ours."

"Is that so?" I reached for my toothbrush. "Their police don't seem that motivated to go in search of any witnesses or the real killer, though."

"This place is a little out of the way, darling. Things are slower out in the sticks. That was always the case. I'm sure they'll catch up." She smiled. "Eventually."

"I'm supposed to be getting married in a few days, Grandmama," I said through a mouthful of minty froth. "Them allowing him to languish in prison until he's sixty years old before they 'catch up' won't help me."

"Sixty isn't old, darling."

"It's ancient!" I argued, and began rinsing my mouth out with bottled water.

"It really isn't. Now, get dressed."

Being out and about with Gwyn is always an interesting experience. Some people can see ghosts and some people can't. Some people think they see something and then, when they look a little closer, whatever it was is no longer there. Naturally, they're the ones who dismiss what they thought they saw as a figment of their imagination.

And so it was this morning. One or two of the assembled throng—and I mean throng; the court was jam-packed with men and women, but mostly men, of all ages—could clearly see my great-grandmother, floating along beside me and wafting at herself with an enormous rattan fan. Several attendees took one look at her, crossed themselves and bolted outside. Among those who paid more curious attention to her was Roy.

"Hi!" I said, pleased to see a familiar face. "This is my great-grandmother, Gwyn, who has turned up just at the ... erm ... right ... time."

"Alfhild Gwynfyre Daemonne," Gwyn corrected me. "I'm the original Alfhild. But you can call me Mrs Daemonne."

"The pleasure is all mine." Roy pressed his hands together and made a deep bow.

Gwyn looked absurdly pleased. "Oh, you're charming," she said.

"Grandmama, this is Roy. He helped me out yesterday." I smiled at him. "I'm very grateful to you."

"Anything for you, sister," he said. "I thought I would pop along this morning before I open up and see whether I can be of any further assistance."

"We may well need a translator," I agreed. Someone jostled me, and I grabbed Roy's arm to keep my balance. "Oops! Beg your pardon, Roy."

Roy's head bobbed as he glanced around. "It's busy today. Lots of cases."

"These people aren't just here to see Silvan then?" I couldn't hide my relief. "I'd been imagining that this was a notorious murder case and everyone wanted to see a man hang."

"So melodramatic, darling," Gwyn murmured, wafting at her face and glaring at the woman who had pushed into me. "Honestly, Roy, Alfhild thinks her life is a movie. Or a series of books or some such."

"That would be the only possible explanation for some of the stuff that happens in my life," I said. "But in any case, I'm glad people are here for their own cases and not Silv—"

Shouts broke out near the entrance. Following a noisy and ill-tempered commotion—complaints and a surge of people into the court—a group of men pushed their way inside, cursing and snarling. They were dressed in worn and soiled clothing, mainly white, and judging by the language they used, I could tell they were sailors. Clearly, given the way a couple of them rolled around, some of them had been up drinking all night.

"Well, really." Gwyn curled her lip. "Such riff-raff. No wonder they're in a courthouse. Who else would you expect to see here?"

"Order! Order!" The tiniest little man had come to the front of the court. Dressed in a smart short-sleeved pale blue shirt, freshly pressed trousers and a bright pink lanyard, he ordered everyone to sit down. There was a fresh scuffle as people leapt for the public seating, mainly benches, scurrying like mice for every available space. Gwyn, Roy and I were left at the front, in splendid isolation, with at least a hundred pairs of eyes trained on us.

"Meep," I said, shuffling sideways.

"Take a seat," the little man squawked. "Take a seat! Court is about to commence."

"Take a seat, where?" I muttered, but Roy took matters into his own hands and began chatting animatedly with several women on the front row. After much head wobbling, covert glances and some complaints, they shifted up, and Roy and I were able to squeeze onto the pew.

"All rise!" came a cry.

My backside had hardly touched the wood and we were up again. The judge hustled out from a side door, a bundle of folders in her arms, to take her place at her high seat, her white curly wig slightly askew. It seemed India had indeed taken instruction from the British judicial system; however, in addition to a long-sleeved black coat, the judge was wearing a white collar over a salwar kameez.

"Unorthodox," Gwyn remarked loudly, as the rest of the court fell deferentially silent. "And yet oddly stylish."

"Shhh, Grandmama," I hissed at her out of the side of my mouth. The whisper travelled around the vaulted space, stubbornly refusing to be soaked up by the bodies pressed together around me. The judge, a woman in her late forties I imagined, glared down at me from her pedestal.

I forced a smile of apology. What a great start!

The judge took her seat and we all followed suit. Cue more shuffling, scraping of wooden chair legs and bench ends, coughing and muttering.

"Judge Bhandarkar presiding," called the little official.

"Good morning, everyone," the judge said. "The day's schedule has been posted, and there is a lot to get through. Let us get straight down to business."

"Dakti Bhoin case number zero-zero-zero-zero-six-three-six-eight-two-one. Maharashtra versus Horace T Silvanus."

"Oh, thank heavens," Gwyn said. "We're first. We don't have to wait around for too long."

Judge Bhandarkar squinted in my direction but

evidently couldn't see Gwyn. I clamped my mouth tightly closed. *It wasn't me, it wasn't me,* I telegraphed, not wanting to find myself chucked out of the court.

"Very well, bring out the prisoner."

Two gentlemen slunk to the front of the room to stand before the judge, waiting patiently as Silvan was escorted in through a side entrance. Dressed in a bright orange jumpsuit, with his long hair tied back in a ponytail and stubble on his face, he still looked beautifully handsome, if a little tired. I half stood, waving at him to catch his attention, but then remembered this would probably be frowned upon and sat down rather heavily. The bench creaked alarmingly beneath me.

Silvan spotted the movement though, and winked at me before turning his attention to the judge.

"State your name for the record," the usher told him.

"Horace T Silvanus," Silvan answered.

There was a growl from the back of the room. I distinctly heard someone mutter, "That's him. He's the one."

"Aaar," came the disgruntled response.

"Occupation?"

A tricky question. I waited anxiously for Silvan to answer. Would he admit to being—

"Handyman for hire."

Handyman? Was he for real?

"State your address for the record."

"Whittle Inn, Whittlecombe, East Devon. UK."

"Your Honour, if it pleases you?" A man dressed in a suit entirely unsuitable for the weather raised his hand.

"Go ahead," said Judge Bhandarkar.

"I'd like it to be known that Mr Silvanus is currently a visitor to this country. He is temporarily resident at the Midnight Flower Luxury Lodge Resort."

"Noted." The judge ruffled her papers. "Mr Silvanus, you are charged with the murder of one Captain Dunley Bloodstone, on the fourteenth of this month at The Monkey Nuts bar in the village of Dakti Bhoin. How do you plead?"

Silvan lifted his chin. "Not guilty, Your Honour."

"Liar!" someone at the back shouted.

"Aar!"

"Order!" The judge glared towards the rear of the court until silence prevailed, before returning her attention to Silvan. "I see. Very well. In the interests of public safety, you will be remanded to the White Water District prison on the mainland until your trial date is set."

"Murderer!" shouted the most vocal man at the rear of the room.

"Murderer!" The call was taken up by his friends. "Aaar!"

"Order! Order!" Judge Bhandarkar banged her gavel. "Order in my courtroom!"

"Hang him high!"

I gasped in shock. Did India have the death penalty?

"There's no need for that," Gwyn remarked, spinning about. "He's a scoundrel, but I don't think capital punishment is the answer."

I jumped to my feet in horror. "Of course it isn't!"

The men at the back were in full flow.

"He don't deserve a trial, he don't!"

"Arrrrrrrr!"

"Set him frrrrrrreeee!" one of the men yelled. "We'll deal with him for you. Pirate justice! That'll sort 'im!"

"Cowardly cur!"

"Bailiffs?" The judge banged her gavel in fury. "Have those gentlemen escorted outside and bar them from returning!"

There was a scurry and a kerfuffle, lots of shouting and swearing, and more than a few threats. By now, the court was in complete uproar. Other spectators were on their feet, straining to see the ruckus as the mob was bundled out into the lobby beyond.

I took advantage of the diversion to hurry closer to Silvan. Only the wooden dividing bars separated us.

"How did you get on with finding Salty Dog?" he asked, keeping his voice low.

"No joy so far," I told him. "But I'll get straight back on it."

"Don't worry, Alfie." He smiled at me. "I have a

court-appointed lawyer. He'll sort everything out, I'm sure."

I glanced over at the man in a suit. He couldn't have been more than twenty-five and was chatting with the prosecution lawyer, a woman, in a friendly and overly familiar way. I couldn't share Silvan's optimism.

"I'm working on it," I told him. "I have a couple of leads."

That was a complete lie, but I wanted to reassure him.

"I have every faith in you," he told me. "And you have Gwyn by your side!" He raised his eyebrows to indicate his astonishment. "What could be better?"

I could think of a couple of hundred things that might be better, but I elected to remain schtum for the sake of any potential earache.

"I'll be in touch as soon as they let me," he said. "And I'm sure you can communicate with my lawyer. Grab him before you leave."

"I will do."

The bailiffs had finally ejected the noisy group from the back of the court, and now the guards were at Silvan's side, ready to escort him away.

"I love you, Alfie," Silvan said. "Don't fret. I guarantee we'll still be able to marry next week."

I really couldn't see this happening myself. As the guards led him away, tears pricked at my eyes. "I love you too!" I called after him.

But honestly? I could have wrung his neck!

Before the next case was called, Roy and I made our way into the lobby where Silvan's lawyer was waiting.

"Ms Daemonne?" he asked, shaking my hand. "I'm sorry for your trouble. I'm Martin Mudakatte. I've been appointed to your fiancé's case."

"He didn't do it," I blurted out. "How soon can you get him out?"

"Obviously these things take time," Martin said, reaching into his pocket. "This is my card." He made a great show of pulling a card from a little faux-leather wallet. "You can call me at any time, madam. I am at your service."

"There are witnesses," I told him. "Have you spoken to Lazar, the bartender at The Monkey Nuts?"

"Lazar?" Martin clearly didn't have the foggiest notion to whom I was referring.

"Have you spoken to anyone at The Monkey Nuts at all?" I asked, suspicion gnawing at my insides.

"Just the owner." Martin pointed at a man standing with a uniformed officer. I vaguely recognised him from the bar the previous evening. He'd been the one who had given Lazar permission to speak to us.

"Who's he with? Who is that man in uniform?" I asked.

"That's the chief of police," Roy told me. "I think this does not go so well for us."

"What do you mean?" I looked at Roy, back at Martin and then at the chief of police.

"I ... er ... Everything will be fine, madam," Martin said. "I will get Mr Silvanus free for you. No problem." With a wobble of his head, he began to pull away.

"Are you leaving?" I asked. "Shouldn't we be discussing tactics?"

"Leave everything to me, madam. I am at your service. Thank you. Goodbye!" Walking backwards, he bowed his head.

I held up my hand as though I could pull him back. "I really think—"

"At your service. Thank you. Goodbye for now." Martin scurried away.

I frowned after him. "*What* is going on? Why's he in such a tearing hurry?"

"Perhaps he has other cases, Alfhild." Gwyn waved her fan at me. I was grateful for the breeze. "Not everything revolves around you, my dear."

"So you keep telling me," I grumbled. Really! If she had no help to offer, what was she doing here?

"I thought you'd be grateful for my company, dear," Gwyn told me, reading my mind as usual.

Roy interrupted us. "I think I may know what is happening." He nodded his head at the chief of police. "That is Goliath Netalkar. He's from a well-known family." He emphasised the words 'well known'.

I didn't really catch his meaning.

Roy lowered his voice. "There are plenty of officials from territories all over India who are known to be corrupt. Families who rule the roost, so to speak. Dakti Bhoin, as beautiful as it undoubtedly is, is no exception. The Netalkars have our district sewn up."

I leaned in a little closer. "What are you suggesting?"

"The other man? The owner of The Monkey Nuts? His name is Nilesh Padukone. He's from the same family. Married Goliath's sister. If for some reason it suited either of those men to have Silvan labelled as the murderer—perhaps to get the case closed more quickly and make Netalkar look good—then between them they could probably arrange that."

"Besides which, the resulting publicity probably isn't good for a tourist bar," I agreed. "But surely it would be better all round, for the chief of police and any local business owner, to bring the right culprit to justice?"

Roy nodded, but more in a placating way than in agreement. "Sometimes it only needs to appear as though justice has been done for the community to be satisfied."

Ugh. I understood. "And the newspapers report everything as fact, and so no-one will ever be any the wiser." I huffed. "Hell's bells."

"Hell's bells indeed, Alfhild. I can hear them ringing," Gwyn said. "But I can tell you now, India is far hotter than Hades! We should go back to the hotel, darling. They have air conditioning."

Air conditioning sounded tempting, but honestly? How could my great-grandmother be feeling the temperature? She was a ghost! "Grandmama, I can't just abandon Silvan this way. If no-one else will help him, I have to!"

"How truly tiresome," Gwyn moaned, flapping her fan at her face. "What are you planning to do?"

I glanced at Roy. "I'm going to the harbour to look at boats."

"I'll leave you to it. It should be plain sailing, at any rate," Gwyn quipped and apparated away.

Chapter Eight

With Roy's help, I was able to speak to the harbour master. In the UK, a harbour master is an official job with proper offices and computer equipment and customs forms and all manner of officialdom. In Dakti Bhoin, the harbour master occupied—that is, he lived and worked in—something that resembled a coconut shy, along with his wife, a son aged seven or eight and three extremely cute little girls, all under the age of about six. They were playing in the sand as we approached, although the eldest daughter seemed to be crushing herbs using a pestle and mortar.

She'd make a fine witch, if she did but know it.

The harbour master, another wonderfully slender man with a rich head of hair—sticking up at odd angles in his case—and a face full of stubble, came out of the hut when summoned by one of his daughters, wrapped only in an orange and gold dhobi.

Roy greeted the man like a long-lost friend and then introduced me to him. Zoze, as he was called, spoke reasonably good English, along with a smattering of Dutch and some German, apparently. I could never fail to be impressed by anyone who had mastery of more than one language, particularly when I couldn't even converse with Monsieur Emietter at home.

"I know *Seawolf*," he told me. "Salty Dog comes and goes. We see him from time to time."

"And he was here the night before last?" I asked.

"Yes, yes," Zoze confirmed.

"Did he leave that night?"

Zoze thought for a moment. "He was gone when I woke up."

"Do you know where he went?" I asked hopefully, but was disappointed when Zoze shook his head. I turned to Roy in frustration. "Don't they have to file ... sailing plans? Like ... flight plans?"

Roy chuckled and spoke in Konkani with Zoze. Both men laughed together.

"I'll take that as a no," I said.

But I wasn't going to give up. "Where might he have gone?" I tried.

Zoze waved a hand vaguely in the direction of the horizon. "Salty Dog is a sailor."

And sailors sail. I glared at the ocean, hating it for being so immense. "I'll just have to go after him," I decided.

That wiped the smile off Roy's face. "What do you mean?"

I lifted my chin. "I'm going to hire a boat and go after him."

"But you don't know where he's gone," Roy reminded me.

"I'll just sail out there"—I pointed into the wild blue yonder—"and take a look around."

"Like a day trip?" Roy asked.

"Something like that," I agreed. Hopefully it wouldn't take too long. In my head, all I had to do was track down Salty Dog and get him to make a statement: Silvan was in the bathroom while the ruckus took place, and it therefore could not possibly have been Silvan who'd stabbed Dunley Bloodstone.

That would clear it all up. And perhaps Salty would know who the culprit was. Although if that was the case, it would have been nice if he'd stuck around to give his statement.

Assuming it wasn't actually *him*, of course.

"Sister—" Roy grimaced. "You're a sailor?"

Staring at the boats moored in the harbour, I considered this. I didn't know one end of a boat from the other. Port? Starboard? That was a game for girl guides. Hull? A football team. Stern? A description of my grandmama.

Plus ... what was the difference between a boat and a ship anyway? And why did some yachts have sails and some have engines?

How thoroughly confusing.

But how difficult could it be?

"I am now."

Unfortunately for me, Roy had to go and open up his little shack shop. He did it regretfully, but I completely understood. I'd taken up far too much of his time as it was. "Don't worry!" I'd sought to reassure him. "I'm a big girl. I can find my way around the harbour and hire a boat ..."

And someone to drive it. Or sail it. Or whatever.

"I mean, it's simply a matter of communicating with someone and then flashing a bit of cash. Right?" I'd asked, donning my sunglasses, and Roy, having regarded me cynically for a moment, finally smiled and wished me luck.

He'd bought me a bottle of water at a small stall before heading back towards his home. "You come and find me if you need me though, sister. I don't want you getting into trouble."

"I'll be fine," I'd blustered, not letting on that getting into trouble seemed to be my default setting.

"Perhaps make your enquiries," Roy had suggested, "and then before you make a decision about hiring a boat, come and talk to me. I know a few decent sailors. You could ask for Wallace. He has a glass-bottomed boat that allows you to see the ocean floor."

"That sounds fantastic," I agreed. "But this isn't a sightseeing trip. I just need a boat that can sail out and come back. Preferably quite quickly. With binoculars on board."

"As you wish." Roy had bowed. "I will see you a little later, sister."

I had waved goodbye and stepped out alone. Grasping my water bottle, I'd approached a clutch of signs at the entrance to the harbour. Faded posters enlightened me about fishing trips and scuba diving schools, sightseeing tours and ocean floor excursions.

Perfect. If everyone was looking to make a quick buck, then I wasn't going to have much trouble hiring a boat and team, was I?

Famous last words.

I approached the first boat with my hopes high. It looked relatively stable. Old, but no obvious holes anywhere. A young man was stacking life vests—which I took as a good sign—but when I enquired about chartering the boat for a trip out, he told me that he already had customers and directed me to the next boat along.

It was the same story there, and at the third one—although here they understood so little English, it was difficult for me to ascertain if we'd really been on the same page—so I kept going.

The fourth chap, the owner of a rickety fishing barge, shook his head in horror. "Foreign," he said, in a way which caused me to question just how much of a crime that could be. "Go see foreign," he repeated, jabbing his hand towards the other end of the harbour.

Ah! The international boat set! This was more like it ... no stinky fishing boats for me.

My first port of call was a flash boat with a sleek frontage, all pointed and aerodynamic and expensive looking.

"G'day." A tall blond Australian, bronzed and muscular, wearing little more than a pair of teeny weeny swimming—well, I'd hesitate to call them 'pants' let alone shorts, but erm ... I'll leave that to your imagination—posed on his sun deck and smiled down at me. "How ya doin'?"

"Great, thanks." I removed my sunglasses so he could get a better look at me—and I at him, to be fair—and nodded back at him. "I wanted to enquire about chartering a boat."

"Is that right?" he asked. "Where are you looking to go?"

"I'm not really sure. Just ... out."

"Like a joyride?" he asked.

"Not really. I'm looking for someone." Even as I said the words, I could hear how ridiculous they sounded. While talking to Zoze and Roy, for some reason I'd imagined that it was feasible to track down Salty Dog despite the absurd number of square miles I would need to cover.

"Maybe you've found him." The Australian waggled his eyebrows at me.

Sheesh.

In the face of his obvious lechery, I said the first

thing that came into my mind. "I'm getting married next week."

Urgh. How stupid did that sound?

"Are you?" The Australian grinned. "Lucky man. Or ..." He chuckled. "Is that who we're looking for? Has he run away?"

"Oh, ha ha, hilarious." I narrowed my eyes. "No, it's not him. I know *exactly* where he is." I decided not to provide specifics.

"Who are you talking to?" A female voice drifted up from the inside of the boat. She appeared a few seconds later. A young woman, tall and toned and willowy, with short reddy-blonde hair and bronzed skin shown off to perfection by her skimpy coral-coloured bikini. "Oh, g'day!" She wound an arm around her charming partner.

"Hi," I said. "I was wondering about chartering a boat?"

"You're a Brit?" She turned her head to study the young man. He arched an eyebrow at her. "Yeah, no, this is a private boat. We don't do hires."

"Fair enough." I began to retreat. "Thanks for your time."

"No problem," she called after me.

As I wandered away, I heard her ask him, "What were you up to, Keith?"

"Nothing, you great drongo. Just making conversation."

"You were coming onto her, weren't you?"

"I was not. She's getting married."

"You love married women! Give you an inch—"

I increased the length of my stride, wanting to put as much distance between myself and their bickering and negativity as possible. I needed to keep my energy high and my hopes alive.

There were two boats left to approach, then I'd be all out of options. The first one was another of those sleek white ones, shaped rather like an iron. Not that I was intimately acquainted with irons. It was my least favourite pastime. In fact, I'd rather spend three hours working on a spreadsheet than standing over an ironing board, so I think that tells you all you need to know.

"Did I hear you say you're looking to charter a boat?" An older gentleman in a dark blue linen shirt, white trousers and pristine deck shoes peered up at me from where he was kneeling beside a tall, stinking collection of lobster traps.

My heart leapt. "Yes!"

He regarded me with interest, his gaze raking me up and down. "Can you afford it?"

I glanced at my pretty green dress with the hidden repairs and my pair of white slides. They at least had been bought new for the holiday. What was he suggesting? "I'm sure I can," I told him. How much could it be? A couple of hundred pounds? Five hundred at a push. And I'd want a full twenty-four hours for that.

"Six grand," he told me. Just like that. As cool as a cucumber. Six. Grand.

I almost swallowed my tongue. "How much?" The strength left my knees and elbows, and I began to feel decidedly wobbly. "Six grand as in rupees? Six thousand rupees?" That was it, surely? Sixty pounds.

"No, love." The more he spoke, the clearer it became that he was a Londoner. I should have known.

"Dollars?" The exchange rate was currently pretty poor for the pound, but dollars would be better than sterling.

"Six thousand pounds," he said, slowly and carefully. "I can take you to some fantastic coves nearby. And I have my own chef."

For one crazy moment, I almost considered it. Silvan was worth more than six grand—of course he was—but ... I didn't have anything like that in my personal bank account. Everything I'd earned was pumped back into Whittle Inn and the Daemonne estate, including all the little cottages in Whittlecombe that belonged to us.

"What do you reckon?" the man asked.

"I don't need a chef," I told him, biding time so I could consider where it would be feasible for me to drag the money from. Which account could I rob?

But no. People depended on me for a living. Charity in particular. And I owed money to loads of small businesses, such as the Whittlecombe corner shop and the post office where I had accounts. And to people like Penelope Quigwell and other suppliers of goods and services. I couldn't jeopardise the inn's financial wellbeing on a cat and mouse chase through the Indian Ocean.

"Yeah, thought so." The man lifted a couple of the lobster pots. "Have you considered finding a job on one of the boats? That's a great way to see the world."

"Are you ... hiring?" I asked. Maybe I could do a day or two.

"Have you ever been to sea before?"

I bit my lip. Did a rowing boat with my dad on the Serpentine count? Or a boat shaped like a swan on a boating lake near the sea when I was very young?

"Uh-huh." The man shrugged and began to walk across his narrow gangway. "No can do. Sorry, love."

He disappeared.

The sun was high in the sky now, beating down on me and burning my lower arms. I folded them across my chest, allowing them some respite in the shade of my wide-brimmed sunhat. I shouldn't stay out for much longer. I was liable to shrivel up like a slice of bacon.

Sizzle, sizzle, sizzle.

But there was one boat left. I might as well try my luck with that one and then, and only then, would I call it quits.

CHAPTER NINE

The last remaining boat in the harbour was a completely different prospect. For a start, this one towered over most of the others, and for seconds it was a proper old-fashioned boat made of wood rather than fibreglass or whatever modern boats are made from. It had an interesting shape—rather like a Spanish galleon, I thought—and the windows in some of the upper sections contained bottled glass similar to the kind I had in many of the windows back at the inn.

I warmed to it straight away. Who wouldn't fall in love with a boat that looked like Whittle Inn?

But on the downside it had rigging, and it looked older than Gwyn. Much older than her. In fact, this boat was probably contemporary with dear old Luppitt Smeatharpe, my Elizabethan bard. Although it seemed intact—*ish*—the paint was flaking off and everything about it was in definite need of a refresh.

A small man, skin the colour of old leather, wearing darned breeches and a loose white shirt with a scarf tied around his hair, was loitering near the gangway. He glanced up as I approached and regarded me with suspicion.

"Hi." I offered him my sunniest smile, unsure whether he would speak English or not. It would certainly be arrogant of me to assume he did.

He grunted a response, which didn't help me decide on his language at all, then produced a clay pipe and proceeded to light it.

I pushed on. "I'm sorry to bother you, and I know this is a strange request"—*given that your boat is older than Moses and probably isn't even seaworthy*—"but I'm looking to hire a boat."

"Oh arrrrrrr?" the man purred. He had a deep, growling voice with a west country accent. I recognised it immediately.

"Do you know Whittlecombe?" I asked. "In East Devon?"

"Arrrr!" I wasn't sure whether that was a yes or a no, or even whether he could say anything besides 'arrrh'. He puffed on his pipe to get it going, sucked in a mouthful of air and then expelled it towards me in a big cloud of perfumed smoke.

I wafted it away, blinking. "That's where I'm from," I told him, trying to elicit a friendly response. Maybe strike up some kind of rapport that would lead me to finally finding someone who would take me out on the water. Even for a few hours.

"Oh, arrr?" *Puff, puff.*

"So, anyway, as I said, I'm looking to hire a boat," I told him. "Just for a few hours."

"Arrr?"

"I can pay." I rethought that. "Within reason."

"Arrr." *Puff, puff.*

"Is that a possibility?" I asked. I was hot and withered and losing the will to live. I began to recognise that I was on a complete hiding to nothing.

"*Poseidon's Curse* is not for hire," the sailor told me.

Poseidon's Curse? I stole a look at the side of the boat and spotted the name painted in swirly curlicue writing. "What sort of a boat is called *Poseidon's Curse*? That's not a very cheerful name."

"Maybe we're not very cheerful people," the sailor said, with a slight curl of his lip. "If I were you, I'd be on my way."

I took a step backwards. There was a definite air of malice in this chap's voice. "Sorry to have taken up your time," I told him.

"Oh, too late." He puffed on his pipe again. "Now you've done it."

"What have I done?" What was this impossibly rude little man talking about? "What do you mean?" I took another step away from him. He arched an eyebrow and nodded over my shoulder.

Spinning round, I spotted a gang of men heading directly for us. As if that wasn't bad enough, I recognised them as the mob from the courthouse a few hours previously.

"Oh dear." I glanced back at the little pipe-sucking sailor. Behind him, the harbour ended. My only options were to try to dodge my way through the encroaching gang of his loutish friends or jump into the sea.

For one moment I considered doing just that. I could swim, after all, but did I really need to get myself wet? I'd ruin my sunhat. At a push, I could take them all, I decided. I slipped my hand inside my bag to grab my wand. It curled reassuringly between my fingers.

I spun around to face them. "Greetings!" I might as well try to bluff my way out of this situation first. "Lovely boat you have here."

"'Tis a ship," the man in the lead told me. He was the largest of the group: round of face, round of belly, with an impressive red beard and long hair, rather like mine, but without the benefit of conditioner and having seen too much sea, sun and salt to my mind.

"It's a ship, is it?" I glanced at *Poseidon's Curse* and, in an act of contrition, nodded.

"Arrrrrr," the gathered throng sang in unison. I reeled slightly away from the onslaught of alcoholic breath. *By the goddess*!

"My apologies." I ducked my head at them. "I was enquiring about chartering a boat—"

"We don't do charters," the big man told me.

"Arrrr!" the others chorused.

"So I gather." I sidestepped around Mr Big Belly Bearded Bloke, trying to politely indicate that I wished to get past them and be on my way.

"Didn't we see you at the court this morning?" one of the other men asked. He was a tall, gangly fellow who would have been lost standing behind a lamppost.

Batpoop! They recognised me! "The court?" I feigned innocence. "Not me."

"Aaar! It was you. You were with the ghost and the guy who runs Roy's Snack Shack."

Oh.

But wait ... "You saw a ghost?" I queried.

"Of course we did. We're not blind!" an old fellow, a toothless wonder, shrilled.

"You were with the murderer," Mr Big Belly Bearded Bloke said.

"Arrrr!" came the chorus. "'Twas 'er, so it was!"

Mr Big Belly Bearded Bloke was obviously the official spokesman. "Who is he to you?" he asked.

I took a breath, thought quickly, and decided the occasion warranted the truth. "He's my fiancé," I admitted, holding my scarred palms up against the torrent of abuse. "We're going to be married next week. But, I should tell you now, he's not a murderer."

"He's a murderer alright," spat the sailor with the pipe.

"No, he isn't—" I glared at him.

Mr Big Belly Bearded Bloke closed in on me. "He murdered our captain, so he did!"

"Arrrr!"

"Dunley Bloodstone was your captain?" That made sense. That's why they'd been at the court this morning, of course.

"Arrrrh!"

"You're mistaken," I told them. "Silvan didn't kill your captain. He was there at the bar right enough, but—"

"We were at the bar too," Mr Big Belly Bearded Bloke told me, and now he was right in my face. I leaned away from him, trying to escape the fumes of hard liquor.

This rowdy mob was the same rowdy mob Lazar had told me about. "Then you must have seen what happened?"

The men looked around uncertainly. There were a couple of non-committal 'aarh's but nothing convincing.

"You didn't see what happened?" I asked.

Mr Big Belly Bearded Bloke pulled himself up to his full height, a rather intimidating seven foot or thereabouts. "We *know* what happened."

"How can you know if you didn't see it?" I argued.

"Because the murder happened outside and your man was outside, not inside, and we found him there holding the captain's cutlass!"

"Let me get this straight," I said. "Captain Bloodstone was killed using his own cutlass?"

"Aaar!"

That was a lie. Silvan had told me that the victim had freed his own cutlass from his belt. "But you didn't see what happened?"

An unusual silence.

"Well, there you have it. Silvan, my fiancé, didn't kill anyone."

"So you say," said Toothless Wonder.

"I do say!" I agreed. "And yes, I'm trying to prove his innocence, but you should be too."

"How do you work that out?" Mr Big Belly Bearded Bloke asked. "He deserves to die!"

"Hang 'im!"

I rolled my eyes. "Simple. If you're interested in the right person receiving justice—"

"Hang 'im high!"

"Aarrh!"

"If *you're* interested in the *right* person receiving justice," I began again, raising my voice, "then surely you would like to have a stake in *finding* that person?"

There were grumbles and some disagreement.

"As far as I'm concerned, we've got someone," a tall whiskery man of my age said.

"Aar." A few murmurs of agreement.

Mr Big Belly Bearded Bloke frowned. "But if it's the wrong person, Smithy, that's not justice."

"I don't care as long as we hang someone," Gangly Man offered.

"A bit of swashbuckling wouldn't go amiss either,"

Toothless Wonder said. "We haven't had any of that for a while."

"Aaar!" The men were more enthusiastic about that, and even Mr Big Belly Bearded Bloke nodded in agreement.

"Look," I said. "I don't think that what I want and what you want are diametrically opposed."

"You what?" Mr Whiskers asked. One or two of the others shook their heads.

"What tongues is she speakin' in?" Gangly Man asked.

"What I'm saying is that you get swashbuckling—whatever that might turn out to be—and adventure *and* the man who actually killed your captain ... and I get my fiancé out of jail so that I can get married."

"What's your plan?" Mr Big Belly Bearded Bloke wanted to know.

"I need to track down the sailor Silvan was meeting the other night," I told them. "He's out at sea somewhere. You could help me do that." I gestured at *Poseidon's Curse*.

"No, no, we couldn't," Toothless Wonder told me.

"Yes you could," I argued. "Why couldn't you?"

"We don't take passengers," Mr Big Belly Bearded Bloke said.

By all that's green! "I don't have to be a passenger," I suggested, striving my hardest not to whine. "I could be a member of the crew!" *Genius*!

The men looked at each other, pulling faces,

picking their teeth, scratching themselves in places where men scratch themselves. For half a second, I really thought I was beginning to get somewhere.

Mr Big Belly Bearded Bloke shook his head. "Impossible."

Dang it! "Impossible? Why?"

Mr Big Belly Bearded Bloke rolled his eyes as though that were the stupidest question anyone had ever asked him. For a moment he looked fifteen again, rather than a mature chap well into his thirties. "We can't take on crew without the captain's say so."

What? I hesitated, but it had to be worth reminding them, right? "But your captain is dead," I said, quietly.

I waited for the look of comprehension to pass over the faces assembled in front of me, but none was forthcoming. "He can't recruit anyone," I emphasised. "He's dead."

Mr Big Belly Bearded Bloke finally seemed to understand. "Then we won't be able to take anyone on," he said, more in surprise than with any malice towards me.

"Aaar," came the chorus, along with a couple of comments such as, "That's a shame, that is."

"It was a good idea for a second, there ..."

"Aar, I thought so too."

The sun and the incredible stupidity of this throng of piratical lightweights had started to give me a headache. I tipped my head back and drained the rest of my water. I needed to stay hydrated or I'd end up as daft as them. Wiping my chin where I'd dribbled, I asked, "Well ... how are you going to recruit a new captain? Can't one of you be the *acting* captain?"

The men shook their heads and shuffled around. "No, no," one of them muttered. "I wouldn't want to be the captain."

"Oooh, no. No. No, no."

"That's not the done thing," said Mr Whiskers.

Gangly Man agreed. "That would be terribly disrespectful."

"What about you?" I asked Mr Big Belly Bearded Bloke. "You seem to be someone the men could follow. Why don't you become the captain?"

He jerked his head back in horror. "Captain Bloodstone never made me second-in-command."

"Did he make anyone second-in-command?" I asked, looking around.

"Wrathful Bob," Toothless Wonder said.

"And which one of you is Wrathful Bob?" I asked, studying the faces that stared back at me.

Mr Big Belly Bearded Bloke shook his head. "He's visiting Davy Jones's Locker."

"Aaaaar." One of the men took off his worn cotton hat and clutched it to his chest. "Rest in pieces, Wrathful Bob."

Pieces? My face must have given me away. "Shark attack." Gangly Man filled in the details. Turns out I didn't really want to hear them.

"This is getting us nowhere," I said, casting around

in my brain for a new plan. These men needed a leader. Chances were, if they didn't find someone who could tell them what to do, they'd be marooned here on *Poseidon's Curse* from now until doomsday. The tides would come in, the tides would go out, and they would forget to eat, drink and wash, until eventually, the ship and the men would sink to the bottom of the harbour and become seafood and bits of sand ...

They needed taking in hand. By someone purposeful and strong.

They needed Captain Alf!

"You have a job vacancy and you need to fill it." I stood to attention. "I would like to apply."

"She wants to apply," Toothless Wonder repeated.

"Pfft." Mr Whiskers wasn't very impressed. "She's a girl."

"I'm a *woman*," I corrected him. "And I bet I can do plenty of things that you can't."

"What, like the washing and cooking?" Mr Whiskers asked.

There were titters.

I whipped out my wand. "I don't cook," I told them. "Unless you count pasta. But let me show you exactly what I *can* do, so there's no mistaking my capabilities." I pushed my way through them and aimed my wand at the pile of lobster traps by their neighbour's boat. I didn't mean any malice, not really.

Maybe a bit.

"*Concitamentum*. Off! Off you go!"

I shot a thin stream of yellow energy towards the tower, and one by one the traps began to topple over the side of the harbour and into the sea. *Sploosh*! went the first one.

And *sploosh*! The second one.

And the third ...

And the fourth.

The Londoner with the expensive deck shoes came running up to his deck. "What the bleedin' Nora is goin' on?"

Sploosh.

Dashing down the gangway, he raced to save the rest of the traps. I increased the intent of my spell and watched with some satisfaction as the rest of them tipped over the side at once with an enormous splash, showering the man's deck shoes in seawater.

Toothless Wonder roared with laughter, so loudly, in fact, that the Londoner turned his attention to us. Seeing me standing there with my wand aimed his way, a look of fear crossed his face, but it was only momentary. Almost straight away he lurched towards us, his eyes burning with fury.

Oopsie.

I had no choice but to 'handle' the situation ...

Handle it in the way that would best serve my immediate needs, that is. "*Concitamentum*!" I repeated. "Bye!"

The man with the expensive deck shoes stopped dead in his tracks, flailed his arms, then began stumbling backwards. Back to the edge of the harbour and then, with a shriek, tumbled away and out of sight.

This time the wall of water that splashed up was higher than ever.

The sailors fell about laughing, clasping their sides and slapping each other on the back. Evidently, any person falling on hard times would prove amusing to them.

"So what do you reckon?" I asked Mr Big Belly Bearded Bloke. "Can I apply?"

"No, no." He shook his head, face completely solemn.

"But—" I began to bluster. What more did I have to do?

"This isn't the Royal Navy, Mrs-nobody-who-would-be-a-Captain." Mr Big Belly Bearded Bloke made a grab for the sword he kept at his waist. "We're pirates!"

"Aaaarh!" The men took up their weapons, a motley collection of daggers and knives, a cutlass and ... was that *a potato peeler*?

"We don't recruit *anyone*." Mr Big Belly Bearded Bloke waved his sword in the air. "No-one at all!"

"Then how do you add new members to your crew?" I asked, keeping a wary eye on where the men were pointing their implements.

"We press-gang them!" Mr Big Belly Bearded Bloke roared.

The pirates bellowed back their response. "Aaaarh!"

"They press-gang people," I grumbled into my thali. I'd left the pirates and *Poseidon's Curse* in despair and returned to The Monkey Nuts, glaring at Expensive Deck Shoe Man and Instagram-worthy Australian Couple—still bickering—in turn as I passed them. "Who, in the goddess's name, press-gangs people in this day and age? It's like the past two hundred years never happened."

Now, sitting on a bench at a wooden table beneath the shade of an enormous parasol, monkeys chattering nearby, parakeets and other exotic feathered beasties twittering and singing in the trees, I was simultaneously in limbo and heaven. The thali, a sensational treat for the stomach, was spread out on a sizable banana leaf in front of me and contained a variety of beautifully spiced vegetarian mini-dishes in little silver pots, a pile of fragrant rice, a heap of chapatis, two baby bananas and a portion of melon. Never a melon fan, I threw those chunks towards some monkeys playing beneath a nearby coconut palm. "You've got more hope of getting on a boat than I have," I told them.

Maybe I should turn myself into a ship's monkey. I considered the ins and outs of this plan, all the while scooping up lentil dahl and aubergine curry with a chapati, before deciding it wouldn't be a good idea. What if someone put a collar and lead on me and I ended up being sold to a man with an organ grinder?

No.

What about becoming a rat, then?

Mmm. No.

The bartender brought me a fresh one-litre bottle of water. I'd been perspiring so much, I think I'd lost all the liquid from the first one I'd ordered. In any case, I was thirstier than a home printer that's run out of ink. "No Lazar today?" I asked him.

"Lazar not work here anymore," the new boy told me.

"He lost his job?"

"He go away."

How convenient. The only person I'd found so far who could tell the chief of police what he'd overheard had mysteriously disappeared.

"You want beer?" the new bartender asked me. "Cobra?"

I considered my options. What did I intend to do this afternoon? I was fresh out of ideas. I could pay a visit to Roy, see if he had any further suggestions. Maybe track down Silvan's lawyer. He'd be thrilled to hear from me so soon, I was sure.

I could go back to the resort and consult with Gwyn.

Or I could have a beer.

Twist my arm. "Yes, please. If you have a cold

one?" I asked. He nodded and disappeared while I stared out at the dazzling ocean. Little shimmering sparkles danced on top of the waves, and I itched to take a swim.

But when my thoughts recalled Wrathful Bob's sticky end, I decided that might not be such a good idea either.

The bartender brought out a large bottle of Cobra beer with a chunk of lime squeezed into the neck. Condensation dribbled down the side of the bottle, and my mouth watered along with it. "Thanks." I smiled and pushed the lime inside. I toasted the ocean and the rest of my thali before drinking down half of the contents. So cool. So refreshing.

By the time I'd finished that bottle, and a second, and my thali, I was feeling pleasantly tipsy.

That feeling—well, the tipsiness aspect of it—seemed to increase rather than decrease the longer I remained seated at the bench. The sun's rays were relentless, even through the parasol, and the day was getting hotter. I really wanted to speak to Roy again before heading back to the resort, so I needed to get a move on, but after paying my bill, fumbling badly with the filthy notes in a currency I was largely unfamiliar with, I stood up and to my astonishment found myself feeling decidedly wobbly.

"What's in that Cobra?" I giggled to myself. "What proof is it?" I picked up the empty bottle, trying to concentrate on the writing, but my eyes were wonky and unfocused. "Or maybe it's me. Maybe I can't hold my beer anymore."

I chortled happily to myself, lurching away from the bar's garden and down towards the shore. "So pretty," I sang. "Sooooooooo pretty. Very, very pretty!"

For some reason, I now decided that a paddle in the shadows seemed like a really good idea. I could cool my feet and play spot-the-minnow ... but as I leaned over to unbuckle my sandals, something clunked me on the top of my head.

"Owwww!" I yelped in annoyance and clamped a hand to my crown. Turning about, I found myself face to face with Mr Big Belly Bearded Bloke clutching an aluminium frying pan. "What did you do?" I asked him, but the words died in my mouth as the strength left my knees.

"Stand by, lads!" called Mr Big Belly Bearded Bloke.

"Timber!" added Mr Whiskers.

And then I knew no more.

Chapter Ten

"Pieces of hate!"

"Eurgh." I turned on my side and instantly regretted it. A wave of nausea threatened to overwhelm me. "Why did I drink so much?" What a stupid thing to do. I hated hangovers. I was getting far too old for them. Except ... *how could I possibly have a hangover after only two beers?*

"Pieces of hate!"

Wait a cotton-picking minute!

I allowed my eyes to flicker open, blinking into the light. The room *was* swaying, but not because of the alcohol I'd imbibed. It was swaying because I was on a ship.

"Pieces of hate!" A brightly coloured parrot, sitting on a perch at the foot of my bunk, regarded me with a beady eye. *Squuaaaaawk*! "Pieces of hate!"

"By all that's green!" I sat up. Too quickly. The contents of my stomach demanded to be expelled. As luck would have it, there was a large basin fortuitously positioned on a wooden cabinet close to the bed, with a jug of water next to it. I made an emergency dash, and …

We'll draw a veil over that.

I used the water in the jug, surprisingly cool, to wash my face and swill my mouth before turning my attention to my surroundings.

"They press-ganged me," I complained. "I don't believe it. They actually pressed me into service."

The parrot kept a close eye on me as I stumbled around the room. I had a headache, probably from being tapped on the bonce, and my stomach rolled. "Maybe I don't have my sea legs yet." Lurching over to the window, I stared out in despair.

Miles and miles of blue ocean. The sun had dropped. I estimated it to be about four in the afternoon. Where were we going? What were the pirates going to do to me?

"The goddess help me," I mumbled, rubbing my head. This wasn't a hangover. I had a feeling that somebody had put something in my drink.

"Pieces of hate!"

"Do you mind?" I asked. The parrot's squawk was going right through me.

"Pieces of hate!"

"Yeah, yeah, I get it."

I stumbled towards the door. It occurred to me that at least I wasn't shackled or tied up, but that didn't mean that the door wouldn't be barred and bolted.

Except it wasn't. The knob turned easily in my hand, and the narrow, squashed-down door opened outwards.

Not locked? Okay. But they'll have stolen all my stuff ... my wand ... my phone ...

I couldn't help but feel suspicious and yanked the door closed again, huddling in the safety of the cabin to give myself thinking time. My bag, hanging on a hook behind the door, bobbed in front of my face.

Oh!

Well, yeah.

Not locked in and they hadn't stolen anything.

My purse was safely stowed inside my bag along with my wand, my suntan lotion and my sunglasses. There was no sign of my sunhat, but perhaps I'd left that at The Monkey Nuts. My memory was addled when it came to those last few minutes.

So I wasn't tied up, and nothing had been pinched. I hadn't been harmed, apart from the bump on the back of my head.

But there was the small issue of being drugged. I was convinced I had been. Two bottles of beer, even on a hot day when I was feeling a little dehydrated, would not normally have done that to me. I swung my bag over my head and pushed the door open once more. This time I marched out, ready to give the pirates a piece of my mind.

"Pieces of hate!" the parrot squawked after me before the door slammed closed behind me.

I found myself high up on a bit of deck, slightly higher up than a medium deck, which was higher up than ... the lowest deck. *Hmmm.* And at the back of the ship. There were probably technical terms for these decks. Proop? Poop? Fore? Aft? But I had no idea what they were. Let's just say that this deck was the highest deck and that I was queen of the castle. Above my eyeline were the big timbery things that held up the rigging and ... stuff. Ooh! A crow's nest. Yes, I knew what one of those was. Below me, the big main deck appeared to be decorated with cannons, and to the front of the ship was another raised area—surely the forward deck?—and the ship's wheel and ... more shippy-type stuff.

I marched across my little bit of deck and navigated—with some difficulty because I realised I only had one sandal on—my way down a ladder, fixed against the side of whatever structure was below my cabin. Halfway down, I heard someone whistle, then cry, "Captain on deck!"

I paused where I was and turned my head in surprise.

The pirates were gathering below me. I spotted Toothless Wonder goggling up at me, and a few of the other younger sailors giggling. Even Mr Big Belly Bearded Bloke seemed to be blushing. I realised with horror that they could all see up my skirt.

"By all that's green," I mumbled and hurried the rest of the way down to the main deck.

"Captain Alf, sir!" Mr Big Belly Bearded Bloke greeted me.

"Aaaar!" the other men chorused, some of them without much enthusiasm.

I regarded them all with some confusion.

"You're not leaving already, are you, sir?" Gangly Man asked me.

"How can I leave?" I started to argue. Weren't we miles out to sea? I pointed at miles and miles of blue ocean.

Mr Big Belly Bearded Bloke glanced to his right. When I followed his gaze I realised, much to my mortification, that just below my eyeline was the harbour.

Of Dakti Bhoin.

We hadn't actually sailed anywhere yet. The natural movement of the ship on the water, even while moored, was making me feel seasick. The fact that we hadn't set sail made perfect sense when I thought about it, because there was no way, Jose, that these sailors would ever venture anywhere without a captain giving them orders first.

"Ohhhhh." I felt like an idiot, but there was still the question of the bang on the head and the drugs.

I wiggled a finger at Mr Big Belly Bearded Bloke. "You press-ganged me."

He nodded and jerked his head sideways. "We thought that was what you wanted, Captain!"

"You didn't have to use violence!" I complained.

"I've got a bump! Look!" I moved closer to him. "Feel that!"

He twitched, then reluctantly held out a hand, his fingers as fat as pork sausages, and gently stroked the top of my head. "That's a good'n," he said, proudly. "It would've been even better if I could have located the iron skillet, but unfortunately I think our last cook ran off with that."

"Thank the goddess for small mercies," I told him. "You might have killed me."

"We usually stop short of that, Captain," Toothless Wonder told me.

"Aaarh!" the men chorused.

Right.

"And there's the small matter of the drugs."

A couple of dozen blank faces stared back at me. "Whatever it was you put in my drink," I reminded them.

A smattering of bemused expressions. Several shakes of the head. Someone asked his neighbour, "Do you think we backed the wrong horse here?"

Mr Big Belly Bearded Bloke puffed out his chest. "We don't dabble with drugs," he said. "Unless you include rum ..."

"AARRR!" The biggest cheer so far.

"I quite like a drop of rum," I said.

"Fetch the captain a ration of rum, Half-Crocked," Mr Big Belly Bearded Bloke told Toothless Wonder, and the little man ran towards a barrel close by. He opened the lid and dipped a ladle into it before scurrying back to me with a small ruby glass full of deep amber liquid.

Wow. I didn't need to bring the glass anywhere near my nose before the smell hit me. My stomach rolled over again.

Mr Big Belly Bearded Bloke leaned in close to my ear. "'Tis mighty good for seasickness, Captain," he whispered.

It was that obvious, was it?

"Somebody spiked my drink," I told him. "That's why I'm sick."

"Rest assured it wasn't us, Captain," he said. "We would never do such a thing. We're honourable scallywags, we are."

"Aaaarh!"

I smiled at the dichotomy of honourable scallywags. "What's your name, sailor?" I couldn't call him Mr Big Belly Bearded Bloke forever, could I? It just wasn't polite.

"Sarn't Michael Morello, ex-Royal Navy at your service, Captain."

"Sergeant Morello."

"I'm better known as The Butcher!"

"Aaarh!"

"How charming," I said.

"You can call me Butcher, Captain!"

I nodded. "Butcher. Okay. Pleased to meet you."

"And this here is Wilfred Noonan." Butcher introduced me to Gangly Man. "But you can call him Scurvy."

I forced a smile and shook the man's hand. "Hello, Scurvy."

"He's the temporary cook," Butcher explained.

I shuddered. Who needed a cook named Scurvy? "What happened to the permanent cook?" I asked. "Please don't tell me he became shark fodder too?"

"Ah, no." Butcher managed to look regretful. "He poisoned himself. Turned out he had a seafood allergy."

"Goodness gracious." I made a mental note to order takeaway.

Half-Crocked, or Toothless Wonder, was in charge of rations. Mr Whisker was Uther 'Smithy' Smith and was the ship's carpenter. In rapid succession I was introduced to and shook hands with Voodoo and Zulu —twins from Newcastle-upon-Tyne who looked incredibly alike and whose names were actually Algernon and Reginald—as well as Smelly, Quarter, Sausage, Doubloon, Blunderbuss, Swab, Beagle and others whose names escaped me.

"Phew," I said at the end of all that. "It'll take me some time to remember everyone."

"You'll get the hang of it soon enough," Butcher told me. "I can remind you in the meantime."

"That's very helpful," I said, touched that he was so understanding. "So, how about we all have a cup of tea and a biscuit now? It would help to settle my stomach."

The pirates conferred among themselves.

"See, sir, if I may," Half-Crocked said, wringing his hands and grimacing up at me, "we don't 'ave no tea, and I'm not sure you'll be wanting our biscuits."

"Not want your biscuits?" How foolish could one sailor be? "Of course I want your biscuits."

Half-Crocked curled a lip and glanced at Butcher. The big man shrugged. "Very well," Toothless Wonder muttered and hopped away. He returned quickly with a handful of biscuits in his grubby mitt. He could have at least arranged them on a plate for me.

"Thanks." I took them from him and stared down. Four rectangular oaty-type biscuits. Or at least they were pale with flecks in that might have been oats. Rock hard but not rock cakes. Something tickled my palm and I turned the pile over. A little face stared up at me. I shrieked and threw them over the side. "Maggots!"

Butcher grinned at me.

"Welcome aboard, Captain Alf!"

Chapter Eleven

"This 'ere? 'Tis the captain's quarters, Captain Alf," Butcher told me, "as recently vacated by Captain Bloodstone." He'd led me back up the ladder —me desperately trying to gather the voluminous skirt of my beloved summer dress around me so that nobody could get another peep at my pants—to properly show me around my new quarters.

"They're lovely," I said. "A little small perhaps—"

"With all due respect, sir," Butcher said, "these two rooms are larger than the quarters I share with Half-Crocked, Smithy and Scurvy. The rest of the men take it in turns to sleep in hammocks below the waist deck."

"Oh, my apologies." I ate my words. Which one was the waist deck?

With the doors open and the window shutters on both sides pulled back, I could see how cramped and untidy the space really was. This first room served as a bedroom-come-bathroom, with a cunningly hidden water closet that opened out to the sea. An intriguing idea. There were several wardrobes in here, chock full of clothes and maps, books and odd items that begged to be explored.

Through the rear of the room, another of those small cramped narrow doors opened into an oak-panelled room that might more properly have been called a library. There was a map table here, a beautiful old globe in an enormous wooden frame, and several comfortable armchairs. It smelled of pipe tobacco and spiced rum and testosterone.

In fact, it stank.

"Do we have any room spray?" I asked. "Lavender, maybe? Bergamot is my favourite."

Butcher shook his head.

"Shame," I said. "But I suppose I can clean it up—"

"I wouldn't do that if I were you, sir," Butcher warned me.

I frowned. "Why not?"

"We're pirates, sir. The men don't want anything too namby-pamby."

"I'll tidy it when they're not watching," I suggested. "I'm not looking to re-cover the upholstery in chintz." *I'm not Florence, after all.*

"There's always someone watching," Butcher ventured, and I took that to mean him. "What I ought to say, begging your pardon, Captain Alf, is that I had to persuade the men that having a girl captain—"

"Woman," I reminded him.

"Female," he said. "I had to persuade the lads that

having a female of the species as a captain would be a good idea. If it turns out ... if they imagine ... Well, sir, if they think you're soft, there'll be consequences."

He let that word hang in the air. Con-se-quen-ces.

I chewed on my lip for a moment, thinking. "Point taken."

"I have every confidence in you and your knowledge. I'm sure you'll lead us all on some fantastic adventures," Butcher said.

My knowledge? What knowledge? Oh, now I was in trouble. "I definitely will," I lied. "Adventure is my middle name." Following 'trouble' and before 'didn't-see-that-coming'.

"Excellent. Shall we cast off, Captain?"

Cast off? For a moment I thought we were going to start knitting, but then I remembered that casting off was a phrase used to untie boats from the side of the harbour. Wasn't it? "Erm ..." I hesitated. "What, already?"

"No time like the present, Captain. We want to catch good tides."

"Of course we do. Of course we do." *Oh, cripes.* Now that it came down to it and I was actually going to be able to get out there and scour the ocean for Salty Dog, I was having quibbles. I had to think quickly. "What about ... provisions? I can't eat maggoty biscuits for days on end."

"The maggots are a good source of protein," Butcher argued, "but I understand where you're coming from. I suggest we call in at Kandla tomorrow and restock, Captain. You can check what we have in the coffers and we'll buy what we need for your first voyage."

My maiden voyage, in fact, but probably best not to tell him that.

Butcher continued, "You'll find Captain Bloodstone's strongbox under the bed. There should be enough to tide us over for a while."

"What about hiring—sorry, press-ganging—a new cook?" I asked. "Someone who can actually ... you know ... cook?" It turned out Scurvy had baked those biscuits himself and had already started preparing the supper. I wasn't holding my breath for a decent meal anytime soon with him at the helm.

Hey! At the helm! Wasn't that a boating term? I was getting the hang of this!

"We could look into that tomorrow too," Butcher agreed. "I wouldn't bother here in Dakti Bhoin. We won't find anyone here."

"We won't?"

"Nah. This is where we picked up Scurvy. Must be a decade or so ago now."

I sighed, out of options. "Well then, in that case, anchors aweigh, eh?"

"Arrrh, Captain Alf!" Butcher pumped the air with his fist. "Let's go!"

I had a little time before dinner to explore. Seeing as I was now a captain of a vessel I knew nothing about, I decided it was incumbent upon me to see how the land lay. Or how the boat at sea lay. Or something.

I can't say I was overly impressed by what I found. The main deck wasn't too bad, although there were so many ropes coiled and flung into the corners that parts of the ship looked like a viper's nest. The rum was stored in sizable barrels here too. I took a particular interest in them. When I bought rum for the bar at Whittle Inn, I bought in bottles, not barrels. The provenance of these barrels suggested the Caribbean, which was fair enough—that's where all good rum comes from—but there was no suggestion of what proof it might be.

It could have been gasoline with a bit of added sugar for all I knew.

My next stop was the galley. Of course, I'd heard of galley kitchens, and when I'd been living with flatmates in London, I'd even shared what the estate agent had referred to as a 'galley' kitchenette but was actually a cupboard with a stove and a sink.

But this was a true galley. There was hardly room for two people to pass unless they were pipe cleaners in disguise. One side of the galley resembled a farmhouse, with all the shelves, and pots and pans swinging from hooks. There were cupboards along the bottom with ingenious clasp devices to keep them closed, and a limited workspace on which to prep food. Lanterns swung above my head to illuminate the work area, while strings of garlic and sprigs of dried herbs clawed at my hair.

I could chop onions here—if I was so inclined, but I wasn't in a rush to volunteer my services anytime soon—then simply turn about and fry them on the stove. Genius.

A few steps down and I was in what passed as the officers' mess.

And mess it certainly was.

The tiny room had a circular table and eight rickety wooden chairs, all of them mismatched. It appeared to me as though a banquet had been held in the middle of a storm because the walls were stained with food, much of which you could have scraped off with a fork and identified. Some half-hearted attempt had been made to clean the floor, but really, the mess had simply been redistributed to the corners.

My poor stomach, still not particularly happy, rolled around in complaint.

I swallowed hard, climbed back into the galley and sought out something else to scrutinise.

The crew's quarters were on the deck below. Once again I had to navigate a ladder to access it. What was with these shipbuilders and their ladders? Why not build a nice staircase?

There were few refinements at all down here. The place was airless, the only light coming in through some round portholes above my head. The timbers creaked more noticeably down here too, and I cast a wary eye about searching for leaks.

Nothing to see, thank the goddess.

However, there were sailors in various stages of undress, so I had to avert my eyes a few times. I was surprised there were quite so many sailors down here doing nothing, but perhaps they worked in shifts. I couldn't imagine a pirate ship would pull up for the night to allow everyone some uninterrupted shut-eye. That wouldn't be particularly bad-ass, would it? Several of the men were asleep in hammocks, others were playing cards; one or two were reading books.

But, phew. It was stinky. Lots of unaired bedding, soiled clothing and unwashed men.

"May I ask where the bathrooms are?" I asked one man, who glanced up from his *Piratyrannical News Monthly* as I wandered past him.

"Bathrooms?" he growled. "Bathrooms are for land-lubbers!"

That would explain it then.

Another ladder took me down into the hold. There were some stores down here, recognisable by the labels on their barrels, but not a huge volume of anything. There was also a variety of odd things that really had no place on a ship at all. A nineteen-twenties Rolls Royce, for starters! An early Edwardian camera on a tripod. A massive wax model of a pirate, complete with hook and eyepatch, carrying a sign that said:

Summer Opening Hours

Monday to Saturday 10 am – 8 pm

Sunday 11 am – 6 pm

Hmmm. Thieved from some attraction somewhere, no doubt.

The most disturbing aspect of the hold was the evidence of rat activity, including items that had been chewed up. Little holes where you wouldn't rightly expect any. I even heard noises coming from a barrel of flour. I didn't bother to pull off the lid and have a look.

Down here, the stench alone was enough to make me gag.

Hmmm. Something was missing ... I slowly turned about, trying to identify what it could be.

It didn't take long. A definite absence of treasure. What sort of pirates were these?

And how the devil had they managed to stay alive this long? They didn't have a decent chef, and the food supplies were rank.

There was no way I'd survive aboard *Poseidon's Curse* unless things improved.

But with me—*me*!—as Captain, I couldn't genuinely see that happening.

Could you?

I was right about dinner. It was an inedible stew. It had meat in it, which might have been chicken but might just as easily have been rat or frog. Whatever it was, it both tasted and felt like shoe leather. There were vegetables, which would normally be great, but the whole thing was both burned and yet sloppy. How it was possible to be both, I had no idea.

The 'officers'—me, Butcher, Smithy Whiskers and Half-Crocked—were served separately to the 'men' in the mess just off the galley. We had the table and chairs and proper silverware, plates, bowls and glasses. Nothing matched, but that didn't seem to matter. Given the way the ship yawed from one side to another, which I found most disconcerting even in the mild swell we were experiencing, I was surprised they had anything breakable left at all. Above our heads, lanterns swung freely. I'd already realised that in a ship, you have perpetual motion. The sea moves. The horizon shifts. Everything around you that isn't nailed down wobbles, slides, or waves at you. Sails flap. Ropes jerk around. Men are constantly on the move.

I badly needed a lie-down.

The 'men'—lower ranks—ate their food either on deck—the big deck—or below deck where their hammocks were. The officers had the pick of what fare there was, and let's be honest here, it wasn't great fare, it wasn't even fair fare, and the men divvied out the rest. Which seemed *un*fair. They were the ones doing the bulk of the work, after all.

I toyed with my stew, keeping a sharp eye out for anything that might have been doing the breaststroke in it. My stomach hadn't really settled, although

Butcher had been right, the rum did help. Eventually, I gave up and opted for an orange and a couple of bananas that had been bought at Dakti Bhoin's market and were therefore fresh and unmaggoty.

After dinner, Smithy, AKA Smithy Whiskers, Half-Crocked, Butcher and me remained at the table chatting. Or rather, the men chatted. I cradled another ration of rum, twisting the little glass around to catch the crystal colour of the liquid, thinking about Silvan and how I could find Salty Dog and his boat, *Seawolf*. It would be like searching for a needle in a haystack.

But ... people would know of him, wouldn't they? Silvan hadn't happened upon him by chance. Salty Dog had a reputation. Stopping at a busy harbour would enable me to ask around.

Or get the men to do it. That might elicit less attention.

That's a plan! "I think I might retire for the night," I said, and necked the remains of my rum.

"Ar, Cap'n!" Butcher said. "And what time shall I rouse 'e?"

"Rouse me?" I considered this carefully. I needed some sleep, but it wouldn't do for me to sleep for too long. I needed to set an example. Would seven be early enough? It gave me a lie-in and—

"For your watch, sir." Butcher waited, his expression full of expectation.

"Watch?" I glanced at my wrist. I wasn't wearing one.

"We do four-hour watches, sir," Butcher explained. "Everyone takes it in turns."

Oops. That kind of watch. But ... surely he was joking? "I'm the captain," I spluttered.

Smithy Whiskers began to fidget in his seat, flicking his eyes at Half-Crocked.

"Everyone takes it in turns," Butcher repeated.

I could tell there was no getting away with it, so I nodded and pushed my chair back. It wasn't quite eight yet. Rather than an early night, I'd have to have a lie-in instead. "No time like the present!" I breezed.

Smithy nodded in approval, then he and Half-Crocked relaxed again with another ration of rum.

I followed Butcher out into the night. In the distance, to the left of me, I could see lights at water level: perhaps that was Naarangi, perhaps it was some other island. I had no awareness of what speed we were doing, but it didn't seem particularly fast. There were a couple of sails up, but the night was largely windless so we weren't zooming anywhere. The ship bobbed gently on what swell there was, probably hardly noticeable for those who were used to such things, but I had the sensation that one leg was longer than the other. Even more peculiarly, the longer leg kept swapping sides. It took all my brain power to prevent myself from giving in and just lying on the deck, allowing myself to wallow and roll around as the ship tipped from left to right.

"So, what am I watching?" I asked as Butcher led

me up to the foredeck where Gangly Man—or Scurvy as I now needed to call him—had his hands on the wheel. "Because there really isn't a lot to see, is there?" I tipped my head back. Nothing to see apart from the big, beautiful sky and a zillion stars and planets winking down at me. "Woah!" I caught my breath. "A shooting star! Did you see that?"

"You'll catch plenty of those, I dare say," Butcher replied, "but Cap'n, you have to keep your eyes peeled—"

"Peeled like a banana," I agreed. Possibly—and I hesitate to admit this—two shots of rum on top of the spiked Cobra beers were too much for me in one day.

"—for dangers to the ship," Butcher finished.

"Such as?" I wanted to know. What was going to harm us out here on a gloriously calm night like this one?

"Other ships. Pods of dolphins. Whales. Coral reefs. Icebergs—"

"Icebergs?" Now I knew he was jesting. "Not in the Indian Ocean, surely. Although ... what with the climate emergency and one thing and another ..."

"If you see anything at all, you ring the ship's bell." Butcher pointed at the chunky brass bell hanging close by. "You'll see Arr Jim Lad up in the crow's nest." I followed his gaze all the way up one of the large timber uprights to see a small basket at the top with a human shape tucked inside. The human shape—Arr Jim Lad, in fact—waved down at me. I waved back enthusiastically.

"If you need anything, I'll be in my cabin. Send for me," Butcher told me and began to retreat.

"Just one thing," I said before he could disappear. "You don't need me to go up there, do you?" I pointed up to where Arr Jim Lad was. "Because I can do heights, but I'm not sure how good I am at shimmying up timbers."

"Masts," Butcher corrected me.

D'oh! Masts! Of course that was what they were called. This was turning into a steep learning curve!

"You won't need to go up there unless we demote you," Butcher told me.

"Ah." I could hear the threat in his voice. Perhaps he'd benefit from a nap. "I'll see you in a few hours."

That left Scurvy and me in charge. *Ohmigerd*!

Scurvy nodded at me. "Cap'n," he said, reaching to his side then handing me a brass telescope. I examined it, working out which end was which, before dutifully taking up my station next to Scurvy and pressing the telescope to my eye, still unsure what I was expected to watch out for given it was full dark. Surprisingly though, because lanterns had been lit and hung around the sides of the boat, the illumination carried a long distance. Added to that, I could make out the shadow of land and the lights from the nearby island. There were one or two other boats about too. I studied those for a while, fascinated to see them gliding around. Several yachts headed inland, travelling at impressive speeds even in the dark, but they all had to slow as they approached land. I supposed there were maritime rules about such things ...

And there would be rocks around the coast ...

Further out to sea, there was less to interest me, but as *Poseidon's Curse* moved beneath my feet and I gradually found a bit of a rhythm to it, I became intensely aware of how fragile she must be, made of wood in a world cast from granite which had then been filled with infinite tonnes of water. It really wouldn't do to crash into anything harder than us.

Hmmm.

"Are there any lifeboats?" I asked Scurvy.

"What's one of them?" he asked.

That answered *that* question but I persevered. "Nothing to, you know, float away on if the ship is in danger of sinking?"

"*Poseidon's Curse* will never sink, Cap'n!" Scurvy roared.

"That's good news." I didn't share his certainty. The whole boat-ship-floating-whatever-it-was thing appeared to be held together with chewing gum and safety pins to my uninitiated eye.

"There's a rowin' boat." Scurvy pointed into the shadows on the bottom deck.

I couldn't see anything, but assumed it had been placed under canvas for protection. "*One* rowing boat? Great!"

"It's not for the likes of you." Scurvy folded his arms, his eyes gleaming with mischief.

"It's not?

"No. See, thing is, Cap'n Alf, if *Poseidon's Curse* goes down, you'll 'ave to go down with 'er."

Over my dead witchy body. "Why?"

"That's what captains do. It's what they *always* do."

I stared at him incredulously. *Time to change the rule books*, dear Scurvy, I thought. This is one witch that no-one gets to drown.

The four hours passed uneventfully. I took my responsibility seriously, moving around from one part of the forecastle—as Scurvy referred to it when I mentioned how much I liked the balustrade—to the other. Sometimes left, sometimes right, sometimes at the front, always straining my eyes into the night, hearing the snap of ropes and sails, the soft creaking of the timbers and the chink of lanterns and bells, the low whistles of the sailors and their occasional muted conversation.

There was something extremely calming about those four hours, alone with my thoughts, watching the world around me, with nothing of modern society intruding on us.

When Butcher reappeared, I was glad to see him,

but only because it had started to turn a little chilly. My lovely green dress was perfect for visiting a courthouse or sitting by the beach and drinking beers, but captaining a ship in the middle of the night probably called for something somewhat more robust.

"I'll take Middle Watch, Cap'n," he announced. "Perhaps you'd be so kind as to do Morning Watch?"

"Of course," I said, stretching. That wouldn't be too bad. A few more relaxing hours of solitude after breakfast. "What time's that? Eight till twelve?"

"Four till eight, sir. See you in a few hours."

"Pieces of hate," the parrot squawked as I entered my cabin. "Pieces of hate."

I realised I hadn't paid much attention to him so far, but I'd inherited Captain Bloodstone's cabin, and by default, his parrot as well. "Do you say anything else?" I asked.

"Who's a pretty boy!"

"Very parrotty," I said. Just what I'd expect. I took a seat on the edge of the bed so we were at the same eye level. "But you *are* a pretty boy."

The parrot squawked and raised its wings and head feathers so I could see all the glorious colours in its plumage, the yellow and green with hints of blue and red. "Very pretty."

"You're a pretty girl," it parroted back at me.

I smiled, wiping my dusty face with the palm of my hand, not feeling particularly pretty. "Do you have a name?"

"Pete."

"Pete?"

"Peter Parrot, Pride of Poseidon."

I laughed. "Now that's an impressive name, my friend. I'm Alfhild. Alf to my friends."

"Captain Alf!"

"Yeah, Captain Alf. I don't feel like a proper captain," I said. "I don't look like one, that's for sure. Some of the sailors probably don't think I should be the captain, and they're right, of course ..." I rambled away, the way I would have done had Pete been Mr Hoo, not knowing whether the parrot was following or not. "I don't speak enough piratey lingo. I don't know my port from my starboard. I can't abide the cooking. Every time I climb a ladder the whole world can see my knickers ..."

My eye fell on the wardrobes where Captain Bloodstone had stored his worldly goods. By rights, I should've been boxing the whole lot up and sending them to his family. If he had one. Jumping up, I pulled the door nearest to me open. A load of stuff tumbled out and landed on my feet. This was worse than my wardrobe back home. At least there, Florence occasionally picked up after me and hung everything nicely. Here, all the hangers were empty and the captain's clothes were piled high in a heap. I rummaged around, picking out a large cream blouse—with only a few stains on it—and pair of worn black breeches. Captain Bloodstone had been a big man, and these would be baggy on me, but it did mean I wouldn't have to bother with my poor dress in the morning. I'm not sure it could stand more punishment, anyway.

Thrilled with my spoils, I stood up rather too quickly and, with all the comic timing I was renowned for, elbowed the wardrobe door hard with my funny bone. Before I could start to groan with painful laughter, the door sprang back and hit me on the side of my face, a hook jabbing me in my eye.

"*OWWW!*" I shrieked in protest, as though the injury had been done to me rather than me doing it to myself. "Ow. Ow. Ow. Ow." Clamping a hand to my eye, I realised it had already started to weep. For a moment I thought it must be bleeding and started to panic, but when I drew my hand away, I only found salty tears. Squinting, I flailed about, seeking the jug of water, and quickly decanted some into the bowl so I could bathe my face. That soothed the eye somewhat and, having dried it on my dress—I'm really not sure anything else in the cabin was clean enough—at that stage I decided it would probably be best to call it a night.

"Goodnight," squawked Pete as I tentatively lay down on the bunk. "Goodnight."

"Goodnight, Pete," I murmured. "Wake me up when they're serving toast."

"Toast! Toast!"

Imagining I'd never be able to sleep, I had to jam the pillow over my head to drown out Pete's chatting. As luck would have it, I didn't need any rocking, although this was an unfortunate turn of phrase given the movement of the ship.

I was asleep in moments.

It seemed as though I was woken almost immediately by a banging on the door. "Cap'n?" Butcher called out to me. "Cap'n? Are you decent?"

I sat up stiffly, muscles aching, and shivering. The night had turned cold and I hadn't bothered to cover myself in a blanket before I fell asleep, mainly because I was wary of bed bugs.

I became aware that my right cheek was wet and I couldn't open my eye. I tapped it gingerly, feeling the puffiness there. *Great …*

"Cap'n?"

"Yes," I called back, my voice hoarse. "I'm decent."

The door opened and Butcher stomped in. "It's time for Morning Watch. I've been trying to wake you for ages."

"I had my head under a pillow," I explained.

"What have you done to your eye?" he asked.

I pretended to be unconcerned. "A bit of an accident. Nothing to worry about."

"Aar."

"What's the matter? Has something happened?" I asked.

"No, Cap'n. It's been a quiet night."

"Oh, good." *What chance a cup of tea?* I wondered as I stumbled over to the forecastle, before remembering there was none on board. I needed to make buying tea a priority when we hit land. "It's still night." I moaned, stifling a yawn.

"'Tis just after four, Cap'n, and it's your watch."

I pouted. "I know. I know!"

"You need to do two per night, sir."

"I know! But ... but ..." *Absurd.* "When do I sleep?"

"You have four hours, Cap'n. That's pretty decent to my reckoning."

Is that so? "How long till we make land?" I asked, following Butcher as he left the cabin.

"Should be there around ten, Cap'n."

Ten. If I did four hours' watch now, I could grab another couple of hours of shut-eye immediately afterwards.

Butcher waited for me to climb down the ladder. I still hadn't had time to change out of my dress, which was a nuisance, and doing everything barefoot was a pain in the proverbial. The weather was definitely cooler out here on the ocean. My toes were cold!

"I don't suppose there's any chance of a hot drink, is there?" I asked, wrapping my arms around myself. "And some socks?"

"If I were you I'd provide your own socks, sir, but Scurvy will serve your breakfast at eight, and then I've arranged muster so you can inspect the crew at nine before we all go ashore."

Nooooo! There went my nap.

"Too kind, thank you," I said. "What do you normally have for breakfast?"

"Porridge, Cap'n."

Ugh. My worst nightmare. "It doesn't have weebles in it, does it?"

"Weevils, Cap'n," Butcher corrected me, pointing up the ladder that led back to the foredeck. "And probably. They're the same oats he uses to bake the biscuits."

I didn't bother with breakfast. I spent the time in the captain's cabin, trying on Captain Bloodstone's boots. They were all far too big, so I had to continue to go barefoot.

At nine I went out, clad in the black breeches and the big cream shirt, tied at the waist with a length of frayed rope that I'd found lying around. I knew I looked a sight, what with my eye swollen shut and weeping, and my hair a bushy, unkempt mess. But what could I do?

And my personal observation concurred with the crew's. "What does she look like?" I heard one of them whisper.

That was rich, coming from this lot.

Every sailor, with the exception of Arr Jim Lad and Scurvy at the helm, was standing to attention on the main deck. I say 'attention'. They were upright. Let's leave it at that. A more obvious shambles of manhood I had never seen.

Dismally, I surveyed them all. No wonder they were pirates. Who else would want them? I filed between their ranks, noting the shabby clothing, the number of men without boots, the emaciated bodies, the bad skin, the lack of teeth.

The stink of them.

Returning to the front, they stared up at me, one or two twitching with the discomfort of standing still for any length of time. "I won't keep you—" I started to say, then spotted Half-Crocked, the man in charge of stores, picking his teeth and leaning against a barrel of rum.

"Half-Crocked?" I called. He looked over at me. "How much fruit do we have left?"

"Fruit, Cap'n?"

"Yes, fruit." I nodded.

"Twenty or so apples. Two dozen bananas. Some oranges. Mangos."

"Splendid." I crossed my arms. "Share what we have out among the men."

The sailors exchanged glances. A couple of them grimaced.

Half-Crocked stared at me, clearly puzzled. "Cap'n? It's for the officers, Cap'n."

"I don't care. Share it out."

Butcher frowned. He met Half-Crocked's eye. They traded silent communication.

"We can always buy more at the market today," I explained. "It isn't fair for us to hoard the fresh fruit and vegetables if nobody else is getting any."

"They're for the officers," Butcher reminded me. "Fruit and vegetables don't keep long at sea."

"Have you thought about hooking up some solar power?" I asked. "Maybe running some electrics to a fridge or cool storage area? Fresh food would keep longer."

There were mumblings, mostly of the discontented kind. What was up with these people? None of them had even a modicum of imagination!

"We don't like fruit," someone piped up.

"Or vegetables," someone else volunteered.

I folded my arms and glared at them. "You can't stand there—all of you together—and tell me you don't like a single fruit or vegetable."

Silence.

I laughed in disbelief. "You must like cherries?" I tried. "The nectar of the goddess?"

Silence.

"Plums?" I asked. "Sweet, juicy, ripe plums from an English country garden?" My mouth watered just thinking about them. "Strawberries? Kiwi fruit? Gooseberries?"

Silence. But a couple of the sailors had brightened at the memory of strawberries.

I moved on to vegetables. "Sweetcorn? Cabbage? Runner beans?" Heavenly. Especially with a Sunday roast! "Oooh, cauliflower?"

There were no takers for cauliflower.

"Naaaaaaaaaaah," someone at the back sneered. "Yeurch."

"I only like chips," Scurvy said.

"A-ha!" I pointed at him. "Chips are potato slices. Potatoes are a vegetable!"

"Naaaaaah, they're not," he said.

"What we want is pies," said a young sailor at the front.

"Yeah, more pies!" agreed his neighbour.

"And puddings!"

"That's enough, men!" Butcher yelled. "Unless you want a whipping for insubordination!" Instantly, all of the men quietened.

I could feel the wave of resentment travelling towards me. I'd been the cause of the unruliness. The sailors were taking the blame. Typical. Perhaps I'd take Butcher aside and have a quiet word with him to go easier on the lower ranks. No need to show him up in front of the rest of the crew.

"Land ho!"

"To your stations, men!" Butcher barked, and every

sailor fled to do whatever it was they did for the ship to sail into port. Sails were raised and lowered, rigging was climbed, ropes were coiled this way and that. It all seemed rather busy. I clambered up to the foredeck, dabbing at my weeping eye.

"Status report?" I asked Smithy Whiskers. I'd seen any amount of science fiction movies, and this was the sort of thing they always asked, so I figured it couldn't be that different for a ship.

Smithy Whiskers gave me a little side-eye. "Everything's A-okay, Cap'n."

"Great." I plucked up the telescope, put it to my bad eye, realised what I was doing and swapped it over, zooming in on the island of Kandla. The harbour was busy with people loading and unloading trunks and crates and parcels and sacks and all manner of things to and from the large boats—including a passenger ferry of all things—as well as smaller boats packed full of goods that they appeared to be selling to the bigger boats, if that makes any sense at all.

I simmered with excitement. This was a shopping opportunity I would relish. The first stop would be for some shoes!

"Cap'n?" Butcher was climbing the ladder. "We need to decide who's going ashore."

"Can't everyone go?" I asked.

Smithy Whiskers snorted.

"Everyone?" Butcher asked. "That wouldn't be the best idea ..."

"Surely everyone's allowed a little R and R?" I asked.

"Not all at once, Cap'n, and we're only staying long enough to resupply—"

"And find ourselves a new cook," I doggedly reminded him.

"Aye, Cap'n," Butcher said. Another snort from Smithy Whiskers. "If we can."

I waved away his concerns. "We will. I'll let you decide who among the sailors goes ashore and who stays. I'd like several of the men to enquire about Salty Dog in the local bars—"

"Cap'n, I really don't think you can expect to let loose a bunch of pirates in the harbour bars and—"

"Sometimes you have to treat people like adults," I argued. "Surely we can trust the men to do what's right?"

Smithy Whiskers began choking. I glowered at him. "Failing that, perhaps you and Smithy and Half-Crocked could make the enquiries while I purchase what we need for a voyage. How would that be?"

Smithy Whiskers rolled his eyes, but Butcher nodded. "Very well, Cap'n."

"Smashing. Now, how do I go about paying for the supplies? I'm great at bargaining." I didn't like to blow my own trumpet, but over the past few years I'd become adept at seeking the best bargains for Whittle Inn.

"In a box under your bed, Cap'n," Butcher told me, his tone suggesting he was resigning himself to disaster.

Honestly! The man had no faith in me.

Chapter Twelve

Clutching a bagful of doubloons, I spent my way around the colourful market, all the while enjoying its frenetic buzz. The money didn't really consist of doubloons—what I'd found in Captain Bloodstone's strongbox was an enormous wad of US dollars—but I was enjoying the fantasy of being a proper pirate with a parrot on my shoulder and a sword at my side.

Actually, Pete had elected to remain in the cool of the cabin, and I was carrying my wand, but you get the gist.

Markets are the same the world over; they just vary in their scents and in the way the locals dress. Dogs barked or slunk around my feet. Men, women, children and donkeys bustled around, carrying baskets of purchases, whereas I, buying in quantity, arranged to have everything packed into sacks and crates and delivered to *Poseidon's Curse*. Goods were plentiful, the sun was shining, water could be bought by the bottle and, best of all, I was able to enjoy a sneaky breakfast at an air-conditioned café while keeping an eye out for any of my crew.

Once I'd finished my double helping of dosas, a triple egg omelette and two pots of chai for good measure, I asked the English-speaking waiter if he would know where I should enquire about a chef. He directed me to a hostel on the road behind the market, to make enquiries at reception there.

As luck would have it, the hostel was utilised by a charity for women who had fallen on hard times and who would otherwise be homeless. Many of the women had been married, and had either been widowed or had separated from an abusive husband.

I explained to the receptionist what I was after, and although she seemed a little taken aback by my slightly unconventional dress, she agreed to let me speak to a couple of her guests.

The first woman, Anner Drake, was a meek and mild, god-fearing Christian woman from Kerala who had been widowed at a young age. Her daughters had grown up and left to live with their husbands' families. Poor Anner had been unable to keep up with her bills and had eventually left her homestead and moved to Katigarrh on Kandla to make a living. She told me she was a good cook and worked in an orphanage preparing meals for dozens of young children.

Like a fool, I didn't opt for Anner.

No, no.

In my infinite wisdom, I decided that Anner was too docile to deal with the inevitable grief that a woman on *Poseidon's Curse* would have to contend with, so instead I decided on Neta.

Neta Marsh, originally from Delhi, was an entirely different kettle of fish. Her hair, like mine, was a mass of curls, but hers was cut to shoulder length. She wore salwar kameez but would have been equally at home in jeans and a t-shirt. She smiled widely and often, displaying a gap between her two top front teeth, and had piercings in her nose, lip and eyebrow that gave her a decidedly punky look, even though she must have been well into her forties.

Oh, and she swore like a navvy.

"Can you start today?" I asked, and she grinned at me in delight.

"Anything!" she said. "Anything to get out of this junky pad."

Her English was decent and she walked with a bit of a swagger. I decided there and then that she would be able to hold her own on a shipful of miscreants and criminals and hired her on the spot.

"Pack your things," I told her, "and go and find *Poseidon's Curse* in the harbour. You'll find a chap named Scurvy waiting by the gangway. Tell him Captain Alf sent you, and he'll allow you on board. You'll find the galley easily enough—just follow the stench of burnt food. I'll see you back there in a bit."

Satisfied with a good day's work—and it was only

eleven in the morning—I took a tuk-tuk to an international supermarket. After carefully counting how much money I had left, I budgeted accordingly and walked around, loading up a couple of trolleys with a cashier's help. I purchased an enormous box of teabags, sacks of sugar, various flours and a magnificent variety of spices as well as a pallet of butter, all to be delivered back to the ship that very afternoon.

For sure, I was enjoying myself, but I didn't take my eye off my main goal. The pursuit of Salty Dog remained my primary consideration. I watched for him wherever I ventured—not that I had any idea of what he looked like except for Silvan's pathetic description, but I scrutinised everyone I came across, especially those in possession of a beard, or who potentially had ties to a boat or the harbour, no matter how remote those ties might be.

In fact, it boiled down to me taking an unnatural interest in all adult men, really.

Eventually, after partaking of some freshly fried samosas—street food at its best—to use up the handful of change I had left, I wound my way back to the ship, eager to find out what Butcher and Smithy Whiskers had discovered.

What met me was chaos.

Porters from the market had been delivering the goods I'd ordered, and now everything was piled high on the quay. There was some shouting and squabbling between a handful of porters and crew members, who were standing around with their arms folded. I rushed up to them.

"What's going on?" I demanded.

"They want tipping," one sailor told me, his face a mask of incredulity.

"Tipping?" I reached into my bag but I already knew what I'd find. The samosas had wiped me out of any remaining change I possessed. There were a couple of teeny copper-coloured rupees at the very bottom of my bag, in the furthest corner with a handful of fluff, the furry remnants of old tissues, a hairy mint humbug and the silver spiral that had been ejected from a broken biro, but I had a feeling none of that would get me very far.

"Don't worry! I'll sort it," I said and rushed up the gangway onto the ship, clambering up the ladder to the rear deck and my cabin. When I reached the deck, I stopped. The door was open. I hadn't left it open. At least, I didn't think so. Not that it would have mattered as there wasn't a lock on it, or, to my knowledge, anything worth taking ...

Except there was, wasn't there? The strongbox. It had been on the bed. I'd left it there in my hurry to get to market. The sweat that broke out on my forehead was nothing to do with the heat, growing in intensity as the day wore on, and everything to do with the fear of what I was about to find.

And my fears were realised. The box was still on my bed.

And it was empty.

Every last penny had gone.

"No-no-no-no-no," I begged. "Don't do this to me."

"Pieces of hate!" Pete squawked. "Doubloons! Doubloons! There's always tears!"

The shouting and caterwauling from outside were getting louder. The porters sounded like a bunch of fishermen's wives who were about to come to blows with the crew. I rushed out on deck to see some of the porters trying to force their way over the gangway.

"Get back!" I shouted, trying to assert some authority. "We will sort this, I promise!" But my words were lost in a cacophony as sailors jumped from their stations, zooming down ropes and ladders as though they were playing a life-size version of snakes and ladders, weapons held aloft and shrieking like cowboys and Indians in one of those old-time Hollywood movies.

"Oh, my life!" I could imagine the ruckus that was about to unfold. The deck would be swimming in blood and chunks of head and arms and ... What should I do? Where was Butcher? He could help me. I cast my gaze around, seeking him, and instead it fell on a pair of figures entwined next to the barrels of rum. One of those barrels had its lid removed. I could see it was less than a third full, when it had been half full the last time I'd checked.

And those figures? Swaying along to music only

they could hear? Half-Crocked—now fully-crocked—and Neta!

My mouth fell open. How dare she! I'd hired her literally less than two hours ago! I'd paid her a hundred dollars as an advance of her salary so she could buy herself anything she would need for a relatively short—I hoped—voyage.

She must have sensed me looking in her direction, because she raised a tankard—full of a deep amber liquid—my way, grinning happily.

"Arrrrrrrh!" An angry roar stopped the crew dead in their tracks. Even my knees quaked.

Butcher had returned to the ship along with Smithy Whiskers. Now he pulled himself up to his full height and expanded that great chest of his.

"What the devil is going on here?" he roared with such demonic fury that every porter in a half-mile radius fell to his knees, prepared to start begging for his life to be spared.

Butcher's gaze sought mine.

By all that's green, I thought, and tried to force a smile, eager to convince the big man that I had everything in hand. Smithy's cold glare told me he saw right through my bravado.

I hurried down the ladder. "I can explain," I babbled as I rushed across the gangway to where Butcher was waiting for me. "I forgot that it's the custom in India to tip the porters. We don't tip people in Britain. Well, just taxi drivers and waiting staff. Oh, and sometimes hairdressers. But *generally*, we don't tip anyone ..." I trailed off as Butcher's nose flared.

"Then tip the porters and let's get going."

"Hahaha." I laughed, making light of my mistake. "The thing is, we"—I gestured around at the ship to show that this problem was bigger than just me—"have a bit of a cashflow problem—"

Butcher's eyes widened, and I noticed that both the crew and the steelier of the porters were creeping closer to see and hear what was going on. "You can't have spent all the money from the strongbox!" Butcher exploded. "Tell me you didn't!"

Oh boy. "Of course I didn't!" I told him. "But I left it unsecured, and someone has stolen what was left." I had a feeling I knew who, but I wasn't sure how to prove it.

Butcher choked. Smithy reached out and slapped his back. "Stolen? You mean we have no money left in the strongbox at all?"

"None," I replied, my voice weak. "I'm really, really sorry. I'll make it up to you all."

Butcher blinked in astonishment. "Make it up to us?"

Smithy roared with laughter. "Enough of this, Butcher! Let's be done with it!"

Numerous crew members, notably those who had been so vocal about not liking fruit and vegetables, began to nod. "Aaar!"

"She's no captain," Smithy spat. "She's no better than a stowaway."

Scurvy curled his lip. "And we know what happens to stowaways on *Poseidon's Curse*!"

"Arrrrr!" roared the crew.

"May I enquire what happens?" I asked, wincing at the expected response. "Just out of interest?"

"We hangs 'em from the yardarm!" sang Scurvy, eyes alight with delight.

Perhaps my face conveyed my confusion. I had no idea what a yardarm was.

Scurvy cocked an eyebrow and pointed up at a cross-beam on one of the masts. The sails were attached there using a complicated system of pulleys and weights and knotted ropes.

"Smashing," I said. "How about I just disemboard instead?"

"Disembark, you mean?" Butcher looked like he might give this serious consideration. I could tell he was dying to see the back of me. But then, wouldn't he have to admit to the men that he'd backed the wrong horse for captain? Or the wrong Alf, seeing as I wasn't a horse.

"Pretty please," I said.

"Oh no!" Smithy Whiskers wasn't having that. "No, no, no, no, no!"

"No, no, no, no, no!" chorused some of the other sailors. They were enjoying this. Even Half-Crocked and Neta were on their feet, swaying along to the music of the rabble.

"No, no, no, no!" reiterated Smithy, in case I was in any doubt whatsoever whether my plea for clemency would be entertained. "There's a proper punishment for a treacherous captain. Hanging's too good for your sort!"

"Alright." I sighed. "And what is it?"

"You'll have to walk the plank," Butcher told me.

My good eye twitched.

"Walk the plank?" I enquired.

"AAARRR!" chorused the men.

Chapter Thirteen

At first, I genuinely thought they would let me walk the plank while we were in harbour, but it turned out that wasn't their fiendish plan at all. They tied me to the main mast while they hauled the supplies on board—between them, Butcher and Smithy had enough ready cash to pay the porters what they expected—and organised them on the main deck. By the time they'd finished, there wasn't much room left for anyone to move around.

"Why did you buy so much?" Butcher exclaimed, sweat running down his brow.

"How else are you going to feed your men?" I asked. "Look at them. It's cruel the way they're kept in that ... that pocket of hell below decks. You should be ashamed."

"That's their quarters! That's what they expect! We can't all live in the captain's cabin, can we?" Butcher snapped back. He was cross. I'd let him down, bless him.

"I don't suppose you could find me a sunhat, could you?" I asked. "Too much sun is really bad for my complexion."

"I'm not sure a bit of sunburn is going to matter too much where you're going," he told me, but his heart wasn't in it.

"It's just my eye," I said. "It's a bit painful ..."

"You should have bought yourself an eyepatch while you were out at the market," he told me. "It does look sore."

"There's one on the wax model in the hold," I said. "Maybe you could fetch that for me?"

Slightly taken aback, he regarded me in confusion. "You are strange. Aren't you scared of what's coming? Your imminent demise and all that?"

I shrugged. "What will be, will be," I told him. He resumed his business, but I caught him glancing at me from time to time and, a little later, one of the young sailors brought me the eyepatch from the dummy and did me the honour of looping the strings around my head and tying it on for me. It carried a faint ratty whiff about it, but given I wouldn't be wearing it for long, I didn't let that worry me.

And no. I wasn't concerned. Not really. The pirates—and I was seriously beginning to doubt any of them were genuine pirates—had tied me to the mast using a thick rope that wound around me from just below my shoulders to just above my ankles. My arms were trapped by my sides. However, my bag was still slung over my shoulder, and the knots were so thick and cumbersome that I'd found that simply by wriggling, I'd garnered myself a little extra room. I could easily slip my hand into my bag and extract my wand if I wanted to.

The only reason I hadn't done so yet was because I wanted to see how far the pirates would go.

Within reason.

I didn't want to free myself and then end up suspended from the yardarm by my neck.

So I stayed where I was, occasionally blowing hair away from my eyes and watching Butcher try to make sense of all the supplies and figure out where to store them. Once everything was loaded on board, Butcher gave the order to weigh anchor and set sail, and we were off again.

I found it rather exciting to be tied to the mast like a damsel in distress. We headed into the wind, and I took deep breaths of clean ocean air and bided my time. Above me, the sails snapped and billowed as they filled up with wind. We raced along the dancing waves, as graceful as can be.

And I concocted a plan.

Once we were well away from land, the anchor was dropped and the sails stowed. A long plank of wood was brought up from the hold, decorated with faint traces of lime and mauve paint. One end was secured to the deck and weighed down with cannonballs, the other left to dangle above the sea. The pirates began to squeeze together on the deck, anticipation on many faces. Not that there was an awful lot of room for them all. The supplies I'd bought were still stacked high. Someone really needed to take things in hand, and poor Butcher seemed to be at a loss.

Smithy Whiskers wasn't backwards in coming forwards, however. He had plenty of ideas of how to get rid of me, didn't he? Now he urged Butcher on to get the deed done. It was he who mustered the men. He who organised the plank. He who did it all with a cheerful countenance while Butcher hung back, his expression dark.

"Untie her!" Smithy ordered, and several of the sailors made to dart towards me. Butcher shooed them away and came forward to do it himself.

"What's up, chuck?" I asked him. "Why the long face?"

He twerked the corner of his mouth and turned slightly sideways so the others could neither see nor hear him. "I thought you'd make a difference," he told me. "I served under Captain Bloodstone faithfully for years, and I'd do it again. But he didn't have the first clue. After my time in the navy, all I wanted was to sail the seven seas and have some adventures, but being a pirate on *Poseidon's Curse*, it's not as exciting as I imagined it would be."

That was similar to what one of the other men had said, wasn't it? When I'd first suggested we go after Salty Dog. They'd demanded some swashbuckling.

"So what were you doing under Captain Bloodstone?" I asked as he reached behind me and easily uncoupled the rope.

"Sailing."

"Sailing? That's it?"

"Pretty much."

"Nothing piratey? No robbery? How did you come by the money in the strongbox?"

"That was Captain Bloodstone's fortune. By all accounts he came from a wealthy family. He didn't speak about it much."

"Oh." Oops. And I'd spent a load of it and managed to get the rest stolen. "What time is it?" I asked, adjusting the eyepatch to make it a little more comfortable.

Butcher consulted a silver fob watch he kept in his waistcoat pocket. "One twenty-two."

"Good. That gives me time." I shook myself. "I have a delivery booked for four, so we need to get back before then."

Butcher shook his head. "I don't think you understand what's about to happen here."

"Oh, I do. I do!" I smiled. "I really do."

"What's keeping you?" Smithy bellowed.

I tapped my ears. "No need to shout," I said,

nodding at Butcher and stepping lightly towards Smithy. "I can hear perfectly well."

"Well, let's crack on, shall we?" he grumbled, with slightly less volume.

"Where do you want me?" I asked, even though it was perfectly obvious.

"Up, up!" He took out his sword, a rapier I believe it's called, long and slim with a sharp, pointed head. It twanged when he shook it.

"Would someone look after my bag?" I asked. "I don't want it getting wet."

"Have you got anything of value in there?" Neta asked, worming her way through the ranks of men.

"Not really. My purse, my phone." I opened it up to show her.

"I'll relieve you of it," she told me, and I let her do so. She giggled and retreated towards her place beside Half-Crocked and the barrels of rum.

Smithy prodded me with his rapier. "Up! Up!"

"Alright, alright! Hold your horses!" Primly—all an act, there is nothing prim about Alfhild Daemonne—I held a hand out, waiting for someone to help me. Several sailors came forward to do so, and I climbed onto the edge of the plank.

I must admit that at that stage, the butterflies began to beat a little in my stomach. I'd conquered my fear of heights when the movie people had visited Whittle Inn, but even so, this was quite a long drop into the sea, and while I could swim, and liked to swim, the ocean was full of the unknown.

And it would probably be freezing.

Smithy waggled his rapier. It made an impressive zipping noise through the air. "Go on!"

"Aren't I allowed any last words?" I asked. He prodded me with the pointy end. I was glad my rump was so well endowed. "Do you mind?"

"No last words."

I glanced over his head at Butcher. I could see what was going to happen here. Smithy would wait until I was seafood, and then he'd stage a coup against Butcher. Smithy would manipulate the men, half-starved and half-crazy from long weeks cooped up on a stinking ship—and he'd lead a mutiny. If Butcher didn't nip things in the bud, he'd end up in Davy Jones's Locker alongside me and Wrathful Bob.

Smithy prodded me again. Harder this time.

"Ouch!" I glared at him. "Okay. Alright."

I shimmied across the plank, one foot in front of the other. I wasn't even halfway across when it began to bend under my weight.

Smithy leaned over, rapier held out. He would run me through me if I dilly-dallied. "Captain Alf, for crimes against the pirates of *Poseidon's Curse*, you will die one way or the other." He jabbed me once more, and this time I felt the pointed end nick the skin on my calf.

"Fine." I shuffled forward a little more, my weight finely balanced now. A few millimetres more and I'd be tumbling into the crystal abyss ... "Adieu!" I cried and took a deep breath, reaching into the deep pocket of Captain Bloodstone's breeches. Once my fingers curled around my enchanted piece of Vance, I took that final step.

The plank bent beneath my weight, and now there was no preventing that downward trajectory. I fell quickly—quicker than I'd anticipated—the wind flying by my face, the colours of *Poseidon's Curse* a blur to the side of me, blue and sparkles in my peripheral vision as I plummeted towards the waves, but! I held Vance aloft and uttered the word "*Mora*!"

My progress slowed until I came to a stop, just in the nick of time, my bare toes paddling in the waves. It wasn't as cold as I'd imagined it would be. Almost enticing, in fact. But I didn't intend to hang around for a dip.

Instead, I twisted, weightless in the air, and shifted towards the side of the boat. Close up, I could see *Poseidon's Curse* was badly in need of a little TLC. Far too many barnacles and other clinging beasties—sea anemones, tubeworms—had their slimy little tentacles in the woodwork, and the paint had faded, chipped and peeled. But that in itself provided the extra texture I needed, because my next task was to climb around the front of the ship and up the other side.

For months and months now, memories of Castle Iadului had never been far from my mind. I experienced that crazy traumatic time over and over in my nightmares. A night when I'd led a badly injured, partially sighted Silvan around the castle, striving to avoid a murderous drop into a steep precipice.

And I'd done that using the now infamous 'sticky spell'.

Well, now I was going to fully utilise it again, and the second time around it would be easier because I knew what I was doing, I'd conquered some of my fears and ... and most importantly ... falling twenty feet from the side of a ship into water was a lot less worrying than running from vampires and then falling into Alfie oblivion in a bottomless chasm in Transylvania.

Or so I figured.

"*Tenax*!" I intoned, directing my wand in a sweeping motion from left to right before tucking it down the front of my shirt. I reached out to stick my hands to the wood. This wasn't particularly pleasant. The barnacles were sharp beneath my scarred palms, and the anemones were horribly squidgy. In fact, the amount of slime on the side of a boat is deceptive. Of course, seaweed plays a part and goodness knows what else. Bio-ickiness!

While concocting this genius plan, I had been concerned about the scar tissue on my hands. For weeks after my run-in with Senan, I hadn't been able to grip much at all. Fortunately, Wizard Shadowmender had been as good as his word and I'd had access to one of the best surgical wizards in the business. After a period of intense physiotherapy and the application three times a day of Wizard Zelinski's marvellous balm, the muscles and flesh had healed nicely. Only the scars that were tough and unyielding, and even they would improve with time. I'd been promised plastic surgery if I wished, but I tended to think of all my physical scars as medals from my various adventures, and so I'd declined that.

"Not that I go seeking adventure," I grumbled, shifting my handhold. "I just want a quiet life. I want to read my books and write my postcards and moonbathe and ... canoodle with Silvan."

And that, of course, reminded me of why I was there. Specifically why I was clinging to the side of a pirate ship in the middle of the Indian Ocean.

At first I couldn't gain any purchase at all.

"*Tenax*!" I said again, increasing the intention. Perhaps I'd been too light-hearted before, imagining this would be a piece of cake. Finally, my hands stuck fast. Forcing my weight through them, it was time to get my feet involved.

"*Tenax*!" I said and lifted my knees. I positioned first one foot and then the other, until finally, much like a spider, or more properly a crab in this case, I was able to scuttle sideways. I moved each limb in turn. Right hand, right foot. Left hand, left foot. Over and over, making decent progress until I was around the front of the ship.

That was the other notable difference to my experiences at Iadului. The castle had been an enormous stronghold that seemed to stretch for miles. In comparison, *Poseidon's Curse* was a garden shed.

No sooner had that thought formulated in my mind than the ship began to move. Castle Iadului had never moved. Once they had weighed anchor, the gentle drifting that *Poseidon's Curse* had indulged in up until now became a more forceful movement. I could tell the exact point at which the sails were raised and the ship was given her head to run with the wind because she suddenly lurched forward ...

And I faceplanted into an enormous pair of boobies.

I hadn't paid attention to the masthead before, but suddenly I found myself face to face with a golden-haired water nymph, or something similar, with her sizable bust covered in a pair of impossibly large decorative shells. To navigate around her, I had to use her ... erm ... appendages as handholds.

Noting her pained expression—she had the permanent appearance of a bulldog chewing a wasp—I hurried to apologise. "I do beg your pardon," I said. "Don't take it personally." As I paused to catch my breath, I added, "You know, I understand that look of pain." I fought to regain my balance as the ship lurched first one way and then the other. "If I was carrying this bunch of hoodlums on my back, I wouldn't be best pleased either." I patted her in a sisterly way. "I'll get you sorted, don't you worry."

Once I'd rediscovered the rhythm of the slap, hold, release, slap, hold, release technique that I'd utilised in Transylvania, I found it easier to manoeuvre and could pick up speed. It was kind of exhilarating, in fact. I rode the ship as she skated through the waves, rather like a princess on a dragon. And all the time I chittered to myself, just to keep myself company, really. "I'm a crab! A crab apple." I laughed. "Or a crab Alfie ... or something. Or ..." I slipped round to the flatter part of the boat where it was easier to hook my hands in the beams or find toeholds to help push myself up. "SpiderAlf!" Giggling, I sang, "SpiderAlf! SpiderAlf! Does whatever a SpiderAlf does!"

I was still humming to myself as I hauled my carcass towards the balustrade, or whatever it was called. Near the top, just before I would expose my continuing existence to anyone on the deck, I reached for my wand, handling it with great care. I didn't want to drop it and then have to dive into the water after it. A SpiderAlf was one thing. A merAlf was something entirely different.

Clamping the wand between my teeth, I resumed the last few feet of my climb, grabbing the railings with great relief and flopping over the top of them to land on the wooden deck with a loud plop.

I sat up, resting against the railings, snatching my wand from my mouth and smiling at the astonished sailors who were striving to organise the chaos of my deliveries.

"Ooh ...er ..." Scurvy darted backwards away from me. "Butcher! Smithy!"

Others took up the call. "Skip!"

Smithy rushed out from the captain's cabin. It hadn't taken him long to ensconce himself in there, had it? Butcher was at his heels. Spotting me, Smithy waved his rapier at me then dashed for the ladder. He didn't bother with the rungs, simply slid. That was a skill I fancied learning for myself.

When he rushed towards me, waving his weapon —*twang, twang*—I lifted my little part of Vance and issued a thin beam of energy. "*Dearmo*!" I intoned. It didn't require much intent. He wasn't ready for me. The sword swung easily out of his hand and flipped pointed end over handle, handle over pointed end, to embed itself in the wooden galley door where it stuck fast.

Smithy slid to a halt, eyes wide, mouth open. "Witch!" he hissed.

I batted my eyelids. "You can't say I didn't give you fair warning."

CHAPTER FOURTEEN

"This is how it's going to be," I said. I was standing on the patio part of the cabin's deck. Okay. It's not a patio, but I figured a couple of containers with some pretty flowers wouldn't go amiss, and then I could have a deckchair out here, read a couple of Captain Bloodstone's books, and keep an eye on what everyone was up to.

The men were arranged on the next deck down. Butcher had referred to it as the quarterdeck, and I took his word for it. He'd been as shocked as anyone else to see me, but I was gratified that the big man had seemed genuinely relieved too.

He really wasn't cut out to be a pirate.

"I can offer you adventure, travel and a certain amount of swashbuckling," I told the men, knowing that I'd want to keep the latter contained until I understood exactly what buckling your swash consisted of, "tasty food and decent accommodation—"

As one, the men pricked their ears up.

"In return for your loyal service."

I indicated the port of Katigarrh. We were arriving right on time. I was pleased to see the people standing on the quay waiting for us. Everything was coming together exactly as I'd planned.

"By loyal service, I mean I expect you to attend to your duties responsibly. You will work hard, but your rewards will be worth it. You scratch my back—not literally—" I said when a couple of younger men began to giggle, "and I'll scratch yours. Also not literally. And also not if you haven't taken a bath in the past year."

Half-Crocked howled. "You'll have us as slaves, is all!" He wasn't best pleased because I'd pointed out to the others how much rum he and Neta had knocked back in the space of the last few hours, which obviously meant he was in everyone's bad books.

"Not at all." I stared squarely at the other men, gazing up at me, hope in many eyes. "We will figure out a way we can operate which will ensure every man has downtime to do with as he wishes, as well as time when he is on watch or attending to his duties. You'll have ample sleep time and, when we make shore, everyone will have a little shore leave. I can't say fairer than that."

I listened to the muttering below. Some were with me, some were not.

"This is a time-limited offer," I told them. "I will only be Captain temporarily. At some stage I have to go home to my own life. There are people who rely on me back in England. But first, we need to find the killer of your previous captain, and I need to find a way to set my fiancé free so we can be married."

Some nods. Not quite enough. They were certainly making me work for it. I could have promised them the moon and they probably wouldn't have gone for it yet.

"But when I go, I intend to leave you in the best hands possible, so, here and now, I am promoting Sergeant Michael 'the Butcher' Morello to my second-in-command."

Butcher did a double take before blinking rapidly, a blush spreading over his cheeks.

"It was remiss of Captain Bloodstone that he never gave Butcher the rank he deserves," I said. I nodded at him. "Richly deserves."

"Aarrh!" one of the men shouted up.

"Aarh!" the others echoed. Here was something they all seemed to be in total agreement with.

"There are going to be many changes in the next twenty-four hours," I told them, "and some of you may find these difficult. With this in mind, once we've docked, any man who wishes to be released from service"—I levelled my gaze at Smithy Whiskers—"is free to go without fear of consequence."

A hush fell over the men gathered before me. They exchanged nervous glances with each other, one or two of them suddenly intent on picking lint from their clothes, or cleaning their ears with filthy fingers, or wiping their noses on their sleeves ...

I could do no more. I had to let them make up their own minds.

"To your stations!" I said. I still wasn't sure whether this was the right thing to say, but again, I was fairly certain I'd seen it in the movies.

The men began to scurry around. I watched them for a moment, fascinated that they knew exactly what to do to line up *Poseidon's Curse* with the side of the quay.

Butcher sidled up to me. "Captain Alf ..."

"I really hope you're not going to give me any trouble, Mr Butcher," I said, without looking at him.

"No, no, Cap'n ... it's just ... I'm not ... I don't know ..."

"*You* don't need to know," I told him. "I've been running an inn for years. *I* know how to make things work, and I'm a good judge of character." Jed popped instantly into my mind. "Usually." I turned to face him. "*You* deserve to be captain of this ship, not me, but I need *Poseidon's Curse* for my own ends for the time being. I'll make a deal with you. You make a sailor out of me, and I'll make a manager out of you."

A broad smile broke out across his face. "What do you have in mind?"

"So much! By the time I've finished with you, if you ever decide to retire from pirating, you'll be hands-on favourite to run any inn or hotel anywhere in the world."

He snorted. "Is that a fact?"

"My solemn oath," I said. "So, what about it? Can you turn me into a sailor?"

He puffed out his cheeks. "I think I got the hard end of the bargain."

I grinned. There could be no denying the truth of that.

He nodded. "Aye, Captain. But you've got a lot of learning to do!"

With the ship moored alongside the quay, Half-Crocked, who had rapidly begun to sober up now that I had my beady eye on him, organised the sliding out of the gangway. I stood at the top of it, arms folded, and glared at Neta as she slunk past me, practically throwing my bag back at me.

"Thanks for looking after it," I told her. "I trust everything is inside."

She curled her lip, ready to have a go at pulling my hair out. I jerked my head sideways. "Be off with you," I ordered, then waited for her to make it safely to the quay before flicking out my index finger and causing her to trip. She landed face down in a pile of donkey poop, coins and notes exploding out of her clothes.

"Oops," I whispered.

Butcher, standing next to me, gave me a bit of a side-eye. I smiled in all innocence. "I believe that's the money from Captain Bloodstone's strongbox," I told him. "Have someone pick her up, shake her down and collect all the cash, will you?"

He gave the order, and I stood by the railings observing as Neta received her comeuppance. Eventually, the sailor marched her off in the direction of the market, and I turned to survey the number of porters waiting for us. Leaning across to Butcher, I said, "Look, this is a little embarrassing, given the circumstances. I don't want to use Captain Bloodstone's money to tip these guys, but erm … I'm strapped for cash at the minute …"

He rolled his eyes. "I'll take care of it, Cap'n."

"I'll pay you back," I promised. "I spotted a cashpoint earlier." It seemed miraculous to me that I could access my bank account from anywhere in the world simply by sticking a piece of plastic in a slither of a gap in a wall, but that was modern technology for you.

I left him to it and rushed back to the marketplace to use my card in the machine. All was well, although I'd have to account for the money with Penelope Quigwell at some stage, but with a *zussss* and a *weeeee*, the Katigarrh computer connected with my British bank's computer, and there I was with a fat pile of rupees in my hand.

Then it was back to the quay, where I intended to elicit ye olde worlde technology. While I'd been in the café enjoying breakfast earlier, I had put in a call to my room at the resort and spoken to Gwyn. I'd figured that, given all that needed to be done on the ship, I could do with her help.

And there she was, dressed in a pretty, pale pink salwar kameez, with a brighter pink shawl wrapped around her head and shoulders. She looked completely at ease among the hoi polloi and the bustle of the quay. I'd known as soon as I'd requested that she join me that she would. She could resist everything except an adventure.

But there was a surprise for me, too.

Standing alongside her, little puffs of steam shooting into the air, a tiny suitcase at her feet, was darling Florence.

I shrieked with joy and bounced along the quay. "What are you doing here?"

"I don't rightly know, Miss Alf!" Florence beamed back at me. "One minute I was organising Chocolate Bomb Rice Pops for Wizard Silverfish, and the next, Mrs Daemonne was telling me to pack my bag, and here I am!" She glanced around. "I don't even know where *here* is, Miss Alf!"

I clapped my hand in excitement. "You're in India, Florence! Imagine that!"

"Oh my!" She clamped a hand to her heart. "If my mother could see me now." She considered this for a second. "She'd probably tell me I was a fool, that I would die of dysentery or be murdered in my bed by a savage, but ..." I watched as she trained an eye over the porters as they called out among themselves and jostled for position. "... they don't seem that bothered."

"Historical misconceptions," I told her. "Totally objectionable. And besides, they're not going to kill you; you're already dead."

"That will save my darling mother more heartache, won't it?" She nodded happily. "I'm looking forward to getting to work."

Gwyn, meanwhile, regarded me with distaste. "What do you look like, Alfhild? What have you done to your face?"

I tapped the eye patch. "I had a little accident. It's fine. I can still see out of the other eye."

"Until someone strikes you in that one, no doubt." She shook her head. "Shall we go aboard? I'd like to see my quarters."

I snorted. "It's not a cruise ship, Grandmama. Or the Royal Yacht Britannia. I don't think you'll be happy when you see our cabin, but thank you for coming anyway!" I smiled at her. "And for bringing Florence. What a brilliant idea!"

"I tried to bring Ned and Zephaniah, but Charity wouldn't let me." Gwyn sounded most put out.

"She still has an inn to run," I reminded her. "If you'd taken all her best workers, she wouldn't have been able to cope."

"And Monsieur Emietter refused point blank to come." She shrugged.

"You did your best, and I am truly grateful!" I was also grateful Monsieur Emietter was a stubborn stick-in-the-mud. I could do without him here, adding to my troubles.

"When you told me what was going on, I knew you'd need additional help. Besides, I don't like to get my hands dirty ..."

I laughed. "Well, it's fortunate you're a ghost and you won't have to touch anything, because the whole ship is rank. Oooh! One second!" I spotted a man with a wicker basket heading our way. "Is that what I think it is?"

It was! I accepted the basket from him, directed Butcher to pay him a tip, then gingerly carried the basket back to Gwyn and Florence. "Look what I've got!" I squealed and lifted the basket to show them. A beautifully sleek, fully grown black cat with two of her kittens.

Florence clapped her hands with delight. "I didn't know you were a fan of cats, Miss?"

"I am," I protested. "I like all animals. But I prefer cats to rats, and this ship is riddled with them, so I figure this little madam and her babies are going to be doing us a favour." A sudden thought occurred to me. "I hope she can tolerate parrots though."

"Parrots?" Gwyn's eyebrows shot up. "Surely you haven't bought a parrot as well?"

"I've inherited a parrot," I said, gently nurturing the basket and leading them up the gangway. "His name is Pete, and he belonged to Captain Bloodstone." I turned to Florence. "He's the man who was murdered. The one who Silvan has been charged with killing."

"So you've stepped into a dead man's shoes, Miss Alf?" Florence asked.

"His breeches and his blouse"—I swept my free arm down my body—"but not his shoes. They were too big for me."

Butcher came back on board, nodded at Gwyn, performed a double take at Florence, and peeped into the basket. "Cap'n? Someone from the electrical shop has turned up. They say they have a fridge for us?"

"Oh yes, great! It's here, is it?" I strained my head to see. Yes, there it was. An enormous silver device with double doors and an ice cube dispenser. I hadn't held back. All mod cons for my ship. "And the solar panels?"

"Apparently so." Butcher had paled.

"Marvellous. Hopefully someone among our number knows how to rig those up, because I certainly don't." I performed a cheerful little jig. My plans were all coming together.

Butcher had turned his attention to my basket. "You've bought cats?"

"I have. We're going to eradicate our rat problem," I told him.

I thought he'd be happy about this, but he frowned instead. "Rats are an integral part of the ship."

He had to be jesting! I grimaced. "Ugh! How so?"

"Once they start diving overboard, you know it's time to follow them."

I sucked in a breath, imagining that. "Oh, crikey! That reminds me! I didn't buy any dinghies! I was intending to buy some of those blow-up lilo-type boats so we could use them as life rafts!"

"I think you've spent quite enough." Butcher recoiled in horror.

"You're probably right, but safety first."

"Perhaps you should have bought lilos instead of kittens then," Butcher said. "Not that we have any room to stow dinghies!"

"We're going to be making room!" I gestured at my companions. "This is my great-grandmother, Alfhild Gwynfyre Daemonne."

"Mrs Daemonne." She dipped her head. "Pleased to meet you. You may call me ma'am."

Oh, my life.

"And this is Florence. She's the housekeeper at my inn, and she's going to organise the men."

Florence, clutching her tiny little suitcase, curtsied, then giggled. "You can call me Florence."

Butcher recoiled. "Organise them?"

I deposited the basket safely at my feet. "Butcher, my friend, once everything is loaded aboard, we are going to have an enormous clear-up!"

We started in the hold. I sent Gwyn down there primarily because she was the most fearsome of us all, and the men were more likely to do as they were told. Florence might look the scariest at face value, but as soon as you had any sort of interaction with her, you realised what an absolute sweetheart she truly was.

Firstly, Gwyn had her team of 'volunteers' empty everything from the hold. They formed a human chain and brought out barrels and crates, piles of clothing, the waxwork dummy—everything that could be carried came up onto the already cramped deck.

With the notable exception of the car. How that had found its way *in* I had no idea but, I reckoned, there it would remain until the ship ended up on the ocean floor.

As soon as the hold was cleared, I sent a rather subdued Smithy Whiskers—yes, he'd stayed with us—down there with a couple of helpers to build some shelves and strengthen the flooring where the fridge would go. Once that was sorted, the fridge was lowered through the double hatch. Again I marvelled at how many men it took to lower the device through those doors, because the car must have weighed two or three times as much.

That done, we found a sailor with some electrical knowledge who began to rig up the solar panels and connect the fridge. While all that was happening, Butcher had his team begin to fill up those new shelves with all the goodies I'd purchased.

Florence and her smaller team were in the galley and ship's mess. She put her sailors to work scrubbing every inch of every surface, and if she wasn't happy, she made them do it again. She took it upon herself to clean the kitchen, and when I popped my head in there, I heard her humming away, sleeves rolled up, soot flying, never happier.

That left me.

I retired to my cabin and began to sort out Captain Bloodstone's chaos. Florence had already offered to launder the clothes and repair anything salvageable so that the men could make use of them, so I created piles. The good stuff in one, the filthy-but-could-be-saved in another, and the rags in a third. Florence would be able to show the men how to make rag rugs to jolly up their quarters, and perhaps even some patchwork quilts. Who knew?

I kept a few items back for my own use. Another pair of breeches in bright red—rather fetching, I thought—and a couple of cream blousons. I also found a waistcoat I rather liked that had ties at the back so I could alter it to fit me.

"Aaar," I said when I tried it on.

"Aaar!" echoed Pete.

Slipping my hands into the pocket, my fingers touched cool metal. Curious, I drew out a silver key, no longer than a pen lid. "I wonder what this opens?" I said, glancing around the room for potential locks to try. Nothing immediately jumped out at me. There weren't many secrets on this ship. Hardly anything was locked up. I suppose if you misplaced a key while at sea, you were in trouble, weren't you? Returning the key to my pocket, I made a mental note to mention it to Butcher.

The next cupboard was full of books. *Treasure Island, Shipwreck, Moby Dick, The Old Man and the Sea,* 20,000 *Leagues Under the Sea, The Voyage of The Beagle, The Log from the Sea of Cortez* and so on and so forth. Classics of the English-speaking world. Captain Bloodstone had had good taste.

I piled them up. If I managed to get a spare five minutes, I wagered that some of these would help my understanding of how to run a ship no end. Butcher would be pleased.

See? I can be a good student.

Of literature, anyway.

I stripped the bed and examined the mattress. It would do. It was luxurious in comparison to what the men were having to put up with, so I had no complaints there. Imagine me in a hammock? What if it collapsed in the middle of the night?

No thanks.

The bunk was fixed to the wall, so to be able to pull out everything stored beneath, I had to lie on my stomach. Some of what I found might have been there for centuries. Not one but *three* chamber pots. I edged them towards the door, not wishing to examine them too closely. There were nightcaps and nightshirts, books and magazines. Newspapers that crumbled when I caught hold of them. Dozens of stray socks and single stockings. Goblets and pewter tumblers. Plates. A sword, rusted and irredeemable.

Just when I thought I'd found everything, I noticed, in the furthest corner, something glinting. Slithering like a snake, I inched forward, blowing cobwebs and dust from my face and getting my hair snagged on the underside of the bed. "Ow. Ow. Ugh. Ugh," I chanted, worried that my backside would become wedged and I'd be trapped here for one of the sailors to find. Reaching with my fingers, I touched the glinty thing and realised it was a hinge and that actually what I was looking at here was some sort of box, like Captain Bloodstone's strongbox.

With difficulty, because the box fitted perfectly in the corner, I worked it free and began to wriggle backwards, dragging the box along with my fingertips until finally I was out far enough that I could get on my knees, wrap my hands around it and pull with all my might.

Bingo! I fell backwards as the box came free.

"Pieces of hate!" squawked Pete. "Pieces of hate!"

"Is that what this is?" I asked. "Doubloons?"

"Treasure!" called Pete. "Treasure. Yarrrrk!"

"I wish."

I wiped the top of the box with my filthy shirt sleeve to reveal an intricate carving on the lid: a large mansion or country house, framed by trees and flowers.

I ran the tip of my finger around the image. Beautifully crafted. Beneath the house were three letters. DBR.

"DBR?" I wondered who that could be? Not Captain Bloodstone. Perhaps a relative? Not his father or grandfather. Some other ancestor?

Turning the box around, I realised it was secured with a lock. It needed a key to open it, but there wasn't one immediately to hand.

Except there was, wasn't there?

"It can't be," I murmured, reaching my hand into the waistcoat pocket and extracting the small key I'd found there.

Fumbling with it, I finally managed to insert it into the lock. It fitted beautifully, like they were made for each other.

I turned it.

Click.

And lifted the lid.

Inside were a bunch of scrolls.

"Treasure!" squawked Pete. "Treasure. Yaaarrrrk!"

Chapter Fifteen

Somewhere, a gong was sounding. Kneeling there on the cabin floor, my clothes dishevelled, my hair an absolute mess, I sat back and listened. *What time is it? Could that be a dinner gong?*

I pushed myself up. I'd been in one position for too long and my muscles were aching. To be fair, hadn't I over-exerted myself today, what with the SpiderAlf efforts and trying to clear up this room? I'd be feeling it tomorrow.

Poking my head out of the cabin, I sniffed. Salty air and beef and ale pie, if I wasn't much mistaken. Florence had been working her own particular brand of magick, had she? Glancing down to the lower deck—which, miracle of miracles, had been scrubbed!—I could see the men queuing up for their supper. Most of them looked how I felt. Dishevelled, filthy and shattered.

I returned to the cabin, regarding all of Captain

Bloodstone's earthly belongings piled up on the floorboards.

"Treasure!" squawked Pete. "Treasure!"

"But is it?" I asked him, wedging the narrow door open so I could begin moving the separate piles to the patio deck.

"Lost family treasure!" Pete told me.

"Is that a fact?" I studied him thoughtfully. "Tell me what you know."

"Favoured son. House. *Aaaaaaaark*! Lost family treasure!"

There could be something in it. I picked up the box and deposited it on the bed. I would talk to Butcher about it a little later. For now, I wanted to clean myself up. With a wave of my wand, I set a broom to sweeping the floor.

Pete sputtered and danced on his perch. "Magick! Magick!"

"Ssssh!" I whispered. "Don't tell anyone, else I'll be casting cleaning spells all day long for the rest of my life."

Once I had a little space, I stripped off and gave myself a bucket bath with my jug of water and basin before drying myself off on Captain Bloodstone's great coat and changing into a cleaner pair of breeches and shirt. I kept the waistcoat, however. I quite fancied myself in it.

There was absolutely nothing to be done with my hair. I wound it into a bun on top of my head and fastened it with string. It was beginning to look like dreadlocks. Added to my increasingly weather-beaten complexion—okay, not so much weather-beaten as a fetching shade of sun-scorched pink—and the eyepatch, I'd have been ill-pressed to look more like a pirate if I tried.

My eye was causing me problems though. I could hardly see out of it thanks to the swelling, and if I did try to force it open, it began to weep. I carefully bathed it, dabbed it dry, and recovered it with the eyepatch.

When the gong sounded again, I plucked up the box, meaning to hide it under the bed, but given that I'd already been robbed once while on the ship—these were pirates, after all—I placed it in the bottom of the wardrobe and pointed my wand at it. "*Occaeco*!" I whispered, and the box vanished from view. I left the wardrobe door open. Anyone stealing into my cabin while I was otherwise engaged would see that the wardrobe was completely bare and would hopefully refrain from riffling around for hidden drawers and secret compartments.

I followed my nose down to the galley, where Florence was flitting about with one of the young crewmen—Voodoo it might have been, or Zulu—serving up supper. I'd been correct. Beef and ale pie with mash and gravy and mounds of carrots and peas dribbled with butter.

"Mmmmmm!" I sniffed the air appreciatively. "Oh, Florence, I've missed you!"

"That's cupboard love, Miss Alf, not true love," she scolded me, and sent me through to the mess. I sat with Half-Crocked, looking positively sheepish, Smithy Whiskers, looking absolutely murderous, and Butcher. Only he looked buoyant.

"How's it going, chaps?" I asked, depositing a bowl of vegetables in the middle of the table.

"Everything is ship-shape and Bristol fashion, Cap'n," Butcher told me.

I wasn't at all certain what that meant, but judging by Butcher's tone, it seemed to be a good thing, so I smiled and exclaimed, "Excellent!"

"The hold is tidy and the stores are well organised, Captain Alf," Half-Crocked told me.

"Super! Let's keep it that way, shall we?"

"Aye-aye, Captain!"

"And Smithy?" I asked, raising my eyebrows in his direction.

"I've sounded the ship and all is well, Captain," he replied, keeping it civil at least.

"Fab."

Voodoo—or Zulu, I still couldn't tell them apart—brought through our pie and set it down in front of me. The golden-brown pastry was thick and crumbly, and when I took the serving spoon to it, it sliced through and released a volcano of steam and rich dark gravy.

All three men moaned in unison.

I giggled. "Hungry, fellas?" I asked, and dished out large quantities of pie to each. "Help yourselves to potatoes and veggies," I told them. "And before you say you don't like vegetables, you have to try these. Florence is a magnificent cook."

They tucked in with gusto. Even Smithy Whiskers seemed to thaw a little. And after everyone had enjoyed seconds—even me—and spooned the gravy out of the jug, and scraped the dried crust from the pie dish, we all sat back and rubbed our tummies.

"That was mighty fine," Butcher said. "If that little lady wasn't dead, I'd marry her. Burned face or no burned face."

"There's a queue," I said. "I've been tempted to marry her myself once or twice."

"But you're getting married." Butcher waved a finger at me. "That would be bigamy."

I faked surprise. "You know, for a bunch of pirates, you're all awfully moral," I told him and laughed. "But you're right. Hopefully I'm getting married. *If* I can ever get Silvan out of prison."

"Why don't you just break him out?" Smithy Whiskers asked abruptly. "You talk about us being moral, but you have all that magick. Surely you could free him with a wave of your wand?"

"I wouldn't need to." I shrugged. "If Silvan wanted to get out of a mundane prison that badly, he could do it himself. The thing is, we have to live partly in the mundane world and partly in the magickal one. We can't afford to be looking over our shoulders for the rest of our lives while the Indian authorities and maybe the international community hunt us down."

I began to stack the plates, knowing full well that pudding would be following at any moment. I could already smell the sweet scent of honey and peaches and caramel. If I wasn't much mistaken, Florence was going to present us with a honeyed-peach crumble.

"He's an innocent man," I reminded them. "Far better for us that we prove it, and then we'll be free to carry on with our lives."

Smithy Whiskers nodded solemnly. "Which reminds me—"

From somewhere up on deck, a bell began clanging. My three dinner companions jumped to their feet immediately.

"What's wrong?" I asked, but they were already leaving. "Hey!"

I followed them in a hurry, pushing past Florence, who spun in confusion—"Oooh, Miss Alf!"—and racing onto the main deck.

Arrr Jim Lad, up in the crow's nest, had sounded the alarm.

"Ship on the horizon!" Butcher told me and handed me the telescope.

I peered through it, not immediately spotting anything at all, but then, after taking it away from my eye, squinting into the distance for the slightest hint of a blur, I returned the telescope and there, fully rigged, was a ship that could have been sister ship to *Poseidon's Curse.*

"If I'm not mistaken, that's *The Red Eel!*" Butcher said.

"Agreed!" Smithy Whiskers looked grim.

"Is this a problem for us?" I asked, because if it wasn't, I wanted to get back to my honeyed-peach crumble.

"It is," muttered Butcher, gesturing me to step aside. "They're our natural enemy, Cap'n. Pirates from the port of Pompey."

"We could try to outrun them," I suggested, but even as I said that, I knew it wouldn't wash. My crew were up for a fight.

"Pirates don't run from the enemy, Captain Alf," Butcher told me. "We run to them."

Oh dear. We were going to get into a fight. I cursed my luck. "I knew I should have bought those dinghies."

Butcher was scratching his chin. "Every time we have a run-in with *The Red Eel*, we come off worse."

"Do you?" I blinked into the distance, trying to establish how long it would be before they were upon us. It was useless trying. I didn't have a clue. "Then ..." I laughed awkwardly. "Can't we just vacate the area?"

Butcher ignored the question. "You need to give the order for the men to stand by their guns."

"Is that what you always do?" I asked. "Pepper them with cannonballs?"

"Aye, Cap'n. But theirs are bigger than ours, so we usually heave to and they board us and steal our supplies and then let us limp away to lick our wounds and patch up our holes and we all live to fight another day."

"I'm kind of grateful to hear that they don't finish us off," I admitted. "I'm too young to die. But ... let's just rewind a minute. You said they *steal our supplies*?"

"That's why we never have any," Butcher admitted. "It wasn't that Captain Bloodstone never bought any fresh supplies, more that he did and we kept losing th—"

"Stop right there." I drew myself up to my full height. "After all the effort we've been through today, nothing and nobody is stealing my supplies." I stamped my foot and hurriedly climbed to my patio deck. Leaning over the railing, I yelled, "Men? Front and centre!"

There was a scurry of feet as the men, full of pie and crumble, assembled below me, their heads craning upwards, awaiting my orders.

"This is how it's going to go," I said, casting a glance at *The Red Eel*. She was sailing swiftly into our proximity. "They are *not* boarding us and taking our supplies. Not today. Not ever. Nobody, least of all a bunch of unwashed pirates—erm, who aren't you—will ever get their hands on the goods that *Poseidon's Curse* has in her hold. Is that clear?"

"Aar!" A rather lukewarm response.

I pulled my wand out from where it had been safely tucked into my belt. "I said, is that clear?"

"Aaaaarhhhh!"

As a kid I'd loved playing Battleship with my dad.

When our torpedoes missed, we would make a 'ploonk' sound, the sound of something heavy hitting the water. If we made a hit, we made a 'pwwwruuuu-urhhhh-kkkkkkkiiiiii' sound, the subdued noise of something exploding. It had always been great fun.

And I'd *always* won.

Whether that was because Erik let me win or not, I can't tell you. But one thing I was sure of today was that *The Red Eel* was not about to steal my supply of ship's biscuits. I'd fully restocked and, having jettisoned the old ship's biscuits with the weevils deep into the Indian Ocean, I'd replaced them with custard creams, Bourbon creams, chocolate Hobnobs and McVities Jaffa cakes.

Thank the goddess for international supermarkets.

And so now I had everything to play for.

And I intended to cheat a little.

Standing on the forecastle with Scurvy at the ship's wheel and Butcher beside me, I barked commands. "Sail into the wind, then track back," I ordered as *The Red Eel* pressed down on us. I could clearly see that her figurehead was bright red with a toxic green tongue and bold black eyes surrounded by ridiculous eyelashes. Our water nymph—despite her impressive chest—was a wimp by comparison.

"We will not be cowed!" I screamed into the wind, one hand hanging onto a rope and the other gesticulating with my wand. "Butcher?"

"Aye, Cap'n?"

"I want you to pass directly behind her. She won't be able to train her cannons on us, and chances are if we're moving fast enough, she won't be able to reorient herself quickly enough either."

"Aye, Cap'n!" Butcher gave the orders and the men moved around their stations like the true professionals they were. They might be pretty poor at pirating, but once again I found myself praising their undeniable ability to sail a ship.

Perhaps *Poseidon's Curse* sensed the excitement because she bucked her head and skated forwards, a sudden rush of speed that threatened to knock me off balance. But that surge was just the ticket. We whooshed past *The Red Eel*, to the astonishment of her crew, who scuttled about trying to turn their ship's head.

With our advantageous position, as soon as we came side on, I gave my next order. "Fire!" I cried.

Whoopmf!

All our portside—or perhaps starboard, well, whatever-board—cannons roared into life. I'd spent a few minutes going around earlier and daubing the piles of cannonballs with a little trusty magick and a pretty nifty spell. You see, the thing is, I didn't want to be responsible for any fatalities, not on my watch, and certainly not with strangers that I had no quarrel with.

But there was no way I was going to let them *steal our supplies* either, and so I had rigged the cannonballs with a kind of phosphorescent glitter, entirely non-toxic and biodegradable, of course. Once catapulted at the enemy, they exploded in magnificent circles of shimmering light, rather like a firework display, raining glitter down on the crew in all the colours of a unicorn's rainbow.

The cannonballs flew out from between our railings and smacked into *The Red Eel*, over and over again. The effect was startling but not particularly dangerous. When the other crew managed to manipulate themselves into a position whereby they could take aim at us, I had to hurriedly shift tactics, otherwise I feared we'd feel the heat of their fire, and theirs wouldn't be as pretty as ours.

Lifting my wand and using the telescope, I sighted the ropes that held *The Red Eel*'s sails in place, then, with precision focus and laser-like energy, I carefully cut through those ropes, one after another in quick succession—but not all the way. That would have spoiled the surprise. No. I just used the command "*Tero*!" to make the ropes fray.

"Ready, men!" I yelled, and a dozen of my fittest sailors grabbed lines suspended from our yardarms.

"Aaarh!" came the answering roar.

"Steady as she goes," Butcher said to Scurvy, who was fighting valiantly to keep *Poseidon's Curse* alongside *The Red Eel* despite the vagaries of the waves and the light wind attempting to push us away.

"Three ... two ... one." I nodded at Butcher.

"Board!" he shouted, and my hand-picked sailors leapt for their ropes and swung across to the neighbouring ship.

At the exact moment they began to cross the gap between the ships, I guided my wand from rope to rope and gently intoned, "*Exsolvo, exsolvo, exsolvo, exsolvo.*" The sails, too heavy for the frayed ropes, were released into space, drifting to the deck and covering the men like an enormous weighted blanket.

There were shrieks and screams as the enemy pirates, not understanding why the lights had suddenly gone out, fought to find their way free.

But the sailors from *Poseidon's Curse* had already boarded *The Red Eel*, and her captain, standing in his place on the forecastle, threw down his sword.

Victory was assuredly ours!

Chapter Sixteen

I must confess I felt a little guilty watching my crew parade backwards and forwards between *The Red Eel* and *Poseidon's Curse*, clutching the spoils of war, but there was no denying the flush on their cheeks and the sparkle in their eyes. It had been a long time since my boys—as I was starting to think of them—had been able to celebrate success of any type.

Even Smithy Whiskers looked pleased.

I surveyed the goods coming aboard: mainly trinkets and weapons, with several barrels of rum, each branded with the same logo I'd seen on our own barrels. I drew the line at personal items, sending back one or two sailors carrying clothing, even though they protested that the robbing pirates aboard *The Red Eel* had been the ones responsible for plundering similar belongings from us in the first place.

"Shall we send 'er plummeting to the bottom of the ocean, Cap'?" Scurvy asked hopefully, waving his sword around, ready to give the order for the cannons to see *The Red Eel* off once and for all.

"Certainly not," I said. "There are international piracy laws we need to pay attention to!" I had absolutely no idea what these laws were, but I was fairly certain that a) they existed and b) the international powers that be would frown upon cold-blooded murder.

Feeling more confident than I probably had a right to, I clambered between both ships to speak to the captain. Captain Holland Rogue was his name and, as I came aboard, he regarded me with narrowed eyes, but still he cowered as I marched up to him. I couldn't help but find it peculiar to have a complete stranger frightened of little old me.

"Good evening!" I breezed. "Awfully sorry about your sails."

"Aaar. Easily fixed," he growled, his eyes flicking left and right. He had long grey hair, curly like mine, and dark eyes like Silvan's.

"Smashing! I wouldn't want you to be marooned for too long."

"Mighty decent of you," he said, but his tone implied otherwise. "Who the Davy Jones are you?"

"Captain Alfhild Daemonne," I told him, thrusting out my hand. He shook it as though it were a soiled dishcloth. "I'm temporarily commanding *Poseidon's Curse*."

"Temporarily?"

"Yes. While I try to find a seagoing reprobate and escort him back to Dakti Bhoin to face justice."

"Poor man." Captain Rogue arched an eyebrow.

"He could have some vital information about the murder of Captain Bloodstone!" I jerked my thumb at *Poseidon's Curse*. "He may even be the culprit. I think my crew deserve answers, don't you?"

"Aaar." He scratched his chin. "I take your point. I must admit I had a fondness for Captain Bloodstone. We've been at each other's throats for nigh on thirty years."

"Besides which, my fiancé has been remanded for the murder, so I need to prove his innocence."

"I see." Captain Rogue dipped his head. "And what's the name of this fellow you're searching for?"

"Salty Dog," I told him, waiting for a reaction. "Do you know him?"

Captain Rogue twisted his face, his eyes hooded, not so much thinking, as considering whether to tell me what he knew.

"I know him," he eventually replied. "He's been around a bit. Run with a few pirate crews in his time. Currently sailing a boat he uses for private charters. It's called *Seawolf*, am I right?"

"That's right." I placed my hands on my hips. "Have you seen him? Do you know where he is?"

Captain Rogue licked his lips. "What's in it for me if I give you any information?"

Hadn't I just this minute whooped this man's backside? How did he even have the cheek to ask me what he'd get out of it? I pulled my wand from my belt and twiddled with it.

Perhaps that did the trick, or perhaps he recognised the scorn on my face because suddenly he grinned, a devilish expression, in truth. "Just kidding, Captain Alf, just kidding!"

"Ha ha ha," I said, entirely without mirth.

"Let me see." He rolled his eyes upward and made a great show of thinking, tapping the side of his face with long, filthy fingernails.

"It's getting dark," I pointed out. "We need to be on our way." I scraped a stray strand of hair from my face with the tip of my wand.

"Oh, that's it!" He chuckled. "We saw him this morning."

I couldn't believe it. I arched an eyebrow. He'd just remembered that, had he? "This morning? Where?"

"On the island of Verasana. We pulled in there to replenish our water."

"Is that far away?" I don't know why I was wasting time asking Captain Rogue. Butcher would know. We needed to get after Salty Dog, pronto.

"He won't be there now, but"—Captain Rogue leaned in towards me—"for a small fee I can tell you where he's bound."

Bloomin' pirates! "How much?" I asked. "I don't have a lot of money!"

He ducked his head, flapping a pretend fan at his

face. "Oh, I don't want money, Captain Alf. I want rum!"

The crew of *Poseidon's Curse* were going to have me hauling the keel. I could feel it. "How much rum?"

"Six barrels."

"I'll give you two."

"Four!"

"Two and a half."

"Three!"

"Done." I gestured at Half-Crocked. "Have the men bring back three barrels of rum," I told him.

He immediately began to protest. "But Captain Alf!"

I waggled my wand. "And make sure they're full."

"Aye, Cap'n." A disgruntled Half-Crocked began to relay my orders.

"So, where is Salty Dog going?" I asked Captain Rogue. He greedily watched the barrels of rum come back aboard *The Red Eel*.

"I asked him that very question," Captain Rogue replied. "He was a little cagey about it. Said he had some family business to attend to."

"Where?" I was beginning to lose patience. I waved at Half-Crocked. "Hold fast there!" I called, and he gestured for my pirates to stop carrying the rum on board.

"No need for that," Captain Rogue whined. "No need at all, Captain Alf. Old Salty mentioned Exile Land."

"Exile Land?" I repeated.

"Aar."

"Okay." I'd never heard of it, but then I'd never heard of Dakti Bhoin or Naarangi or Kandla or Verasana before travelling out here with Silvan. We'd find it on the maps, I was certain. "I'll check it out. Thanks."

"Good luck," he said, and turned to begin supervising the fixing of his sails and the consumption of his rum.

"Did you have to give him our rum?" Half-Crocked was still moaning as we set a course due west. Butcher, Half-Crocked, Scurvy and myself were poring over various documents on the map table. So far, our search hadn't revealed anywhere named Exile Land.

Butcher was wielding a magnifying glass. "Are you sure he wasn't making it up?"

"I've never heard of it," Scurvy agreed, "and I've been sailing this ocean my entire adult life."

"It's a good name for an island," I said. "It sounds feasible to me. Kind of romantic. Like a place where the French would have sent political or royal prisoners. Marooned them forever more. Left them to rot in stone towers ..."

Scurvy grimaced. "Yes, that does sound romantic."

"Flights of fancy," muttered Butcher.

"'And now their ghosts haunt the rocky outcrops, crying for justice'," I finished. "That's definitely what he said. Exile Land."

Half-Crocked pulled a face. "Since when are we trusting Captain Rogue? He'd barter away his own mother for a barrel of rum!"

I ignored the jibe, although secretly I feared I might have been had. "Wherever it is, we're not far behind Salty Dog. We need to press on."

Butcher looked up. "Gentlemen, could I have the room please?"

Half-Crocked and Scurvy nodded and walked out, talking between themselves. I stared expectantly at Butcher.

"If you don't mind me saying, Captain Alf," he started, slowly and carefully, "it's all very well saying we're not far behind Salty Dog, but given exactly where we are in the world"—he jabbed a fat sausage finger at the middle of the map—"that does display a certain naivety on your part."

I pouted. "How so?"

Butcher positioned a small wooden boat on the map, not a million miles from Verasana. "That's us." He placed a red one close by. "That's *The Red Eel*."

"Okay." I leaned over, wondering what his point was.

He took a pencil and a compass and drew a large circle. A very large circle. "With our current winds, that's a day's sailing."

"Wow," I said. "But we're not going in all those directions at once."

He chuckled. "And that's my point, Captain Alf! We have no way o' knowing which way Salty Dog has gone. There be no road signs out at sea. He could have gone in any of these directions, and we may be moving in the opposite direction—"

"I get it," I said, feeling like an idiot.

"We can only assume that if Captain Rogue bumped into Salty Dog this morning, he won't have too much ground on us."

"Let's just take our best guess," I suggested.

"Best guess?" Butcher coughed. "That's no way to command a boat, Captain Alf."

"It's the only way I know how to," I told him.

"Ship ahoy!"

Arrr Jim Lad, up in the crow's nest, was sounding an alarm.

I clawed my way through multiple lines hung with damp washing. Florence, along with half a dozen helpers, had been scrubbing clothes and dirty linen all morning, and now we had breeches and shirts and sheets and holey underpants and all manner of things hung on lines to dry. You couldn't see from one side of the ship to the other.

Racing to the forecastle, I lifted the telescope to my

good eye, confirmed that there was indeed a ship to the north-west of us, and turned excitedly to Butcher.

"What do you think? Could it be him?"

Butcher took my telescope and peered carefully towards the horizon.

"It's not making any ground," he said. "Looks like it might be struggling."

"Get the men to their stations," I said. "We don't want to be caught on the hop. Perceptions can be deceptive."

"Aye, Cap'n!"

Smithy was at the helm. "Head towards the ship," I said, "but don't bring us too close. Not yet."

I gripped the rails, my knuckles white with excitement, willing *Poseidon's Curse* onwards. Perhaps we'd get lucky! Perhaps this was Salty Dog! Perhaps I was finally getting somewhere!

"What's going on?" Gwyn apparated beside me.

"We may have found Salty Dog!" I told her, but as we drew closer, even I could see there was something wrong with the ship we were approaching. It listed to its side, its sails ragged and rigging destroyed.

"I think you may be out of luck, Alfhild," Gwyn remarked. "And so are they."

"That's *Rose's Revenge*!" Butcher cried.

"Oh wow," I said. "They look like they're in need of our help."

"Steady as she goes, Cap'n," Butcher cautioned. "You never can tell—"

I nodded, but it seemed to me *Rose's Revenge* was taking on water judging by how one side of her was being pulled into the ocean. As we finally closed in on the ship, a figure appeared on the main deck and waved frantically in our direction. "Take us alongside," I instructed.

Butcher was ill at ease with this command. "Captain Alf, that could be dangerous. If the ship is going down, we'll be sucked into the maelstrom."

"I get that," I said, "but we can't leave the crew on board if they don't have life rafts. We have to save them!"

Smithy Whiskers spoke up. "I think we have a little time. But I would advise we're quick, Captain Alf."

It was the first time he'd volunteered anything to me. I nodded. "Take us close. As close as we were to *The Red Eel* yesterday. We'll get the crew off and then back away as fast as possible. Smithy, you see to that. Butcher? You get a rescue party ready."

"Aaar!" they chorused.

Thank goodness for relatively calm seas. Smithy expertly brought us alongside, while Scurvy and Voodoo tied *Poseidon's Curse* to *Rose's Revenge.*

"Ahoy there!" I climbed onto the railing like a full-size Peter Pan, one wrist wrapped in a rope to save me from going over if the two ships suddenly parted ways.

"Ahoy there, Captain!" one of the sailors, wearing a blue cap and a striped shirt, called back.

"What's your name, sailor?" I asked.

"Whistling Sam, ma'am. We were boarded by hostiles."

I craned my head to see a little better. "Was anyone hurt?"

"Aye! Our captain is in a bad way."

I didn't think twice. I leapt over to *Rose's Revenge* to see if I could help. The sailor hadn't been lying; the decks ran with blood. Two men lay prone, both swaddled in sheets. What I'd feared would happen to *Poseidon's Curse* had come true here.

"Can we get them over to my ship?" I asked.

One of the other crew members wrung his hands. "We shouldn't move them!"

"Well, it's that or drown," I told him, "because this ship is going down."

Half-Crocked and Butcher appeared next to me. "Let's get these two injured men off this ship," I said, and Butcher began giving orders. Working in pairs, they carried the injured men over to the railings to be met by another pair on *Poseidon's Curse*. The transfer proved difficult because *Rose's Revenge* was listing heavily. We didn't have long.

Keeping a careful eye out for Smithy's signal, I asked Whistling Sam, "How many crew?"

"Only seven of us ..."

I counted heads. The two injured men, Whistling Sam, four sailors. Seven accounted for.

"There's absolutely no-one else on the ship?" I

asked, casting a swift glance around. "No parrots? Cats? Owls?"

"No, ma'am."

I pointed at my eyepatch. "That's Captain Alf to you, sunshine."

"Aye, Captain!"

I gave him a push. "Let's go!"

Not before time! Smithy sounded the alarm as *Rose's Revenge*'s stern suddenly dropped lower, her bow tipping upwards. "Captain Alf! We need to leave now!" he yelled at me.

I waved my understanding, nodded at Whistling Sam, grabbed his elbow and flung him towards the railings. As I did so, the deck beneath my feet fell away and I lost my balance, tumbling down the incline towards the stern. A cannon, fortunately fixed to the deck, was the only thing to break my fall.

Clunk.

"Ouch!" I tried to right myself, but the deck was slippery and the poor ship was beginning to dip beneath the waves. I struggled to find a handhold and suddenly, there seemed to be an awful lot of water around me. Until you're faced with the reality of the ocean, I'm not sure you ever fully appreciate how vast it is. Water all around, and miles of it below you too.

"Captain Alf!" Butcher yelled. "You have to get off there. We have to get *Poseidon's Curse* away, otherwise she'll be dragged down too."

"By all that's green!" I muttered. "Obviously I have

to get off, you great bearded nincompoop. Do you really think I'm hanging about here for the good of my health?"

I stood on the cannon—the side of the cannon, that is, because the ship was now listing at a sixty-degree angle—and tried to make a jump for the railings. If I could pull myself up there, I'd be able to reach for—

The ship tipped back on its axis, almost horizontal to the water once more, but lower than before. I wouldn't be able to reach *Poseidon's Curse*, not in a month of Sundays, but not to worry, I had my wand tucked into my belt, I'd just metamorphosise myself into Jumping SpiderAlf and—

Perhaps it was because my fingers were wet, perhaps because they were cold, but as I fumbled for my wand, it flew out of my hand and landed on the wet deck.

"Butterfingers." I scolded myself and leaned over to pick it up.

"Captain Alf!" Butcher roared above my head.

Just as my fingertips made contact with my much-cherished piece of Vance, the ship rolled. I flew one way and my wand bounced the other. *Plink, plink, plinkity-plink ...*

Bloop.

Into the sea.

I clambered to my feet, with difficulty, gaping in astonishment at the place where the wand had vanished. "That didn't just happen," I said, but it had.

Without a second's hesitation, I jumped after it. I'd like to say I performed a beautiful swan dive, but no, I didn't do anything as gracious as that. I simply leapt into the sea, arms and legs akimbo.

Fortunately for me, after flailing around for a moment, trying to catch my breath and blinking salt-water out of my good eye, I remembered that wood floats. I splashed around until I spotted my wand, grabbed it and held it aloft in triumph. *Rose's Revenge* picked that moment to begin her final goodbye. She tipped back on her stern, twisted slightly, much like a corkscrew, the bow towering high above me. Incredulous—because how many of us can say we've ever seen a pirate galleon from this angle while taking a dip in the Indian Ocean?—I stared up at it before belatedly recalling the imminent threat to *Poseidon's Curse*.

However, when I manoeuvred myself to check on her, I realised Smithy had already allowed her to drift away, leaving me behind.

"There's gratitude for you." I watched her smooth departure in disbelief.

"Just me then?" I asked the universe. "Are you really that determined that I don't get married?"

In a fit of sudden indignation, I began to swim towards my departing ship. "*Poseidon's Curse* my backside," I growled. "Bigger and better things have tried to kill me in the past. I'm not letting a bunch of snotty pirates ruin my big day—oop—oop—ooooooo! Whooooooo!"

A wall of water swamped me from behind, initially pushing me forward and then dragging me back. I sank beneath the waves, fighting to find my way back to the surface. The ocean swirled around me, and I briefly imagined this must be what it was like to take a ride in a washing machine. First I rolled one way, then I tumbled another, head up, head down, not really sure which direction was north and which was south. I swallowed the threat of panic. If I allowed it to take hold, I'd be a goner. *Get a grip*, I told myself.

Get a grip!

I held my wand in front of me. "*Aaequor*!" I demanded, but only in my head. Even I wasn't sure of the precocity of opening my mouth to intone spells, not when I was underwater.

A thin beam of sparkling pink light began to float from the tip of my wand, cutting through all the turbulent bluey-green. I kicked with my legs, following the energy up ... up ... up ... until I thought my lungs would burst if I didn't break through!

Right at the moment I started thinking *oh-my-goddess-it's-time-to-meet-my-maker*, I popped out of the water like a cork out of a champagne bottle. Coughing and spluttering, I kicked around, trying to get my bearings, and there, joy of joys, was *Poseidon's Curse*, sails down, waiting for me.

But *Rose's Revenge*?

Alas, she was gone forever.

To my immense gratification, a cheer went up among the pirates as I, half drowned, flopped onto their deck like a prize catch of the day. They'd been hanging over the railings, mainly because they wanted to see SpiderAlf in action. I'd have preferred a hand up, but they seemed to think I could manage on my own. Truth to tell, by the time I made it up onto the main deck, I was exhausted. If someone had put a blanket over me, I'd have lain right where I was and gone to sleep.

"Oh, Miss Alf!" Florence flapped around me. "Thank goodness you made it back. I never did learn to swim! Who'd have saved you?"

"I'm fine, Florence," I told her, probably unconvincingly, and, without a blanket immediately forthcoming and aware that we had two injured sailors aboard *Poseidon's Curse*, I had to get my rump in gear once more. I dragged myself to my feet, purposefully ignoring Gwyn's look of exasperation at the state of me—"You have seaweed in your hair, dear"—and stumbled over to where Butcher was tending to the captain.

"How is he?" I asked, trying not to drip on the man lying on the deck.

"Poorly," Butcher told me. "We need to make land as soon as possible."

"Do it." I nodded at Smithy Whiskers, who was

hovering nearby waiting for orders. "Take us wherever is closest."

"Aye, Cap'n!" He raced back to the helm, shouting orders. The pirates of *Poseidon's Curse* rushed to their stations, shinning up the masts, climbing the rigging, dropping sails and preparing for us to make haste.

"Do you know the men of *Rose's Revenge*, Butcher?" I asked.

"Aye," he answered, his face grim. "Captain Ivor Wilde and his men."

"What happened?"

Butcher beckoned Whistling Sam forth and repeated the question to him. The sailor twisted his blue cap in his hands, his face pale, but his eyes alight with anger. "We were attacked!"

The other sailors huddled around him, casting a wary eye at any of my crew who came close, but more concerned by Gwyn and Florence, who was smoking like a chimney, probably from the stress of my lucky escape.

"Can we organise some refreshments for our guests?" I asked Florence, hoping to take her mind off what she'd seen.

"Of course!" She floated happily away. "Some nice sweet hot chocolate and the mango and banana upside-down cake I've been experimenting with ..."

"What's your real name?" I asked Whistling Sam.

He pulled his cap off. "Samuel Drake, ma'am ... Captain, I mean."

"Well, Mr Drake, who attacked you? Do you know? Was it random?"

"Was it friend or foe, you mean?" he asked, and his tone was bitter.

I didn't understand. "Why would a friend attack your ship?"

"That's what I want to know. The *Seawolf* hailed us and came up alongside—"

"Wait!" My chin jerked backwards. "Did you say *Seawolf*?"

"Aye. Salty Dog, an old friend of ours, supposedly. He came aboard with his crew, told us he was short of supplies, that there was a target on his head—"

There certainly would be if he was within magicking distance! I'd put it there myself!

"Captain Wilde told him he could have half of our supplies, but only half because we didn't have much ourselves. We're heading for, pardon me, we were heading for Baratnang in a few days to reprovision there. But that wasn't enough for Salty Dog!"

The other pirates growled.

"Murdering cur," said one.

"Treacherous tyrant," said another.

"You're saying he took what he wanted?" I asked.

"He and his crew overwhelmed us," Drake said. "There were only the three of them, but ..."

"It was like they had it all planned," one of his comrades noted. "They took out the captain, and then Simple Soloman ... and overwhelmed us."

"He threatened to cut the captain's head off," Whistling Sam told me, his eyes bleak. "He would have done too."

I glanced at Butcher. "He's heading for this Exile Land and he wants to keep his head down, but he needs supplies. He must have heard that the police are interested in speaking to him—"

"Or he has an inkling that Captain Alf is on his tail," Butcher reminded me.

"There is that," I agreed. "At least we know we're on the right track." If you can be on track while you're at sea. "Let's move Captain Wilde and the other injured sailor to the captain's cabin," I suggested. "We can look after them better in there."

As Whistling Sam turned to assist the other sailors in relocating his captain, I stopped him. "You wouldn't happen to know where Exile Land is, would you? Or Exile Island?"

His forehead creased. "Exile Land? No, Captain. Can't say I've heard of that at all."

"Okay, no problem." I let him go, watching the care with which the sailors navigated the ladder up to my patio deck.

Standing next to me, Butcher murmured, "Maybe Exile Land doesn't exist, except in Captain Rogue's imagination."

"You could be right," I agreed. "But I'm not ready to give up yet."

CHAPTER SEVENTEEN

The weather changed overnight.

In between watches I slept in a hammock, which was every bit as bad as I feared it would be. For one thing, the sound of all the other men snoring and muttering and singing in their sleep kept me awake, and, on the other, I had the sensation that I'd been folded into two rather like a concertina, that my knees were in my chest and my backside was scraping the floor. But, given how exhausting the previous day had been, I did manage several hours' sleep.

I was awoken at four by Half-Crocked to undertake my next watch. I could tell by the keel of the ship that we were driving hard on the wind. When I made it up to the deck, I stood in awe, staring at the sails billowing above me, catapulting us towards land.

It might have been exhilarating, but with that increasing wind came squalls, cloud bursts that exploded upon us without warning. As I crouched by the helm—holding on for dear life—the rain lashed against me, stinging the stings of a million bees. And oh, those high seas! Not high in comparison to the other storms my sailors had endured in the past, apparently—so I was told numerous times —but certainly nothing like I'd ever seen on a day trip to the beach in East Devon, even during the winter.

Memories of *Rose's Revenge*'s swift descent to the seabed played on my mind as I squinted into the dark. There was nothing to see; the clouds were low, the darkness complete, and dawn still at least an hour away. But I did my duty, remaining in place, my stomach lurching all over the place until I spotted the faintest wedge of silvery light on the horizon.

The sun. At last.

"Bracing, isn't it?" Gwyn said, standing alongside me, wearing some polar expedition's arctic greatcoat, probably made of polar bear fur or something equally as heinous. Her hair whipped long and free, whereas mine, tied up with a piece of old string and so saturated in salt that it barely moved, could have been used to clean an oven.

"You're lucky you don't get seasick," I told her, grimacing as the ship crashed into the well between two waves and then rose again.

"I never did," Gwyn told me. "Did I ever tell you about the time I joined an expedition to Mexico?"

Gwyn never ceased to amaze me. "I don't believe you did," I replied. She glanced sideways at me, probably not appreciating my tone. "Tell me," I added in a hurry.

"We were undertaking a study into the migratory habits of blue whales. I went along because I was friendly with one of the scientists."

"That must have been interesting," I said, wondering how she managed to fit in all these adventures. She'd enjoyed a full life. Not like me. Nothing interesting ever happened to ...

Oh.

"Yes. We did a dive in a little ocean-exploring submarine—"

Now I knew she was fibbing.

"And I rode on top of a whale named Dilys."

"You rode a blue whale?" Was I hallucinating? Or perhaps she was.

"They're really rather friendly, you know. I do wish people would stop hunting them."

I risked peeking over the railings. "Do you get blue whales in the Indian Ocean?"

"You'll find them in most oceans, those that are left, but they're not so prevalent around here." She sounded impressively knowledgeable!

"I wonder what they make of storms ..." I pondered as we lurched down and up again. This was like riding a rollercoaster at an amusement park, but less predictable. And far less enjoyable.

"They probably barely notice them, my dear. Rather like when it rains at home."

Ah, home. Whittle Inn seemed a million miles away. I found myself suddenly feeling awfully homesick. Or maybe I was just travel-sick.

"Look!" Gwyn pointed to the horizon, where fingers of orange were spreading out above the deep blue waves. "Bright blessings for another beautiful day!"

"Indeed! And let's hope we make land soon so we can find medical assistance for our two passengers."

"The goddess will provide, Alfhild. Doesn't she always?"

Above my head the sails flapped loudly, and then, just like that, the storm had passed.

"She certainly moves in mysterious ways," I said.

"And I truly appreciate that," Gwyn told me.

I grinned. "So do I."

With Captain Wilde and his band of pirates safely ashore and being properly cared for at some basic but purpose-built medical facility, I returned to my cabin to help clean up after them. Once we'd collected up the detritus of makeshift bandages and sponges, ripped shirts and breeches, I set about sweeping the floor ready to mop—probably one of my least favourite chores besides ironing, so perhaps I'd magick the mop and bucket but only if nobody was watching—and remake the bed.

Anything to avoid sleeping in a hammock again!

Florence was inside with the clothes we'd washed and dried the previous day, hanging them in the wardrobe and tutting about lack of space and the general absence of mothballs.

"I'm not sure you get moths at sea, Florence," I said, hoping that would offer some consolation.

Florence wasn't having it. "Have you never seen a sea moth, Miss Alf?"

"They don't exist." I pulled a face. "You're making that up."

"Great big things, they are!" She pulled her arms wide apart and dropped the blouse she'd been trying to hang up. It draped over the invisible shape of the box. "Ooh! What's that there?"

"Crikey! I'd forgotten all about that!" I hurried over and tossed the blouse aside, much to Florence's chagrin.

"Miss Alf! I've just ironed that!"

"Soz." I felt around the chest with my fingers, then lifted it and carried it over to the bed. "*Manufesto*!" I intoned, waving my still-slightly-damp piece of Vance over it. The air sparkled for a moment before the chest shimmered back into view.

"Look at the state of that!" Florence tutted and rushed over, clutching her duster. With three or four well-practised swipes, the colour of the wood really began to show through.

"It must have been an expensive chest in its day." I

swirled my fingertips around the carvings. "And I'm absolutely sure this must have meant something. Someone's house maybe."

"A posh house, that," Florence said. "Not like the cottages in Whittlecombe."

I laughed. "Very posh." I lifted the box again, checking I had the key. "I ought to show this to Butcher. I would need to find Captain Bloodstone's next of kin. Can you manage to clean the rest of this cabin without me?"

Florence blinked at me, steam rising in rapid little puffs. "What do *you* think, Miss Alf?"

"Hmmm." I grinned.

As I made my way along the patio deck, I distinctly heard her say, "Thank heavens for small mercies. I'll get everything as shiny as a new sixpence twice as quickly now!"

It's nice to be appreciated, isn't it?

Butcher, Half-Crocked, Smithy Whiskers and Scurvy gathered around me for the grand re-opening of the box.

"Ye found it under the bunk, ye say?" Scurvy asked.

"Tucked right in the dark corner where nobody else would have noticed it," I told them. "I meant to show you when I found it, but everything has been happening so quickly." I eased the lid open, and we all leaned closer to take a better look at the pile of envelopes in faded parchment and a bundle of small scrolls sealed with blobs of red wax.

"Did you go through the contents?" Butcher asked.

"No." I shook my head. "I didn't feel it was my place to do so. This should be handed over to a relative, shouldn't it?"

I flipped through the envelopes. All addressed to Bloodstone. Letters from a lover a long time before. From his parents ...

Half-Crocked pulled out one of the scrolls. "They should be handed over, unless they're related to *Poseidon's Curse*, in which case, maybe the chest belongs to the ship."

"Arrr." Smithy Whiskers was in accord.

Scurvy showed us the wax blob. "If I ain't much mistaken—and I rarely is about these 'ere things—this be the Captain's seal."

"Aar," the men agreed.

I glanced at Butcher, unsure. He shrugged. "I know there was a brother somewhere, but the captain never really spoke of him. Apart from that, we were his family."

"So that's two votes for us to go through the contents," I acknowledged.

"Hey!" Smithy Whiskers held up a scroll. "This has got Half-Crocked's name on it!"

"What?" Half-Crocked snatched it out of his hand.

"Let me see that!" He broke the seal, unrolled the parchment and straightened it out.

"'Tis a map!" The pirates elbowed me out the way to get a better look.

Smithy Whiskers pointed out the edges. "Part of a map—"

Scurvy grabbed another scroll. "This one here's got the name Robert Reargelt. Who's he?"

"Wrathful Bob," Butcher said, taking it from Scurvy. "That was his real name." He broke the wax seal on it and rolled this one out too. "Looks like they're all sections of a larger map."

"Treasure!" enthused Half-Crocked.

"Aar!" Butcher cried. "The Captain always said there be treasure in these islands."

"Aaar!" The men began pulling the rest of the scrolls apart.

I watched them in bemusement. "If he knew there was treasure around, why did he never go and find it?"

Nobody chose to answer that.

Hands fumbled as they lined up each part of the map. There were nine sections, so it was rather like one of those games you play where you switch out parts to make a whole. I enjoyed those, although *Castles and Crones* was much more fun. But I'd play anything if it meant avoiding filling in spreadsheets.

"This be a treasure map if ever I saw one!" enthused Scurvy when the whole thing had finally come together.

"There's the south-west coast of India—" Butcher showed me, his thick finger tracing the outline, before jabbing at an island on the map. "And see? There's Naarangi ... and Dakti Bhoin is that little dot."

I nodded. "Where are we now?"

Butcher showed me a chain of small islands. "This is Baratnang, the largest of the Coral Islands." I followed the sweep of his hand further north and slightly to the west, where an island sat all alone with a huge X daubed over the top of it.

Half-Crocked could hardly contain his excitement. "X marks the spot!"

"We're going to be rich, gentlemen!" Scurvy agreed.

"But—" I tried to break in.

"We should set a course straight there!" Half-Crocked cried. "What say ye, Butch?"

"I think—"

Butcher shifted uncomfortably. "It's not up to me. I'm not the captain."

Scurvy peered expectantly at me. "Cap'n Alf?"

I sighed in exasperation. "Listen to me, fellas. Tell me why Captain Bloodstone didn't take you there before?"

Half-Crocked lifted his chin in defiance. "He was busy."

"He was busy doing what?" These sailors were deluded. "According to—" Oops. I'd better not drop Butcher into hot water. "According to rumours I've heard, you never used to do a lot, just sail around and get into the odd scrap with Captain Rogue, which"—I waggled a finger—"you hardly ever won. Then you'd all sit in port fixing your sails and your rigging and drinking the bars dry." I was making things up now, but I'd been on the ship long enough to know exactly what these men would do. "Then off you'd go and do the whole thing again."

I gave an enormous shrug. "Meanwhile, the ship is falling apart around your ears, the masthead hasn't had a lick of paint in years, the hold is full of rats and there are weebles in your flour—"

"Weevils," Butcher inserted.

"—*weevils* in your flour, and you never have a penny to your name. So why," I asked again, stabbing my finger on the bright red X, "didn't he take you to X island before?"

I stopped, realisation dawning on me.

Butcher's mouth dropped open. "X island."

"X island," I repeated.

"According to Captain Rogue, that's where Salty Dog was heading," Butcher reminded me, not that I needed it. I was all too aware.

"Set a course!" I said. "That's where we're going!"

The men jumped to it. For once, we were in full agreement.

CHAPTER EIGHTEEN

What followed next was an interesting few days of sailing. We stuck all parts of the map together using ancient sticky tape that didn't have an awful lot of stick, and Butcher and Smithy Whiskers put their heads together to plot the best course. Ironically, they decided they didn't want any more run-ins with pirates—especially Salty Dog and his crew—so they opted for a loop away from the Coral Islands, further out to sea than I'd ever been.

You've heard of the term 'plain sailing'? Well, that would be an apt way to describe those few days. We had a decent wind that kept the sails full, pushing us along at a respectable pace. Occasionally there was a lull, and the sailors would work harder to catch the merest breath of a breeze and utilise it in some magickal way that kept us going.

In between, Florence kept up a regime of cleanliness and cooking workshops. Every sailor who wanted to was given instruction in basic cooking techniques.

Those who showed a willingness and an aptitude were able to progress to more complicated recipes, and within twenty-four hours we had rock cakes and fairy buns coming out of the tiny galley kitchen by the score.

Not to be outdone, Gwyn began to offer crochet lessons.

Yes, crochet.

Until this moment, I had remained blissfully unaware that Gwyn possessed crocheting skills, but something about the way the sailors worked with fishing nets and rigging had evidently caught her attention, because she suddenly found skeins and skeins of yarn from somewhere—perhaps she conjured them—in every colour of the rainbow, and set about teaching the men to crochet.

I looked on with some scepticism, I must admit. There was no way these big hefty sailors with all their tattoos and their bushy beards would be the slightest bit interested in creating flowery doilies, and yet ... they were!

So interested were they, in fact, that many of them progressed from crochet squares and pretty but basic doilies to other shapes in less than forty-eight hours. One particularly beefy chap took great pride in the pale pink baby bootees he created for his granddaughter, leaning in towards Gwyn and watching avidly as she demonstrated a technique he hadn't yet conquered.

He soon did, and the next stage was a matching bobble hat and cardigan.

I began to feel a little bit left out. I'd been hanging around Butcher and picking up as much as I could about sailing a ship ... and pirating ... and I now knew a few more useful terms. Sadly, it turned out that my personal deck wasn't a patio deck but the poop deck. I infinitely preferred my name for it. The one below it was the quarterdeck. The back of the ship was stern—like Gwyn—while the front was fore, of course, and the very front was the bow. The bottom of the ship was the keel, and the lowest deck was the waist. There were yardarms and mizzen masts and rudders and all sorts ... so it transpired that I need never misname anything again.

Butcher also demonstrated some basic sword techniques, much to everyone else's alarm. He showed me how to thrust and parry, and I, with all the arrogance of someone who wields a wand and has taken a few magick defence and attack lessons, assumed I was quite good at it.

"I really don't think it's a good idea to let my great-granddaughter loose with anything sharp, young man," Gwyn told him. "She cuts herself on paper. She'll probably end up lopping her own head off with a sword."

"Don't interfere, Grandmama!" I scolded. "It's a great additional skill to have." I swung my sword through the air and deftly sliced through a rope neatly tied to the main mast.

"Heads!" yelled a sailor. Everyone scattered as a huge pile of rigging crashed to the deck.

"Oopsie." I smiled.

Butcher slowly reached out and took the sword away from me. "Maybe stick to your wand," he suggested quietly. I scowled and flounced away to my cabin.

But it occurred to me that I could at least tell stories—if anyone wanted me to—and I shyly offered to do that later in the evening as the men sat around after a supper of Florence's delicious beef cobbler with green beans and buttery mash. Later still, I found myself sleeping in a hammock again, purely because the men wanted 'just another chapter' of *Treasure Island* read to them, so I ended up hunkering down with them for the night.

Such is the life of a wonky sailor.

It would all have been immensely enjoyable had I not, at the back of my mind, continued to worry about Silvan. I'd been away for days now, out of contact with Silvan and his lawyer, with no awareness of how he was faring, and so, despite laughing and joking and enjoying the company of the pirates aboard *Poseidon's Curse*, I willed the ship to hurry to its destination with every ounce of my being.

At the end of the third day, we made landfall off the coast of X Island. With no obvious sign of *Seawolf*, we elected to put back out to sea for the night and then land the following morning. I curbed my impatience and entertained the men by reading Faulkner's *Moonfleet* as they crocheted by candlelight and pigged out on the cinnamon swirls that Voodoo and Zulu had baked.

I slept fitfully and woke, after a few days of good weather, to find a thick mist swirling all around, with low skies so grey they were almost black.

My fellow pirates were less than thrilled by this new weather phenomenon. I heard murmurings of how ominous such conditions were, about how perhaps it was unlucky to have witches aboard—almost a certainty, I'd say—and how some dark enchantment had woven around the ship. Surely we'd be marooned for days?

Never one for staying silent, usually to my detriment, I raised these concerns with Butcher.

"Aar," he muttered. "It's never good when we're marooned at sea. Sailors are naturally superstitious. They fear all manner of sea creatures rearing up from the deep and swallowing the ship whole in fog as thick as this."

"Good job I haven't started reading them *Jaws* then," I joked, but perhaps Butcher had never heard of either the film or Peter Benchley's novel because he didn't crack a smile.

Smithy Whiskers joined us on the forecastle. "Not looking good for a landing today, Captain."

Taken aback, I cocked my head. "Why on earth not? Surely today is as good as any other day?"

"Now, Cap'n." Butcher attempted to put me straight. "We can't find our way into an inlet in these conditions. We'll never see the rocks."

"Aren't the rocks recorded?" I asked.

"Not on our charts," Smithy Whiskers told me.

"And not on Captain Bloodstone's map either," Butcher added.

"Oh." I couldn't help but feel deflated. "So we have to wait for the fog to lift?"

Butcher nodded. "I think it would be wise, Cap'n."

"And how long will that take?"

"How long's your face?" Butcher asked me.

"Pretty bloomin' long, I should imagine."

"Well, there you have it then," he said, chuckling.

I walked away, in a sulk, swearing blind my second-in-command must be related to Gwyn somewhere down the line.

I managed to wait for nearly twenty-four hours before having a meltdown. When I awoke the following morning to an even more impenetrable wall of fog, I decided I wasn't having it any longer. Hanging around was dull, particularly when the sailors were down in the dumps. Virtually all crocheting had come to a halt. Nobody wanted to tell or listen to stories. There was no shortage of cookery class volunteers, but that was mainly because bored sailors eat more. Plus, the sailors were beginning to wind each other up with tales of monsters in the deep and mermaids who bit off people's heads and sucked their brains out.

I mean ... really?

I'd met a mermaid, and while she'd not been the nicest being I'd ever come across, she would have drawn the line at sailors' brains. Architects and mathematicians? Fair do. But not sailors.

I called a meeting almost before we'd finished breakfast. I wouldn't be able to cope with another day of doom-laden pirates crossing themselves and touching wood and stroking a rabbit's foot or whatever else they were doing in order to avoid the ship sinking and us all dying a thousand deaths by seafaring piranhas and such like.

"We have to find a way onto that island," I told the men assembled before me. Half-Crocked, Butcher, Scurvy and Smithy Whiskers. "I can't afford to waste any more time."

"That's as maybe, Cap'n, but the men will take some convincing," Butcher told me, his voice flat.

"They don't know about the supposed treasure yet," I reminded him, feeling more than a little short-tempered but trying to control my annoyance. "Once they know, they'll want to land as badly as I do."

"We don't want to get on the island and for it to turn into a free-for-all," Butcher said.

"You must know that the men will follow orders," I replied. "Those who you expect not to will have to stay aboard the ship. Just take the men you trust."

"We can't navigate close enough to the island," Smithy Whiskers began to argue. "The rocks—"

"Da rocks! Da rocks!" I mocked lightly. "We'll sound the surface of the seabed out as we go using the drop-stone technique—"

Butcher arched an eyebrow. "Drop-stone technique?"

"You know what I mean!" Surely I'd seen it in a movie somewhere. "Maybe it's not called the drop-stone technique, but ..." I grappled with an explanation. "You drop a weight on the end of the rope to make sure you have enough depth to sail the ship in—"

"Ah." Butcher pursed his lips. "Mm-hmm."

"We don't even know exactly where the island is," Smithy Whiskers argued. "We've drifted slightly."

I gaped at him in disbelief. "Are you serious? It's the twenty-first century! Don't you have instruments on board that tell you exactly where we are?"

Smithy's reply was firm. "We use a sextant and a compass, and neither of them works well in fog this thick."

"Well, blow me down," I grumbled. "Let me introduce you to something that will change your insular little lives." I patted my pockets. "One sec. I'll be right back." I raced out of the mess and back to my cabin, shinning up the ladder like a monkey—in my imagination, at least—and searched my bag before sliding down the ladder and hurrying back to the pirates, lounging in their chairs waiting for me.

"Would you like any more tea, Miss Alf?" Florence asked as I passed her in the galley.

"Aar!" I said, because who wouldn't want an endless supply of tea? "And are there—"

"Any biscuits? Yes, Miss. We've been experimenting with shortbread. I'll bring those through right away."

"Excellent!" Feeling chipper, I sashayed into the mess and held my mobile aloft. "Say hello to Google maps, chaps!" I sang.

Chapter Nineteen

And so it was that *Poseidon's Curse* edged towards land. We inched our way forwards, Voodoo—or it might have been Zulu—hanging off the bow with a long rope, testing the depth of the sea beneath the ship, calling out his estimated readings. Zulu—or it might have been Voodoo—sat beside him, keeping his eyes peeled for the slightest shadow that might indicate rocks or indeed anything that could prove detrimental to the keel's integrity. Meanwhile, I stood triumphantly on the forecastle, one foot raised on the railings, brandishing my mobile in the air ... amazed that the signal I could find in the middle of the Indian Ocean was better than the one I had in Whittlecombe.

And they call India a developing nation!

"We're nearly there!" I called in excitement. "Take it slow!"

"We can't go any slower!" Smithy Whiskers grumbled; we were drifting as it was, slipping in with the tide. The world was eerily grey and oddly silent. I couldn't hear the waves. There were no sea birds. Not the slightest sound. The thick fog soaked up everything.

Until ...

"Whoa!" yelled Voodoo, and we all rushed to peer over the bow, nearly knocking poor Zulu into the water.

"Report, Voodoo?" Butcher asked.

"That's as far as I think we should go," Voodoo replied, glancing at me warily. "We just don't have the clearance."

"That's fine!" I nodded with enthusiasm. "Let's get the rowing boat in the water and erm ... organise a landing party." Is that what you called it? Or was that only in *Star Trek*? "Let's be on the safe side. Nobody wear a red shirt."

Butcher shot me a quizzical look. I wafted my hand in his direction. "Never mind. Who do you think we should take with us?"

"Volunteers?" Butcher glanced around. "Half-Crocked should stay on the boat to take command. Smithy Whiskers, you come along with me and Cap'n Alf. Any other takers?"

Voodoo slowly raised his hand. Butcher nodded. "Zulu?" he asked.

Zulu, sneaking an exasperated glance at his twin, reluctantly agreed.

"I will," said Scurvy, and that was it, the landing party decided.

Time to visit X Island.

I'd never realised the idiosyncrasy involved in landing a rowing boat. Much like *Poseidon's Curse*, there came a moment when the boat—with me, Butcher, Smithy Whiskers, Voodoo, Zulu and Scurvy aboard—was too heavy to float in the water. At that stage, we had to get out and push it ashore.

I mean, think of that. We had to get wet in order to push *the boat* ashore.

Bizarre.

I sloshed through the shallows, my breeches soaking up the cold seawater, thoroughly underwhelmed by the slimy feeling of seaweed as it wrapped itself around my calf muscles and insinuated itself between my toes. We heaved the boat—how the rotten thing had remained afloat, I had no idea—onto the sandy beach, higher than the evidence of the tideline just to be safe, then huddled together, glancing around, trying to discern our surroundings. Much like Naarangi, this was a jungle island with mangroves lapping at the water's edge. I could imagine that once the mist cleared and the sun began to shine, it would be beautiful, with monkeys chattering in the trees and parakeets singing from every available branch.

"Do we have a plan?" Butcher enquired politely.

"We have to find Salty Dog. That's our plan," I reminded him.

"No offence, Captain Alf." Scurvy put his hand on the hilt of his cutlass. "I'm here for the treasure."

"Oh, that's right," I said and placed my hand on my wand. "But we don't have the foggiest—excuse the pun—notion of where the treasure is, or if indeed it exists."

"X marks the spot," Scurvy growled.

"X is the name of the island," I countered. "I guarantee that's all there is to it."

"But there had to be a reason why Captain Bloodstone wanted us to come here. He left us those map pieces."

I couldn't deny there was some truth in that.

"In that case, we need to look around anyway," I said. "We either find the treasure or we find Salty Dog."

"Or we find neither." Butcher shrugged.

I thumped his arm. "Or we find both!"

"Which way?" Smithy Whiskers asked.

"Let's go this way." I pointed north for no other reason than it led directly away from the beach. "And let's go quietly," I reminded the men. "We don't want to alert Salty Dog to our presence."

"If he's here," muttered Scurvy.

"Pardon?" I turned to face him and raised my eyebrows.

"Nothing," he said, but then changed his mind.

"Hey! You're a witch. Why don't you disperse the fog using magick?"

"I can't do weather magick," I told him, *although I know a witch who can.* "That's specialist."

"What's your speciality then?" Scurvy asked, falling into step beside me as we all shuffled up the beach. Golden sand, as beautiful as it is, is annoyingly difficult to walk on.

"Ghosts," I said, trying to save my breath.

"Ohhhh." He nodded. "That would explain those two back at the ship."

"Nothing explains those two," I told him. "Least of all my grandmama."

We walked in silence for about six or seven minutes, always heading north and always climbing uphill. Occasionally one or more of us would pause to take a breather, but the others would keep going, driving us slowly and relentlessly to whatever was at the centre of this small island. If I'd been worried that we would find ourselves in impenetrable jungle, I needn't have been. While there was indeed jungle, and plenty of it, it seemed we'd been lucky enough to stumble upon a path. No tarmac or anything to make the going easier, of course, just stone and sand and dust, but nevertheless it was a road, and as they always tell you, all roads lead to somewhere.

The other thing that became abundantly clear was that the island had at one time been inhabited. On either side of this track were flat open spaces that must once have been fields. They were overgrown now, self-seeding with plants I didn't recognise, but not too long ago, someone had tended them.

We found some of the answers we sought when we finally rounded a curve and happened upon a small settlement. I wouldn't have called it a village as such, because there were no more than half a dozen small dwellings there. Each of them was dilapidated, not to the falling-down-at-any-moment stage of dilapidation, but certainly the been-abandoned-for-a-few-years stage.

We moved carefully, Butcher and Smithy Whiskers wielding rapiers, Scurvy a cutlass, Zulu a dagger, and Voodoo a ... potato peeler. I cast a sideways glance remembering the day I'd first met this bunch of pirates.

"Is that the only weapon you have?" I asked.

"It's deadly," he reassured me.

"If you're a potato," I said. "And even then the wounds are only skin deep."

"That's fine by me. I don't like the sight of blood," he confessed. "I've been a vegetarian most of my life."

"Why are you even a pirate?" I asked.

"Seemed like a good job opportunity at the time."

"How wrong you were," I said, and left him to begin poking around one of the little dwellings.

"It's all clear," Butcher called out, and we reconvened in the centre of the circle of shacks.

"No hint of treasure here," Scurvy whinged.

"And no sign of Salty Dog." I turned to stare up the hill and, at that moment, the goddess smiled down on me. Kind of. The mist temporarily thinned. One hundred or so yards above us was a house. A house I'd seen before. The house on the front of Captain Bloodstone's chest. Not a country mansion after all—well, not an *English* country mansion—but a plantation house.

All roads do indeed lead to somewhere, I thought.

And then the earth moved.

Chapter Twenty

Only a few short weeks before, I'd imagined the earth moving in a very different way. By now I should have been married to my beloved and we ought to have been enjoying our honeymoon in peace and tranquillity. But here I was, in the middle of the Indian Ocean, on an island that didn't have a proper name, with a bunch of smelly, crocheting, cake-loving, treasure-hunting pirates, one of whom was armed with a piece of kitchen hardware.

Each of us stood and stared as, in front of us, giant molehills began to erupt from the baked soil. Granules of dirt spat forth like popcorn from a frying pan. Voodoo stepped closer to get a better look, then shot backwards as a bundle—there's no other way to describe it—of bones leapt out of the mound it had created and shook itself—melodically, I thought, because the bones clacked together like slightly flat xylophone pieces—into some semblance of a human skeleton. I say semblance because there might have been a few bones out of place or missing, but I'm not an anatomist, so I wouldn't know.

It just didn't look quite right.

What was instantly apparent, however, was that each bundle of bones—there must have been a dozen of them—was armed with an impressive falchion. Yep. There were no potato peelers on show here, just sharp and shiny swords.

As Butcher and Smithy Whiskers drew their own, ready to fight to the death, presumably, Scurvy shrieked and retreated towards the nearest shack. I pulled out my wand and moved alongside Butcher.

"What is this place?" I asked.

From behind me, I heard Scurvy shriek. Pivoting, I realised his progress indoors, ostensibly to hide someplace safe, had been impeded by the arrival of an additional skeleton. It pushed Scurvy towards us, pricking him with the tip of its falchion to make him move faster.

"We're surrounded!" Voodoo shouted, holding his makeshift weapon up and away from himself at chest height, squinting and batting his eyelashes as though on one hand, he didn't want to see what we were up against—and on the other, needed to see so that he could take aim with his potato peeler.

"Hold fast, lads!" Butcher cried and launched himself at the nearest skeleton, swiping the skull clear of the vertebrae. The creature shrieked as its head shot sideways and, like a cannonball, took out the unfortunate bag of bones standing alongside it. This one's bones exploded like scattershot and, because I was closest, the fingers and ribs rained down on me.

"Oi!" I ducked away. "Careful!" Oh, the irony of being impaled by a funny bone this far away from my wonky inn.

The headless skeleton, arms out, lurched sideways, like a blind man in an open field who has lost all sense of direction. I might have been amused, but I was still trying to figure out how big a threat to us these creatures might be.

"Ugh!" Scurvy shouted in horrified disgust. I turned to see what he was pointing at. The bones from the skeleton that had exploded had begun to draw themselves together. All those scattered ribs and pieces of the fingers—phalanges, metacarpals, whatever they are—were sliding across the ground like leeches on a heat-seeking mission. Meanwhile, the errant skull, which, given how hard the skull is, had sustained no apparent damage, was rolling back to its own body.

As we stood by, watching the melodrama unfold, the headless skeleton leaned over, picked up its bonce, dusted it off and reattached it to the top vertebra.

"I've seen it all now," I muttered.

The skeleton, happily fully compos mentis again, lurched towards Butcher. My second-in-command swiped left and right with his sword, this time through the rib cage. The skeleton jiggled but didn't fall.

"We can't kill these things!" Smithy Whiskers

yelled, trying to run one through. It shrieked, but the bones simply pulled apart, then, when his sword was withdrawn, they came together again.

I decided to have a go. Targeting the previously headless skeleton that had taken umbrage at Butcher's antics, I took aim with my wand and unleashed a stream of toxic green energy. No messing. I didn't have time to feel sorry for multiple bags of bones! "*Annihilare!*"

This time when the skeleton exploded, it instantly crumbled into a cloud of ash that sparkled gently, billowing in the air briefly before sinking to the earth to be lost among the dust of the dry soil.

"Hahahaha!" Scurvy laughed hysterically. "Take that, you—whoa!" Several skeletons began to advance on him. "Captain Alf! Captain Alf!" he shrieked.

"*Annihilare!*" I repeated. "*Annihilare!*" Over and over again. As each skeleton turned to dust, others sprang up. From all parts of the village, as far as we could see in the swirling mist, the molehills would push their way up, followed by the raising of the disparate bundles of bones that would then take their more recognisable shape and begin advancing on us. Sometimes they grouped together; other times they simply staggered towards us one by one.

Scurvy took shelter behind me, while Voodoo danced just out of each skeleton's reach. The problem with each member of my crew doing their own thing was that I couldn't keep an eye on them. "Stand closer to me," I urged the men.

"I don't have a problem with that!" Scurvy was stuck like a limpet to my wand arm.

I shook him off. "Not that close! I need to be able to cast my spells!"

"Tetchy! Tetchy!" he grumbled, but took half a step away.

"Butcher! Smithy! Zulu!" I called out again. "Stand with us!"

They drew around me, swiping away with their weapons.

"Bows and arrows would have been preferable," Smithy Whiskers moaned.

"Cannons would be even better!" Butcher replied.

Only Voodoo, dancing around like some half-crazed shaman, remained outside our grouping. I made a dash for him, firing my wand as I went and rapidly taking down three beasties in quick succession, before grabbing Voodoo's arm and yanking him back towards the others.

"I'll get them!" he told me. "Leave them to me!"

Once our circle was formed, with everyone safely inside it, I began to target the skeletons by shifting round and round. In a tight group, we slowly and surely moved backwards towards one of the dwellings.

"What's the plan?" Scurvy asked, eyes wide with terror. "If we go inside there, we'll be trapped!"

"I can't spend the rest of my life taking out skeletons, only for two more to generate every time I obliterate one," I told him. "We need to get inside and hole up."

"I'll go in and check it out!" Butcher yelled, making a run for the door before anyone could object. I covered him, shooting left, right and centre, clearing the path for him. I heard the sound of pots and pans scattering and the thud of something heavy. I turned in alarm, half expecting a skeleton to appear at the door carrying Butcher's severed head, but instead the man himself called out to us. "All clear!"

One by one the men began to dive through the door, until only me and Voodoo were left. Voodoo grinned, his big happy smile, and for one awful moment I thought he would sacrifice himself to the skeletons to create a diversion so that I could get inside, but at the last second, he ducked through the entrance himself and I quickly followed him.

Scurvy slammed the door behind me as Smithy, Zulu and Butcher began barricading it with every item of furniture they could move. The skeletons were massing on the other side—I could distinctly hear the clicking and clattering of bone on bone and the rattle of teeth as the jaws clacked together—but no matter how hard they battered, they weren't getting in.

That left the window. Fortunately there was only one, and a small one at that. I edged towards it and peered through at exactly the same moment that the head of a skeleton did the same thing. We stared at each other for a few seconds—or rather, I stared into the holes of its sockets, not seeing anything of interest, and it stared into my green eyes ... with probably the same result.

I stepped gently away, and it did exactly the same but in the opposite direction.

I watched and waited. It gradually lost interest and wandered away to be replaced with another one, but again, it couldn't 'see' us, and this seemed to bore it. It, therefore, stumbled away in search of excitement elsewhere. When the mist cleared momentarily, I spotted a pair of skeletons fighting each other with ferocious intent, but the weather closed in again before I could tell what the outcome was.

Scurvy had begun to pace. "Now what?"

Butcher glanced at me. I shrugged. "Now we wait," I told them. "I can't see what other choice we have."

The goddess knows I am not the most patient person in the world, so hanging about with the pirates, with no books or yarn to provide a distraction, proved to be a challenge. After about the three hundredth round of 'I Spy', I was almost considering stepping outside for a while to feed myself to whatever waited out there, but, just as the sun began to set, we noticed that the immediate vicinity of the dwelling had fallen silent.

Clamping my finger to my lips, I slowly climbed to

my feet and peered through the window. The fog had thinned so that only thin tendrils of mist threaded their way through the trees. The disturbances in the earth—the molehills—had disappeared, along with the skeletons.

"What do you think?" Butcher asked, keeping his voice low.

"I think it's worth risking," I told him.

He nodded and joined Smithy Whiskers to quietly remove the furniture barrier from the door. When we were finally able to pull the door open, I led the way back out into the real world, my wand at the ready.

The house—the one carved on top of the chest—could clearly be seen on the top of the hill now. A narrow track wound all the way up to it, and I imagined that at some stage the people who had worked in the house had lived in this small settlement. With the sky glowing a bright radiant orange behind it, the house was an impressive silhouette, modelled on the English country style. No wonder I'd mistaken it for a country estate.

Perhaps more importantly, my sixth sense told me someone was at home.

"Let's go," I said, gesturing up the hill.

"Must we?" Scurvy whined.

"Thar be treasure," I told him, and he fell into step behind me.

CHAPTER TWENTY-ONE

As we trekked up the hill I noted more open ground to our right. There were wooden crosses and stone statues suggesting some kind of cemetery. Perhaps this was the home of the creatures we'd been fighting earlier in the day. I pointed the grave markers out to Butcher and he pursed his lips. "All sleeping soundly now," I told him and carried on, but all the while keeping a wary eye out for the slightest hint of movement.

Finally we summited the hill. The top was flat, with far-ranging gardens surrounding a plantation house that might once upon a time have been grand and well kept, but now, like everything else on the island, had been left to ruin. When we paused to catch our breath, I turned to look back down the way we'd come. Now that the fog had lifted, we could make out the small inlet where *Poseidon's Curse* was anchored and the beach where our rowing boat had been left.

We were also able to gain some sense of the size of X Island, and found it was disappointingly teeny.

"Look at it this way," I said after Scurvy had expressed his disgruntlement. "If there *is* treasure here, there'll be less island to search."

"After seein' all those things come out the ground, I'm not sure I want to be digging anything else up," Scurvy remarked.

"You'd better hope your treasure comes in a large crate labelled with a big 'T' then," I told him. "And a large arrow on the shelf saying, 'take this'."

"No need for the sarcasm," Scurvy grumbled.

"We-elllll, really!" I scolded him.

"I spy with my little eye—" Voodoo began.

"Not now, Voodoo!" we chorused as one.

"No, really!" the young man protested, pointing off to the left. "Down there."

I squinted down the hill, among the trees, then further ... to a little bay. With the failing light I nearly missed it, but there, moored close to a beach, was a small ship.

I gasped. "Salty Dog!" It had to be.

"Could be," Butcher agreed.

"He must be in here!" I pointed at the house behind us.

"He could be anywhere," Smithy Whiskers interjected. "Literally anywhere. Any dwelling we haven't come across. Up a tree—"

"Why would he be anywhere else but here?" I

asked. "Why come to this island but not come to this house? The whole *point* of this island is this house!"

We stood and stared at each other, tired and more than a little stressed.

"If we return to the ship now, we'll be doing so with what light we have left," Butcher reminded me. "The going will be easier. Plus, if those ... things ... are out in force again, we'd see them rather than flailing around in the dark if we leave later."

"Why would we go all the way back to the boat when it's taken us most of the day to climb up here?" I argued. "Who's to say that things will be any better tomorrow?"

"The fog has lifted," Butcher pointed out. "We could bring more men."

"I like that idea!" Scurvy raised his hand. "I vote we do that."

I tutted in annoyance. "Well, fine. You lot trot down to the boat with your tails between your legs and leave little old me to go in search of Salty Dog and the treasure! Why not?"

The sailors exchanged glances.

"When you put it like that," Smithy Whiskers said.

"Good." I clapped my palms together. "Decision made! Let's go!"

I led my merry band of petty pirates through the open front door of the house and into the colossal hall. Quite obviously once beautiful, even now the faded grandeur had an eloquent charm. The walls were covered in pale blue silk and decorated with hummingbirds. A chandelier the size of a small car hung from the ceiling—which was itself covered in classical illustrations of men and women wrapped in silk sheets and cherubs wearing nothing at all—and a winding staircase carved from teak led up and away, curving to the second and third floors. But the plaster was cracking and the wallpaper had patches of mould, bits of masonry were scattered over the tiled floor, and the smell of damp pervaded the whole area.

We grouped together, blinking under the light of the chandelier. Somewhere, somehow, electricity was still feeding this place, and someone was waiting for us.

Instantly, and despite our growing weariness, we were all cautious. I drew my wand, and with that movement, Butcher, Zulu and Smithy Whiskers hefted their weapons once more. Scurvy tensed. Voodoo held up his potato peeler.

I craned my neck, listening for any sounds coming from the floors above, but there was nothing. Shrugging, and treading quietly, I cautiously moved from the hallway to the nearest open door. This was a sizable main room to our left, some kind of lounge or something, with half a dozen sofas, some hard-backed chairs covered in what might once have been red velvet, and long drapes at the window. There was a massive fireplace in here too, although why anybody would need a fireplace this size on an Indian island was beyond me. When would it ever be cold enough?

Movement out of the corner of my eye startled me. I whirled, ready to exterminate whatever threat I found, but it was only a tiny lizard with black eyes, scuttling behind the portrait hanging above the fireplace. The portrait depicted a man with a long red frock coat, a curved sword hanging from his belt, the coat pulled back to demonstrate the weapon to its best advantage, and a tri-pointed hat sitting on a glorious bush of long black curls, à la Charles II.

"Well, as I live and breathe!" Butcher had followed my gaze, and now he stepped closer to the grate. Pointing with his sword, he turned to Smithy Whiskers.

"What?" I asked.

"That chap there's the spit of Captain Bloodstone!" Smithy Whiskers marvelled.

Scurvy tipped his head to one side to regard the painting with interest. "Ha. Now that you say that, I see it too."

"The hair's different—" Butcher stood on tiptoe to use his sword to outline the head. "Our old Captain didn't have quite the ... er ... the ..."

"Volume?" I suggested. As a woman with a lot of hair, I knew all the terminology.

"Volume, yeah!" Butcher nodded in satisfaction.

"And it wasn't as black. Dark in his younger years, grey later. But the nose—"

"And the eyes!" Scurvy agreed.

"Definitely Captain Bloodstone," Smithy Whiskers nodded.

"Or a long-dead relative of his," I suggested, because surely that's how portraits worked. I should know. I had a fair few of them at the inn hanging on the walls in some cases, in storage in the attic in others.

"Wow! Are you suggesting this was his grandpa's place?" Scurvy asked. "I didn't know he came from money!"

Butcher raised an eyebrow. "I always thought he had some tucked away. I mean, we never did a lot of swashbuckling, nor much in the way of pirating, not in the twelve years I sailed with him ... and yet, he always had enough money to see us through the slow times."

"True, that." Smithy Whiskers nodded. "I often wondered where he found those pieces of eight."

Somewhere a door slammed. We all started, then turned about, I for one holding my breath.

"What was that?" Scurvy hissed.

"There's someone here," Voodoo whispered.

Butcher lifted his sword once more. "It might have been the wind."

"What wind?" I asked, purposely striding towards the grand hall. The men traipsed after me, albeit somewhat unenthusiastically.

"Could be a ghost," Scurvy muttered.

"Then I'll soon find out what its business is," I retorted.

"What if it's a poltergeist?" Voodoo asked.

"It's not a poltergeist!" I rolled my eyes. "It's not creating nearly enough disturbance for one of those." I pointed at the door on the other side of the hall. "Let's go and see, okay?" Without waiting for an answer, I charged at the door—oak panelled but painted white, thereby throwing the blue silk of the walls into pretty relief—and thrust it open to reveal a drawing room.

I say drawing room like I actually know what one of those is. I don't. I imagine once upon a time, long before gramophones and rock music were invented and saved us all from dying of boredom, ladies sat in the drawing room and sketched. This particular room had sunny yellow walls, another fair-sized inglenook, and half a dozen upright and uncomfortable-looking armchairs with those sexy, shaped legs that the prudish Victorians always covered up with their flowery flounces and frills.

In front of the window, looking down the gardens towards the islet where *Poseidon's Curse* was anchored, was a chaise, and splayed out on the chaise was the most piratey-looking pirate I'd ever seen. Long bushy black curly hair—much like the portrait in the main living room—an eyepatch, in much better nick than the threadbare and tattered one I was sporting, a striped blouson and a dashing frock coat. He lifted a goblet in my direction as I skidded to a halt on the rug. "Ms Daemonne, I assume," he said.

I frowned. "You have me at a disadvantage."

"I'm sure that's not the case." He tipped a wink and pushed himself up to an almost sitting position before taking a slug from the goblet and dropping down again. "You've caught up with me at last. I knew you would."

I took a step closer, wanting to see him properly in the flesh.

"This weather," he moaned. "Not a bit like dear old Blighty. It's exhausting, don't you find? So close."

"Salty Dog?" I asked, fighting to quell my fury. How could he lie here in front of me, talking about the weather, so nonchalant after what he'd done?

"That's what they call me. It's tiresome. I never wanted to be a sailor, let alone a salty one. I'm much happier on the land." He wafted an arm around. "Do you like what I've done to the place?"

"This is your house?" I asked.

"It is now. The whole island."

The other men had shuffled in behind me.

"Butcher!" Salty Dog raised his goblet. "Come and join me. Help yourself to a drink." He struggled upright, his eyes rolling slightly. I couldn't tell how long he'd been drinking, but he was clearly steamrollered. "Scurvy! My man!"

"I could do with a drink after climbing up that great

hill," Scurvy agreed, and practically skipped over to the drinks cabinet. There were half a dozen bottles of wine on top of it, and Scurvy shook a few before finding one with something in it. "Butcher?" he asked. "Want one?"

"Aar, I'll take one," Butcher said, reaching for a glass. Scurvy poured out a few more and served everyone. I looked on, lips pressed together in disapproving silence.

"What about you, Ms Daemonne?" Salty Dog asked. "Can I tempt you?"

"I have no intention of fraternising with the enemy," I told him.

"Oh, get away with you, my girl." He crinkled his nose. "You look like you could do with something strong. Slightly fraught, I would say."

Scurvy attempted to hand me a tankard full of red wine. I grimaced. "No, thank you."

"No? Oh." Scurvy shrugged. "That's a shame." He took a mouthful himself.

"It is a shame," Salty Dog agreed. "You've been working so hard, seeing off my skinny friends out there."

The skeletons? "They were down to you?"

"Yee-eeees. Ye-eeees." Salty Dog tipped his head in some vain attempt to look coy. "They come with the house. They're the long-dead remains of the sailors my ancestors press-ganged, I believe. That's how the story goes anyway. If you come in on the south beach, for some reason it annoys them and they get upset. That's what we were told as boys."

"We?" I didn't even need to ask. I knew exactly what was coming.

"Yes—me and my bigger, uglier, more favoured brother, Dunley *Bloodstone* Rutland."

"Captain Bloodstone was your brother." I sniffed. "Is that why you killed him?"

"Oh, come now." Salty Dog pushed himself off the chaise and staggered a few steps towards me.

My blood pressure was so high I could hear popping in my ears. "Are you denying it?"

"Denying what?" He affected an air of innocence. "I may be drunk, but I'm not singing—"

"You don't need to sing," I told him. "But you do need to come back to Dakti Bhoin with me because the police need to hear you tell your side of the story. Only you can exonerate Silvan—"

"Ah yes, your beloved fiancé. So handsome. The perfect stool pigeon. If only he could hold his drink without needing to visit the facilities—"

"I know you set him up!" I spat. "I can feel it."

"I have no idea what you're talking about." He began to dance to music only he could hear, a kind of jig that involved lifting his knees. His goblet jerked around, spilling red liquid over the dusty old rug.

"Drink up!" I ordered. "You're coming with me."

He giggled and slid closer to me. "Make me," he

said, leaning right into my face. "M-m-m-m-m make me!"

I pushed him away.

"Perhaps you think my brother's crew will help you take me in?" He cast sly eyes at Scurvy. "We all go back a long way."

I studied the others' expressions. Nobody met my eye. Butcher gazed studiously into the bottom of his glass, with the appearance of a man who is contemplating the meaning of life but not partaking of it.

"You see?" Salty Dog asked me in wide-eyed wonder. "My brother's men are not yours to control."

My fingers itched to lift my wand and eradicate the smug genes from every male in the room. How dare this ennobled pirate make light of Silvan's situation? How dare he treat us this way—so cavalier, so heartless! How dare he ... how *dare* he!

"That's the way it's going to be, is it?" I asked, my voice low, and now I wasn't addressing Salty Dog, even though it was him I was glaring at. "After all we've been through together? This man murdered his brother—"

Salty Dog started to jig again. "Poor Dunley. Doomed Dunley!" he sang.

"Your captain!" I reminded them. "Any loyalty you felt towards Captain Bloodstone is misplaced if you transfer it to his sibling! This man intends to ruin my life, my fiancé's life ... he ... he ..." I struggled for the words. "What about *Rose's Revenge*?" Now I turned to face Butcher. "You saw what he did to Captain Wilde!"

Butcher finally met my eye and swallowed.

"He almost killed him! In fact, he may well have managed to do so for all we know. Think of his crew ..." I turned to beseech Smithy Whiskers. "Remember how you felt when Captain Bloodstone was killed? Remember how you rampaged through the court because you wanted to get at the man you thought had killed your skipper? You swore vengeance?"

Smithy Whiskers nodded. His eyes roamed across the room to where Salty Dog was now filling up his goblet. "I do."

Salty Dog paused, his eyes flicking back to Smithy Whiskers. "Come now, lads!" he cried. "What gives? We're friends, aren't we? We go way back!"

"I never knew you and the captain were brothers," Butcher said, and I could see the pain in his eyes. "He was a good man, our captain. Perhaps Captain Alf is right. Perhaps—"

Salty Dog tipped his head back and laughed. "Butch, my old mate! You're really going to let this woman tell you what you should and shouldn't do? What with all the water that's run under our respective bridges?"

"She's not *some* woman, Salty," Butcher said. "She's *our* Captain. And a brave one at that!"

"Aar!" agreed Voodoo. "I saw how she jumped onto *Rose's Revenge* to help save Captain Wilde!"

"And she saw off all those skeletons far better than we could," Smithy Whiskers agreed.

"And she never backs down," Butcher finished. "She fights till the end."

I could feel my cheeks getting warm.

"Yeah, but at the end of the day she's just a girl, and girls have no place on pirate ships," Salty Dog told them. "You're not going to take me in, are you fellas? Which one of you would dare do that?"

There was a long silence during which my heart declined to beat. This was it. Make or break.

Scurvy necked the rest of his wine, took a deep breath, then let out the longest belch it had ever been my displeasure to witness—and remember, I've worked in hospitality my entire adult life. Reaching over, he plucked Voodoo's potato peeler from his hand and wielded it himself. "I reckon I'd dare," he said.

And that is the story of how we placed Salty Dog under citizen's arrest.

Chapter Twenty-Two

Poseidon's Curse landed at Dakti Bhoin four days later.

It had been a long four days. Interminably so. While the sailors had been busy enough—and thankfully easier to keep engaged—we'd had to keep Salty Dog in the hold, where his incessant howling and protestations of innocence had driven me to distraction. He seemed hell-bent on turning the men against me and tried to spread vicious gossip whenever one of my crew went anywhere near him. Fortunately for me, the sailors had fallen in love with Florence's cooking and Gwyn's no-nonsense attitude to the world as a whole, and perhaps they were a little scared of me and the powers of my wand—and so, for the large part, they pointedly ignored Salty Dog spitting bile about me. If ever there was a moment where that didn't seem to be the case, Florence simply served up fresh lemon juice with cinnamon and cardamom cake.

"I wouldn't worry about it," Butcher told me every

time it happened, his confidence growing—mainly because we were inching closer to our destination with every moment that passed. "The men are on your side."

I was grateful for that, but even so, I felt frustrated that Salty Dog wouldn't tell us what had happened between him and his brother or why. He held his tongue, steadfastly refusing to spill the beans. I had an awful feeling that we'd drag him all the way across the Indian Ocean and still he would decline to answer the police's questions. Without any further evidence, how could I ensure Silvan's liberty? Would he ever be freed?

And so, I kept the telescope plastered to my good eye, scanning the horizon for potential enemy attacks, knowing I wouldn't hesitate to use the cannons this time in order to ensure that my prisoner ended up where he needed to be. I was also adamant that no idiot should accidentally make the mistake of attacking us for personal gain, because they most certainly *would* end up sleeping with the fishes. Besides which, I wanted to be the first to catch sight of Dakti Bhoin, even if Butcher did keep reminding me we were still an awfully long way away!

Day four couldn't come fast enough. I hardly slept for anxiety and excitement. What if we were becalmed? What if a mysterious fog fell again? What if we were attacked by peculiar sea serpents from the deep? What if the Indian Navy took exception to pirates in its waters?

I needn't have worried. Those four days—as dull as they were—were an example of how wonderful life on the ocean wave can be. The waves lapped against the boat, the water sparkled, pods of dolphins swam alongside us, the sails caught enough of a breeze to compel us forwards, and Florence kept the snacks right on coming.

Finally ... finally! Day four arrived, and just before midday we sailed into the harbour at Dakti Bhoin, where a small crowd had gathered to greet us. The police formed one group, and Roy led the other. I'd alerted him by phone that we were due into port and, in turn, he had gone to the police to let them know that their prime witness was arriving and they would be able to interview him straight away.

I could hardly contain myself as Voodoo and Zulu let down the gangway. I wanted to run across it and begin telling my story, but Butcher held out a restraining arm and advised caution. "Chances are you won't have your sea legs," he explained, and he was right. The moment I set foot on dry land, my head wobbled and my knees began to buckle. I held onto Smithy Whiskers for dear life, while behind me my pirate mates laughed and cheered.

"Mrs Demon, ma'am?" The station chief walked over. I was pleased to see that neither the chief of police nor the owner of The Monkey Nuts was in attendance. Maybe we'd get somewhere without corruption ruining any chance of arriving at the truth.

"Yes, hello." I gestured behind me. "Salty Dog, the man who killed his brother, is aboard the ship. Are you going to arrest him?"

"We can't arrest him as yet, ma'am. We need to talk to him first."

I regarded them with weary bewilderment. I could see exactly which way this would go if they decided to speak to him at the station. The chief of police would be there. He would find Salty Dog's story plausible and let him go. Salty Dog would disappear and find his way back to X Island, *Seawolf* and his crew—and I would be no nearer to setting Silvan free.

"You can talk to him on board," I said, gesturing up the gangplank.

"Ma'am—" the station chief began.

I cut off his protestations. "I insist. You must also avail yourself of the finest English breakfast tea there is and some of our cook's incredible coffee and walnut cake." I wrapped an arm around his shoulders and led him to the gangway. He stepped, shakily, onto the plank, and for one awful moment I thought he would fall in. Half-Crocked hurried down to help him. Once the chief was aboard, the other officers followed.

I waited until it was just me and Roy. "Hey!" He smiled, he bowed, then reconsidered and wrapped me in a hug. I was glad to see him too. He pointed at my eye patch. "You look like someone who's had a few adventures."

"You could say that." I snorted.

"But I sense that Alf's skies aren't as blue as they might be," he said, his eyes shining with wisdom.

I appreciated his gentle probing. "There's no way Salty Dog is going to cough to what he did. It's not so much that he's in denial as that he simply intends to lie. The thing is, with the lack of any evidence at all, he'll get away with it!"

"I have no time for liars." Roy shook his head. "It's my biggest bugbear. Hey! Nikel!" He called out to a little boy on a bicycle. If I wasn't much mistaken, it was the harbour master's son. The child stood to attention as Roy approached him and leaned over to speak in his ear.

"I have a plan," Roy told me when he made his way back to me. The little boy had raced off on his cycle at breakneck speed. "All you need to do is hold off serving your English breakfast tea until Nikel gets back."

"Are you having any tea, Miss Alf?" Florence queried as I paced around the quarterdeck.

"No, no," I told her. "Just make sure that Salty Dog gets a second cup from *that* teapot." I was referring to the large stainless steel one she had on the tray that had floated out of the galley with her. "He did drink the first cup, did he?"

"Don't be so impatient, Alfhild," Gwyn shrilled. "It's probably too hot for him to drink straight away."

"He has to drink it, Grandmama! It's a matter of life and death!"

"You're so dramatic, darling—"

"It's the difference between my wedding and my heartbreak!"

Gwyn quirked an eyebrow. "Hmm. If you put it like that, maybe I'll see to it myself."

She spun about and disappeared into the galley. I shot after her, nearly upending Florence's tray. "Grandmama!" I hissed, but she'd already made her way into the mess. I crept forward. With no door between the galley and the mess—you wouldn't want that swinging around during a dinner service while a storm was raging, would you?—I had to press myself against the stove and flatten my gloriously ample self as much as possible to avoid being seen.

I craned my neck as far as I dared, further than I wanted to because my eyepatch meant I needed to see with my left eye, and spotted Gwyn with her wand out, sprinkling some magick dust around Salty Dog's end of the table while the station chief began to quiz him regarding his whereabouts on the night that Captain Bloodstone had died.

"We need to ask you a few questions," the chief began.

"Fire away!" Salty Dog smirked. "I have nothing to hi—" He stopped mid word, then coughed and began choking. One of the police officers hurriedly stood up and thumped him on the back as Salty Dog clasped his throat. Her intervention was largely ineffective, so Gwyn mimed hitting him herself, and he rammed into the table. "Ooof!"

He coughed up a fly.

"Ewww." The police officer grimaced.

Salty Dog retched and hurriedly reached for his tea, downing it in one. I nodded at Florence, and she floated down the steps with her tray. "Can I offer anyone more tea?" she trilled, quickly refilling Salty Dog's cup before he answered one way or another. "Cake?"

"Where were we?" the station chief began again.

"I was nowhere near The Monkey Nuts!" Salty Dog swore.

"Well, that's a lie!" Butcher said from directly behind my shoulder. I jumped and put a hand out to steady myself, burning my palm on the ring that had recently been used to boil the water for tea. *Yowzer*!

"SSssh!" I hissed.

"He was there," Butcher told me, refusing to lower his voice. The station chief glanced our way. He frowned and seemed about to say something when Salty Dog piped up again.

"What I mean to say ... no, I don't mean to say ... what I was about to say was that I wasn't there when my brother was killed ... but actually ... what I don't want to say ... but I don't seem to be able to stop myself saying is ... that I was there ... what the—"

The station chief sought clarification. "Are you telling us you were at The Monkey Nuts on the evening of the fourteenth?"

"I am saying that. I don't want to say it, but I can't seem not to." Salty Dog rubbed his head. There was a hitch in his voice. He might start to cry at any second.

"And Captain Bloodstone ...?"

"Was my brother."

"Did you meet with Horace T Silvanus?"

"I wasn't there ... except I was ... and yes ... I was meeting him because he wanted to charter a boat so he could marry his fiancée at sea." Salty Dog caught hold of his lips, trying to stifle the words.

"And did you see what happened to your brother?" the station chief asked.

I clenched my teeth and my hands, no longer feeling the smart of the burn on my palm. *Please*!

"Of course I saw what happened!" Salty Dog erupted. "I killed my brother. I killed him! I stabbed him with my father's cutlass! I wanted him dead so that I could be the sole inheritor of the island left to us by the old man when he passed away last year!" He clamped a hand to his mouth, but he couldn't stop Roy's truth serum as it took hold.

"He had these grand plans, did Dunley," Salty Dog continued, tears springing into his eyes. "He wanted to divide up the land among me and his pirates. I mean … there are dozens of them. We'd have had a postage-stamp-sized farm each. What use is that? He had a dream—stupid Dunley—to reward his sailors with a retirement. To weigh anchor for the last time. They'd have to work, sure, but they could work together, just as they always did, to make the island a working agricultural paradise … that was his plan."

"You killed him because—" the station chief asked.

"I wanted it all. All for myself."

My mouth dropped open and I turned to gape at Butcher. His eyes were wide.

"And Silvanus?" the chief asked.

"Made the mistake of visiting the bathroom," Salty Dog told him, tears streaming down his face. I sensed that these weren't tears of remorse, merely tears as he faced up to where the truth would land him.

"He wasn't involved," Salty Dog confirmed. "It was all me."

It might have been easier to take a plane back to the mainland—certainly it would have been faster to do so—but we were already on *Poseidon's Curse* and we could get to the town where Silvan was being held in a relatively speedy six hours. So it was that once again I set sail with the pirates and we headed into the sunset over the Indian continent. Night had fallen by the time we made land. I grabbed a tuk-tuk and sped to the local prison, urging the driver to put his foot down, until we found where Silvan was waiting for me, sitting on the kerb clutching a bottle of water, looking a little thinner and a little less tanned.

"Silvan!" I shrieked, throwing myself out of the tuk-tuk before it had even properly pulled up and almost falling to my knees in a cowpat. He sat up taller and grinned, that slow lazy grin of his, black eyes sparkling as they always did.

"Alfie." He eased himself up and held out his arms. I flew into them, wrapping him tightly in the biggest bear hug I could manage. "A one-eyed Alfie." He pulled away and stared down into my face. "A one-eyed Alfie with a bit of a tan going on." He kissed my forehead. "And freckles." He kissed my nose. "With hair of straw—"

"Oh, don't," I groaned.

"Who tastes of salt." He kissed my lips. "And who has never looked more perfect and more beautiful to me."

"Oh, you," I said, squeezing him tightly once more.

"Someone's been having adventures without me," he murmured into my ear.

"It's your fault," I told him. "Always in the middle of something you shouldn't be."

"I knew you'd find a way to sort things out," he told me. "My Alfie never lets me down."

"And I never will," I promised. "But come on." I

broke away and tugged at his arm, indicating the tuk-tuk. "We need to get back to the harbour. My ship awaits!"

"Your ship?" Silvan's eyes glittered.

"Oh yes, I'm Captain Alf now. Just you wait and see."

We celebrated that night while *Poseidon's Curse* remained in harbour, waiting for the currents to change. We drank rum cocktails and ate Florence's party food and sang and danced under the stars. Even Gwyn joined in, singing a couple of sea shanties she knew. Scurvy arranged tiny lights all around the deck and we shared tall tales and ghost stories and sea monster stories, told jokes and laughed till we cried.

It was a marvellous setting, just the kind of thing Silvan must have envisaged when he thought to surprise me with a wedding ceremony on a chartered boat—but when he suggested we marry aboard *Poseidon's Curse,* with Butcher officiating, I broke away from his loving grasp and made my way to the starboard railings, turning my face north-west, towards Europe. Towards England. Towards Devon ... and Whittlecombe.

"No," I said, shaking my head, trying to convey the pain in my heart. "No."

His eyes filled with tears, and I reached for his hands.

"It's fine," he told me, wrapping me into his warm embrace once more. "I understand."

We stayed that way for some time, rocking with each other under the sparkling stars. I lay my head on his chest and listened to the slow and steady beat of his heart.

"I know you do," I told him. "I know you do."

EPILOGUE

"Hooo-ooo-ooo. Hoo!"

Turning on my side, I yanked the duvet over my head. "I don't care what time it is, I'm tired," I grumbled.

"Hoo! Hoo! Hoooooooooooo-ooooo. Hoo-ooh. Hoo-ooh."

Meh. "You do go on a bit. I need my beauty sleep. I'm not getting any younger ...."

Seconds later, I felt Mr Hoo alight on my hip, his deadly talons pinching the good cotton of the duvet. "Oi." I tried to shake him off, but he wouldn't be shaken. When he reached my shoulder, he tugged lightly at the top of the cover and began to pull the whole thing away from me. I rolled onto my back and opened my eyes—just a crack—to accustom them to the light.

"It's still dark!" I complained. It wasn't at all; I just wanted to make the point that it was the middle of the night. Except it wasn't. Around me, I could hear the sounds of Whittle Inn coming to life. The radiators were clanking as the boiler began its morning routine. The heating wasn't on, but the ancient boiler liked to pretend it had to reach each room regardless of what time of year it was. I fancied it wouldn't be long till I had to switch the central heating on, but for now, any morning or evening chilliness was briskly alleviated by one of Florence's fires.

As in one of Florence's fires in a fireplace, as opposed to one about her person.

"Hooo-oooh-oooh!"

"Alright, alright." Reluctantly, I hauled myself upright. Above my head the ceiling creaked. One of my guests was restless. That meant people would be going down to breakfast soon. I had to be ready to meet them.

"Hoooooooooo-oooooooooh!"

I cocked my head to listen. "You're right. It is raining." I stretched and grinned. "I love a bit of rain!"

Feeling cheered, I danced into the bathroom and dunked my face in the sink. No time for a shower and hair wash—I would sort that later. For now I rolled my hair into a bun, checked in the mirror, scruffed it up a bit, slapped some moisturiser onto my face and jumped into some robes.

"Catch you later." I dropped a kiss on Mr Hoo's feathery head.

"Hoooo!"

I hadn't made it more than three feet into the corridor outside my room when I was waylaid by

Wizard Eleghast. "Ah! Miss Daemonne!" He smiled up at me through slightly rheumy eyes, his hand wobbling his stick a little. "I can't seem to reach Colonel Peters on reception. Would you be able to help me?"

For some unfathomable reason, Wizard Eleghast had an obsession with poor old Archibald. "I can certainly try," I promised him.

"I can't seem to locate my lucky underpants."

I raised my eyebrows. "Is that the red pair you lost the last time you were staying here?" I asked.

"Yes. They're the ones I'm after. Did Colonel Peters tell you about them? Have you found them?"

"Have you checked under your bed?" I asked.

He blinked at me. "Is that where they are?"

"Probably." That's where I usually retrieved found them from. I caught myself uttering my first prayer of the day. *I hope you're feeling patient today*, I silently told the goddess. *Because you just know it's going to be a full-on madhouse here in the land of wonky.*

Even so, the thought of what lay ahead made my vexed little heart skip.

"I'll have a look for you," I said and led him back to his bedroom, five doors up from mine. Using my master key, I opened the door and let myself in while Wizard Eleghast trailed after me. The room smelt vaguely of sage, wood salt and something altogether too chemically ... I paused and checked out his dresser, where a crow was sorting through a tray of silver trinkets. If I wasn't much mistaken, despite the muted light in the room, the item in a jar surrounded by green liquid was a brain.

Deciding not to look too closely, I fell to my knees instead. Feeling around, I quickly located a soft item and, withdrawing my hand, confirmed these were indeed Wizard Eleghast's lucky underpants.

"Here they are!" I shuffled around to hand them over, but Wizard Eleghast was nowhere to be seen.

"He's off again," squawked the crow. "Hold on to your hats."

"Mmm." I couldn't help but agree.

"Ooh!" Florence apparated next to me. "Miss Alf, we've run out of soap powder!"

"Have we, Florence?" I asked, cocking an eyebrow. "Could you just use carbolic soap today?"

Her puffs of steam began to speed up. "All the guest rooms are full, Miss Alf! Surely you don't want me to scrub the towels by hand?"

I giggled. "I was kidding, Florence. I'll give Stan a ring and see if he has any—"

"*Kidding*, were you?" Florence didn't sound amused. "Really! As if I don't have enough to do ..." Her feather duster sprinkled sparkles in the air and then she was gone.

Tittering to myself, I retreated backwards in the direction of my office, meaning to make a note of our need for washing powder. I could phone Stan, but not yet; it wasn't even six. As I pushed the door open, Ross

Baines, a techno-wizard ghost I'd found on the Tube line in London's Canary Wharf, glanced up.

"Morning, Ross!" I greeted him. "You're up early. What are you doing?"

"Running software updates." He tutted, his transparent fingers moving at light speed across my keyboard. "You really need a new system, Alf—"

"That sounds expensive."

"It'd be worth it in the long run."

I chewed on a fingernail. What had I come into the office for? I'd forgotten. It wasn't to discuss software updates, though, I knew that much. "You know, you say that," I said, "that it will be worth it in the long run. But then, before that run has been particularly long, you'll be wanting me to update to a newer system that will also be expensive and will also be worth it in the longer long run."

Ross shrugged.

"And the cycle is never broken!" I told him. "Meanwhile, I have other priorities."

"But it keeps me in business, ergo, it's worth it," Ross told me and went back to whatever he was doing.

I tutted, then belatedly remembered I had a breakfast service to see to. "I'll catch you in a bit," I told Ross —not that he was listening—and made a beeline for the back stairs.

"Alf!" Venus was sprinting up the stairs towards me, long ponytail swinging, dressed in black lycra leggings and a skin-tight black vest top, showing off her stunning figure to incredible effect.

"You're up early!"

"I thought I'd do my workout first thing before it gets busy. Famished now. Are you going down to breakfast?"

I pulled a face. "I am going down, but I'm serving breakfast, Venus. *Serving* it. There's a difference!"

Venus seemed taken aback by that. "I would have thought you had other people to do that for you! You know ... staff!"

"It takes a few of us, especially when we're fully booked," I explained. "You could help me out if you like?"

"Dirty plates?" She gave an exaggerated shiver. "No thanks."

"Fine." I laughed. "I'll see you a bit later."

"Toodle-ooh!" She waggled her fingers and jogged away. I resumed my descent downstairs.

Perdita Pugh was just sticking her head out of The Hug as I passed. There was no mistaking her with her crazy hair that wouldn't recognise conditioner if she bathed in it and the thick spectacles perched precariously on the edge of her nose. "Oh, Alf! Morning, lovey."

"Morning, Perdita." I tried to slink past her but Perdita wasn't having it. "You really must come in and check out the electro-endoquaero, Alf. It's working overtime. There's been so much spirit activity overnight!"

"Really?"

"Come see, come see!" She gestured excitedly inside the room.

I stepped away. "Sorry, Perdita, but I have to do the breakfast service. I'll pop in afterwards, okay?"

"Oh." Her face fell.

"I promise," I said. "Besides, you must be hungry."

She wobbled her head from side to side as though trying to work out if she was or not. "I might be." From inside the room came three sharp little barks. "Chi definitely is."

"Well, there you are," I said. "I shall save Chi a sausage all of her own."

Perdita beamed. "I'll do some printouts just to make sure you get to see what I've found ..." She disappeared inside, and, thanking the goddess for small mercies, I started along the corridor for the kitchen.

The door burst open just as I reached it. I reared back in shock, then ducked as a meat cleaver flew past my nose, missing me by a whisker. A nano-second later, a stream of pixies rushed out of the kitchen giggling, Crookshank bringing up the rear.

Spotting me cowering there, he paused, stuck his tongue out, then flipped me the bird and raced off again.

"That's nice, that is," I mumbled and, taking a

breath, walked into the madhouse that was the kitchen first thing in the morning.

"Good morning, Alf!" Charity beamed. "How are we today?"

"Well, *I'm* fine." I smiled. "I'm not so sure about everyone else." I snuck a glance at Monsieur Emietter, expecting him to be red-faced and bug-eyed with fury, but he was busy stirring something on the stove.

Wafting at my face, I complained, "It's hot in here." Every ring on both the stove and the range was in use, as were the ovens and the chiller. In addition to Monsieur Emietter and Charity, there were half a dozen members of the Wonky Inn Ghostly Clean-up Crew dotted around, peeling vegetables and stirring jellies and measuring ingredients, plus a young boy carrying used bowls and utensils through to the washing-up area.

"You're late, darling." Gwyn apparated in front of me. "Why do you have a pair of underpants in your hand?"

"Why do I ...?" I stared at my hand. Wizard Eleghast's red underpants. "Ugh!" I chucked them on the floor. Monsieur Emietter gave me a sidelong glance, so I kicked them under the counter.

"Shall I wash those for you, Miss Alf?" Florence asked, sweeping past me with a pile of laundry. "I'll use my carbolic soap, shall I?"

Rats! I knew I'd meant to write down a reminder

about the washing powder. "All in hand, Florence," I lied. "You can trust me."

Everyone in the room—even Monsieur Emietter, who doesn't speak a word of English—paused to study me for a second. I frowned and rubbed my nose. Just in case. "What?"

"You'd better start serving breakfast," Charity suggested. "And for goodness sake, keep away from the toaster. We don't want to call out the fire brigade again!"

"Ah, Alf!"

I cursed my rotten luck. I'd been attempting to sneak up the back stairs with a plate of toast, but Penelope Quigwell stopped me in my tracks.

"Hi, Penelope." I tried to hide the mammoth pile of buttered toast behind my back, but that was a really bad idea. I hadn't accounted for the pixies. I felt the plate tilt, and in less time than it takes to say homicide, my breakfast had disappeared along with Crookshank and his motley crew.

"Finbarr!" I shrieked in fury, but to no avail, because the little Irish witch was nowhere to be seen. He'd be out in the grounds where he should be. It was just a shame his blasted pixies weren't with him.

Penelope pulled a face and took a step back.

"Miss Alf!" Florence appeared beside me, swiping

at the wall where a number of buttery, pixie-sized palm prints had been deposited, and the stairs where glops of creamy butter had fallen. "Look what you've done to my good carpet!"

"I think you'll find it's Alfhild's good carpet," Penelope said. "I distinctly recall her paying for it. I considered it rather an extravagance at the time."

Florence began to steam. She deemed all the inn's décor hers, because she was the one who was constantly cleaning and tidying and, let's face it, if she didn't, it would all wear out far quicker than it did.

Oops. "So sorry, Florence." I found myself apologising for the hoodlums—and Penelope. Anything to keep the peace. "Erm ..." I shepherded Penelope back along the corridor towards the bar. "Is everything alright for you so far, Penelope? It *is* lovely to have you staying here with us."

"It's wonderful," Penelope told me. "Exemplary service and a beautiful building. Shame the rooms are a little small ..."

This coming from a woman who inhabited one floor of one of the tiniest buildings on Celestial Street. I bit my tongue. "Did you need to see me?"

"I wanted to ask you about the accounts for last month."

"Didn't I send them to you?" I asked, knowing full well I hadn't. Having been in India for three weeks, I hadn't quite managed to get my act together so had yet to finish them.

"No, you didn't." She pressed her prissy lips together.

"I do apologise," I said. "I'll go upstairs to the office and ... oh ..."

"Problem?" Penelope quirked an eyebrow.

I rolled my eyes. "Ross Baines is up there doing something with my software ..." I waved vaguely at the ceiling. "As soon as he's done, I'll get onto it for you ..."

"Very well." She wasn't happy, but what could I do?

From beyond the door into the bar, I heard what sounded awfully like bagpipes. No, not bagpipes. The crumhorn. I caught my breath. "Could you excuse me for a moment?" I asked Penelope and smiled politely before dashing for the door and bursting into the bar.

The Devonshire Fellows were congregating by the bar, tuning their instruments.

"La la la la la la la!" sang Luppitt Smeatharpe, not so much tuning his lute, although he was strumming it, as his voice. "La la la la la la la!"

"My lady!" Napier Harrow, the small, balding percussionist, shook some bells at me. "I marvel at your beauty today!"

"As do we all!" Robert Wait—he of the silvery hair and the crinkled eyes—beamed at me.

"You can't be in here!" I reminded them, glaring at Stephen Arcott until he removed the crumhorn from his lips.

"But my lady! 'Tis drizzling something awful

outside," Luppitt complained. "I fear I shall take a chill, and mayhap this evening's performance would have to be cancelled."

Oh dear. What a shame. Never mind.

"Luppitt, regardless of whether you catch a chill or not—and to be honest, that doesn't seem likely seeing as you've already been dead for the best part of five hundred years—we have a pact!" I stuck a finger in the air, intent on reminding the Fellows of the rules. "No practising in the inn when I have guests." *Or just not in the inn, at all, ever, would suit me, to be fair.*

Luppitt pouted. "Harsh."

"They're not really guests ..." John Bond attempted to prevaricate, his fingers dancing over his fiddle strings.

I pointed at the door. Sheepishly, the musicians gathered their instruments together and trooped out. I watched them go, then turned back to the bar. Zephaniah was trying to catch my attention.

"What's up?" I asked.

"The drayman delivery is late," he said. "We have enough beer, but we're out of tonic and short of whisky."

Short of whisky? That would never do.

"I'll follow it up," I promised.

"Thanks." He returned to his bottling up. "Oh, and Perdita Pugh is looking for you!"

"Is she?" I dashed a glance at the door to the rear of

the inn and moved towards reception instead. Time to make myself scarce.

Bwuk-bwuk-bwuk-bwuk-bwuk.

Oh no.

"If you'd had any love for me, you'd never have disappeared that way!" My mother's bitter tones rang out as I strolled along the first-floor corridor.

"Yasmin ..." my father's plaintive voice responded. "You know very well that I had little choice—"

"Choice? *I'm* the one who had no choice!" my mother bellowed. "No choice at all!"

"Erm ... Mum?" I popped my head into the office. Ross Baines was still at my desk, concentrating all of his attention on the screen in front of him while my parents bickered back and forth like a pair of six-year-olds. "Dad?"

"Hello, darling!" My father, partly in the spirit world, partly not, smiled at me, relief written all over his semi-transparent face. I'd become more accustomed to his presence over the past few years because we'd reconnected soon after I'd inherited the inn.

Yasmin, however, who'd become a reclusive, crazy chicken lady before her death, had been a stranger in spirit to me until recently. It was nice to have both of them around.

But only in small measures.

And never together in the same spot at the same time, because I don't think my mother was planning to forgive my father for his disappearance any time in eternity.

"The whole inn can hear you," I told them. "Can you *not* argue in front of my guests?"

"Well, why is he even here?" my mother sniped. "He doesn't have the right!"

"I like him here," I told her, attempting to keep calm. *I'm allowed to have a relationship with him*!

"He doesn't deserve to be," she said. "I do. I was there for you through all those years when he wasn't!"

This wasn't strictly true. She'd been an abject nightmare to live with after Dad's disappearance. I couldn't wait to leave home.

"Regardless," I pleaded, "for my sake, can you please keep it civil?"

Yasmin sniffed. "If you insist."

"Absolutely." My father nodded and drifted past me.

"Where are you going now?" my mother snapped at him.

"Out to play cricket with the lads," he told her.

"Oh, that's right. Run away—"

"I thought you'd prefer me out of your sight!"

"So typical of you—"

"Hello?" I thundered. "Do you mind?"

"Sorry, love!" my dad said and promptly disappeared.

"Really, ladies!" Gwyn poked her head through the door. "The whole inn can hear you shouting, Alfhild. Keep it down."

Ross met my gaze without even moving his head. I saw the amusement there. Gritting my teeth, I stalked out of the room, brushing past Gwyn and experiencing the quick chill you get whenever you pass through a spirit.

"Honestly!" Gwyn muttered. "No manners."

"Florence, would you mind setting an alarm for Kat and Marc, please?" I asked, lifting a knife and sinking it into the soft flesh of one of Florence's marvellous sponges. The kitchen was a hive of activity: baking, cooking, roasting, boiling. There were ghosts everywhere. Perdita would be having a field day with her electro-endoquaero.

"What are you doing, Miss Alf?" Florence asked crossly, floating up to me to peer over my shoulder.

"I'm having a piece of cake, Florence. I'm absolutely famished!"

"That's for later, Miss! You know it is!"

"You are awful." Charity laughed at me as I extracted an enormous piece of what looked like blackberry sponge with apple icing.

"The pixies stole my breakfast," I told her, "and I didn't make it to lunch because I was busy trying to get

Penelope her dratted spreadsheet with last month's accounts! It took me three hours to sort out!"

"Oh, you should have asked," said Charity, pouring herself a cup of tea. How come no-one had offered me one? "I've got a copy of them on my machine."

"You what?" I couldn't believe my ears.

"I did them while you were away—" Charity shrugged.

"Three hours!" I repeated. "And you had them all the time?"

"Soz."

"Where will I find Miss Kat and Mr Marc?" Florence asked, snapping the cake tin firmly shut. I noticed the rapid puffs of soot; Florence was feeling a tad stressed. She wasn't keen on vampires.

"In the attic," I said.

"No, I had their coffins sent down to the beer cellar," Charity said. "It's cooler below at this time of year."

"Fair enough." What did I know? I was only the boss. "Is everyone else accommodated?"

"Yep. No problems. Frau Kirsch has elected to wild camp in Speckled Wood, but I don't suppose you object?"

"I don't object." I smirked. "The faeries might do, but it's only for one night."

"A very important night," Florence confirmed. "Perhaps you ought to have a nap!"

The instant she said that, I yawned. "You know what," I said, "that's not a bad idea."

"Could you drop into reception before you go up?" Charity asked. "There's a problem with the computer there."

"There's no problem with the computer," I told her. "The problem is Archibald."

"Give him a break!" Charity giggled. "He's about a hundred and sixty years old!"

Pfft. What kind of excuse was that? "Alright." I stuffed the rest of the cake into my gob and waved as I hotfooted it away, slinking past The Hug so Perdita wouldn't hear me, then dashing through the bar in case I was stopped by any of our guests. Dealing with a multitude of problems was my daily lot, but today of all days, I just wanted to do one thing at a time.

"Darling?" Gwyn's imperious tone stopped me dead. I smiled and turned about. She and her best friends Phyllis Bliss, Onnalee Mason and Sybil Torkelson were having a cosy afternoon playing bridge. *It's alright for some, isn't it?*

"You couldn't organise a couple of sherries, could you?" Gwyn asked.

I switched my gaze from her to the bar, all of fifteen feet away, and raised an eyebrow.

"I can hardly stop what I'm doing in the middle of a hand, can I?" she asked. "You need more staff."

"Everyone is working flat out, Grandmama," I reminded her. "But of course I can organise some sherries for you." I narrowed my eyes. "Just don't any of you ladies overdo it! The day is young!"

There was a chorus of giggles as I made my way over to the bar to ask Zephaniah to attend to the sherry dispensing.

"No sign of the whisky yet," he told me.

Oh, batpoop! I'd forgotten to phone the wholesaler. "I'm on it!" I told him, and whisked round to race for reception—there was a phone there—only to bump into Mouse—a woman the size of a brick outhouse—who had crept up behind me.

"Boo!" she yelled.

"Waaah!" I shrieked before I realised.

She wrapped me in a huge, squishy hug. "I'm so pleased to see you!" she laughed.

Barely able to breathe, I managed a muffled, "I thought you'd never get here!"

"I wouldn't have missed it for the world. I should organise your bookshelves while I'm here, Demon."

"Ah, yes." I had let her standards slip, rather.

"To be honest, I could do with the peace and quiet away from that lot!" She gestured sideways with her head. Fleashee and Heshee were standing awkwardly to one side, their numerous children positioned in a line ranging from tallest—not very tall, they were goblins after all—to shortest, all waiting to be received. I hugged each of the little goblins in turn, and no sooner had I suggested they run off and explore the inn and grounds than they were gone, chasing each other and running through everyone else's feet.

Chaos.

Never mind.

They were sweet, in a kind of gruesomely ugly goblin way.

"Fleashee not keen on taking train," Fleashee told me. "Too expensive. Too spread out. Too stuck up. Need cram people into cattle truck, more profitable, more sociable. Keep warm. Good smells."

"That's ... an interesting idea," I agreed. "I think maybe they used to do that and they called it third class."

"Should bring it back," Fleashee said. "Fleashee run company for human. Make ginormous profit. Fleashee full of good ideas."

"Sounds great," I said, making a mental note never to travel on goblin transport. "Grab a drink and make yourselves at home," I said. "I need to sort out one or two issues ..."

And grab a nana nap.

"No problem. We see later!" Fleashee said.

"Looking forward to it." As I moved away, Wizard Admiral Jellicoe caught my arm. "Is that a goblin?" he asked.

Oh dear. "Yes," I told him. "A family of goblins. They're *friends* of mine."

"Friends? How very treacherous!" He pulled

himself upright in his armchair. "Back in my day, we weren't friends with goblins—"

"Back in your day, you weren't friends with anyone," I muttered.

"Beg your pardon?" he bellowed, inserting his hearing trumpet into his right ear. "Speak up, girl! You know I don't hear so well anymore."

I raised my voice. "I was just saying times have changed. Goblins are welcome here at Whittle Inn. We like to be inclusive."

"You'll be telling me you allow vampires to stay here next!" Wizard Admiral Jellicoe grumbled.

"Ah. About that—"

"Or fae!"

Now he'd overstepped the mark. "Good goddess, no! What do you think I am?"

"Quite right, girlie. Quite right! I should think so! We didn't fight The Great Wizard Wars just so ..."

I finally made it to reception sometime later. Archibald was slumped in his chair, fast asleep. I reached over and grabbed the phone, then quickly dialled my wholesaler, requesting an urgent delivery of whisky, tonic water and washing powder before slapping the receiver down slightly harder than was necessary.

"Uh. Uh. What? Oh, there it is!" exclaimed Archibald, hastily retrieving the stapler from the drawer and pretending that I hadn't caught him snoring his head off. "Good afternoon, madam. So sorry, I didn't see you there. Do you require assistance at all?"

"No, I think everything is in hand," I told him. "Any messages?"

"Miss Ballicott dropped by. She left you a little parcel. I took the liberty of having it delivered to your bedroom."

"Thank you. Have all the guests arrived?"

"Mostly, yes." Archibald scanned the paper copy of expected arrivals he kept on a clipboard in front of him. He preferred to do things the old way, with quill and ink and parchment. "Mindi Blockweg and Raoul Scurrysnood will be arriving later. They've been held up on a set." He blinked down at the paper, trying to decipher his handwriting. "It doesn't say a set of what."

"Just on set," I told him. "They're involved in The Great Witchy Cake-Off."

"The Great Witchy whatty?" Poor Archibald looked most perplexed.

"Never mind. Ah!" I spotted Wizard Eleghast coming down the stairs, palm greased and ready to begin smacking the reception bell. He'd be looking for his lucky underpants. "That's my cue to be going!"

I hid around the corner, pretending to tidy the French dresser, until Wizard Eleghast had navigated the stairs, then I rushed by him like a gazelle on performance-enhancing drugs.

Ting! went the reception bell behind me.

"Wizard Eleghast. How may I assist you?" Archibald asked, with all the patience of a saint.

Ting!

"I'm right here, you know ..."

Ting!

The sound of the bell followed me all the way down the first-floor corridor until I came to my bedroom and, shutting the world outside, threw myself on the bed.

I luxuriated in a bath full of fragrant bubbles. Millicent had sent me up a luxurious pamper pack. I could have ventured out, perhaps to Honiton or Durscombe, or even to the nearest big city, but I'd lost interest in chemical peels and facials after my last stay at a luxury hotel courtesy of Phyllis Bliss.

Millicent's products were so much kinder, entirely organic, and smelt completely natural. The soft milky bubble bath was lovingly made using my favourite bergamot scent; the face ointment consisted of mashed apple, clotted cream, a little pressed olive oil and banana. The shampoo and conditioner were rhubarb and blackberry, picked from Millicent's back garden. She sure knew how to spoil me.

Mr Hoo, sitting on the window jamb, blinked solemnly at me. "Hoooo!" he said. "Hoooo-ooo!"

"No, you can't eat me," I told him.

I'd purposely left the window open to allow the steam to escape—along with Mr Hoo, of course—and now I stared through the gap, taking in the darkening sky, remembering how a few years before I had cast a spell, stencilling my intention in the condensation on the window.

For a long time afterwards I'd rued that moment, but now?

Not so much.

It wouldn't be long.

All things must pass.

In a dress of green—spring green with hints of English oak leaf, threaded with moon-blessed silver thread—I strolled barefoot through Speckled Wood. I would never suggest that all of my life I'd dreamed of this, because this moment was not where my life would culminate. Not here. Not tonight.

And yet, perhaps, this was where my heart would find peace and serenity.

The dirt beneath my toes was moist from the morning's rain, but not mud bound, and besides, the carpet of pine needles provided a soft covering on which to walk. I trailed the fingers of my right hand across the bark of every tree I passed, gently stroking time itself and feeling the beating heart of the planet's life force, the essence of the goddess that breathes life into all things.

Branches waving above my head showered me with their goodwill—the first leaves of autumn— while the breathy song of the forest serenaded me. Mr Hoo flew from perch to perch, hurrying me along.

Because I was late.

Wasn't I always?

But there comes a time when living in the moment and experiencing the joy of the simplest of things extends that instant of time until you become lost in it … and time, as the mysterious Mr Wylie had once explained to me, is both a simple and a complex matter —at once endless and finite, flexible and unbending …

Behind me, giggles.

Pixies? Possibly. Faeries? Hmmm. Also a possibility. But perhaps it was only Freddie and Gertie trailing somewhere just out of sight, playing at being spies or secret agents …

The moon was high above Speckled Wood, so that I only caught glimpses here and there beneath the forest's heavy canopy, but Finbarr had thoughtfully been out and cast his own spell, hanging pretty balls of colour-changing energy from the lower limbs of the oaks and beech trees so I could easily find my way.

Most magickal of all, though, were the orbs of vitality I spied here and there. Dozens of them, the spirits of those who have gone before, my ancestors, the ancestors of others who had sought solace in Speckled

Wood, from the time before the wood had a name, a time before land was owned ... before it was tamed ...

The air shimmered with their good wishes. Go forth. Be content. Breathe love. Allow happiness. Be joyful.

And even had I not been able to see, I would have found my way. I'd walked this path a million times, and perhaps another million times in my dreams. It was a path I'd always know. Not to the clearing. Not this time, but to Vance.

Tall and magnificent, this wondrous oak drew himself up from the waters of the marsh, his branches swaying, leaves delicately shaking; this was his welcome as father of the forest.

My *own* father stood before him, smiling at me, the look in his eyes one I'd rarely seen before. Pride. He reached his hand for me as I approached, and though I couldn't feel it, I knew it was there and I recalled his touch and I understood his love.

Beside him, my mother, wearing an old maxi cream and floral number straight from the seventies and a straw hat that had seen better days, dabbed at her eyes, spirit chickens roosting around her feet.

Wizard Shadowmender's silvery beard, magnificent in the moonlight that filtered through the trees here, appeared to have been threaded with shimmering stars. He shone out at the gathering, illuminating his deep purple robes and the faces of those who turned to watch me arrive.

My family, my friends, they smiled at me, whispered greetings and best wishes ... winked, gently pressed my arm as I slipped past them. On any other occasion, I might have felt bashful—I hated being the centre of attention—but not today. Not tonight. Tonight, I felt ...

Invincible.

Powerful.

Confident.

One particular pair of eyes—shining eyes as dark as the night—sought mine ... tugging my gaze the way he did my heart, always drawing me closer, no matter how far away he was, no matter the distance between us.

But for now, there were mere inches ... and we were only seconds from entwining our lives and hearts for all time.

Wizard Shadowmender raised his staff, an old gnarled beast of a thing, much used. "On behalf of Vance, the Great, Wise One, I invite you all, friends and family of Horace Theodore Silvanus and Alfhild Yasmin Daemonne, to come gather round."

Those who were a little further away shuffled forward, all the better to see and hear. Charity, her hair dyed various shades of green to match my dress—she and Florence had helped me choose the material and we'd had it made up by *Ember Embroidery and Couture* in Celestial Street—grinned at me and gave me a double thumbs up. Beside her, Florence steamed and puffed with excitement.

"Oh, Miss Alf!" she whispered. "You look glorious!"

"Isn't her hair beautiful?" I heard Phyllis comment to Gwyn, standing next to her in an incredibly grand Edwardian green evening dress with a high bust and pinched-in waist, diamonds dripping from her ears and throat.

Gwyn preened and replied. "It was my idea to have the flowers threaded through her curls. I did that at my wedding, you know!" In a loud whisper, she added, "Plus I made her use twice as much of Millicent's First Aid Hair Conditioner. It was such a dry mess after India!"

Wizard Shadowmender arched his eyebrows in Gwyn's direction. "If it pleases the congregation? In honour of the union between our dear friends Horace and Alfhild, there will be a gathering in the Speckled Wood clearing immediately after the ceremony. I am given to understand that there will be music and singing—"

I'm so sorry, everyone, I mentally telegraphed. *I'd have liked a rock disco, but the faeries wouldn't give permission, so, no, I had to settle for the Devonshire Fellows*!

"Along with a midnight buffet—"

Thanks to Monsieur Emietter and his assistants, there were vol-au-vents galore—particularly prawn mayonnaise because they were my favourite—nibbles, speciality tapas dishes and the like, and thanks to

Rob Parker there would be a banger of a barbecue too.

And not forgetting Florence! Her wedding cake creation was masterful. A four-tiered woodland scene depicting Speckled Wood during the seasons—with winter as the top tier, dripping white icing that graduated into blossom on the 'spring' tier—resplendent with fondant leaves in an array of stunning seasonal colours, flowers, fungi, bracken, berries and animals. Mr Hoo's likeness, naturally, could be found on each layer.

"And a free bar!"

There was a unanimous cheer.

"But first—" Wizard Shadowmender's tone grew solemn. "Silvan and Alfhild have asked that we keep the ceremony on point, a simple exchange of vows—"

"All the better for us. We can get to the free bar sooner!" quipped my father.

Wizard Shadowmender waited for the roar of laughter to die down before nodding at me. I stepped before him, and Silvan joined us.

"Join hands," Wizard Shadowmender instructed, and we did so, each of us crossing at the wrists to make a knot. Silvan's palms were a little moist, but I could sense the strength of his intent. His fingers tangled in mine, my warmth meeting his cooler skin.

Millicent and Venus stepped forward, each with multiple-coloured strings of ribbons and lace. They had been raiding boxes in the attic, seeking fabrics they could rip up or borrow, and so here I was with multiple strands of wonky history draped over my wrists.

Clasping hands with the man I loved, I barely heard Wizard Shadowmender's words. He bound us tightly together and I noted the intricate threads of the slithers of fabric that interwove to create a kaleidoscope of colour ... until suddenly, Silvan was speaking. We'd chosen to keep our vows simple and heartfelt.

He spoke softly. "Come what may, in lightness and darkness, my love is yours, forever and always."

I echoed him exactly. "Come what may, in lightness and darkness, my love is *yours*, forever and always."

Wizard Shadowmender stamped his staff hard into the ground. Vance shook his branches. Finbarr's lights softly spun. "What nature has joined together, let no *thing* put asunder!"

"Aaarh!" Half a dozen pirates let out a hearty roar. I'd invited the crew of *Poseidon's Curse* along, and they'd anchored in Brixham a few days previously. I was fairly sure my alcohol bill for this event would be astronomical.

After thanking Vance for his hospitality and receiving his blessing, Silvan and I, freed of ties, led the procession to the clearing. The Devonshire Fellows were already in full swing, Luppitt belting out a peculiar and endearing Elizabethan version of Cream's *Sunshine of Your Love.*

Silvan twirled me around, showing off my dress to

maximum effect, and then pulled me close. "I'm with you, my love—"

I rested my head against his chest as we swayed gently to the music, to *our* music, to the music we were making ...

Which is different to the music *you* make, and your neighbour makes, and your parents make and the rest of the world makes.

But there, in the clearing, in Speckled Wood, where the trees swayed in time to the melody and my family and friends began to pour the wine, and sailors danced a jig with Florence, and wizards and witches reined in the antic of their familiars ... where Gwyn and Wizard Shadowmender traded secrets about love spells with Frau Kirsch, Wizard Admiral Jellicoe, Archibald and Wizard Eleghast ... there where the pixies dressed in black and white, circled among my guests offering finger food and only stealing one in three items ... where Charity showed Manc my wild-flower bouquet and made eyes at him ... there where my owl hooted down at me from above, where my father asked my mother to dance and she blushed a pretty pale pink ...

There ... I understood more clearly than ever, that the greatest magick in all the known worlds ...

Is love.

WONKY CONTINUES

Wonky Continues in the 2022 Christmas Special

The Faery of Witchmas Past

Christmas at Whittle inn? Sounds faery nuff ...

This year Alf, our favourite British witch, finds herself in hot water with Gwyn when she tries to sell off some of her great-grandmother's ugly, vintage Christmas decorations.

It transpires that Gwyn has more than a passing attachment to the faery that has traditionally topped the inn's main Christmas tree. Without this particular gargoyle, sorry—precious angel—in its habitual place, the inn is cursed.

Or so legend has it.

Alf is not convinced ...

Until the faery's new owner is found dead.

With chaos and catastrophe unraveling all around her, Alf has her work cut out if she wants her guests to enjoy a faery, merry Christmas!

The ***Wonky Inn Series*** is a sequence of paranormal cozy mystery books that readers from across the globe have fallen in love with.

Clean and cozy, ***The Faery of Witchmas Past*** is the fifth Christmas special in this wonderful series, and as usual is it stuffed full of quirky characters that fans consider a second family.

Giggles, ghosts, chaos and catastrophe abound as usual! Pull on your warmest, snuggest socks, curl up with your eggnog and a mince pie and dive, headfirst, into this festive feast of witchy fun. Lose yourself in the Christmas wonkyverse.

OUT NOW

Dead as a Dodo: A Paranormal Cozy Witch Mystery (Wonderland Detective Agency Book 1

From the Amazon bestselling author of the Wonky Inn books comes a brand-new magical fantasy witch detective series.

Dodo was dead. And there the matter should have rested.

At least for DS Elise Liddell.

Emotionally burnt out, she considers herself retired from police work.

By rights it has nothing to do with her, but someone

killed the poor man and, as Elise can resist everything except a good puzzle (and a shot of Blue Goblin vodka), here she is tangled up in a murder case.

When a petty thief hands himself into the Ministry of Witches Police Department, Elise's ex-colleagues consider it an open and shut case.

She's less convinced.

Revitalized by the investigation, she takes the suspect on as the first client of her new paranormal detective agency. What would this insignificant wretch have to gain by murdering the cantankerous old wizard? Elise knows full well, by uncovering the motive she can reveal the true killer.

But she forgets, in Tumble Town even the shadows are alive ... and now someone or something is hunting her.

The Wonderland Detective Agency Series is a paranormal cozy mystery series, set in the same Wonkyverse that readers have already fallen in love with. While some of the characters and places will be instantly familiar, Wycherley effortlessly casts her spell so that her zany new friends quickly become ours too.

OUT NOW

Packed full of witches, wizards, warlocks, ghosts, shadow people and more, you'll love this glimpse into the dark side.

Take a walk in Tumble Town today!

THE COMPLETE WONKY INN SERIES

The Complete Wonky Inn Series

(*in chronological reading order*)

The Wonkiest Witch: Wonky Inn Book 1
The Ghosts of Wonky Inn: Wonky Inn Book 2
Weird Wedding at Wonky Inn: Wonky Inn Book 3
The Witch Who Killed Christmas: Wonky Inn Christmas Special
Fearful Fortunes and Terrible Tarot: Wonky Inn Book 4
The Mystery of the Marsh Malaise: Wonky Inn Book 5
The Mysterious Mr Wylie: Wonky Inn Book 6
The Great Witchy Cake Off: Wonky Inn Book 7
Vengeful Vampire at Wonky Inn: Wonky Inn Book 8
Witching in a Winter Wonkyland: A Wonky Inn Christmas Cozy Special

A Gaggle of Ghastly Grandmamas: Wonky Inn Book 9
Magic, Murder and a Movie Star: Wonky Inn Book 10
O' Witchy Town of Whittlecombe: A Wonky Inn Christmas Cozy Special
Judge, Jury and Jailhouse Rockcakes: Wonky Inn Book 11
A Midsummer Night's Wonky: Wonky Inn Book 12
Halloween Heebie-Geebies: Wonky Inn Book 13
Owl I want for Witchmas is Hoo: A Wonky Inn Christmas Cozy Mystery
Oh Mummy!: Wonky Inn Book 14
Pieces of Hate: Wonky Inn Book 15
The Faery of Witchmas Past: A Wonky Inn Christmas Cozy Special
A Barbarous Band of Blood Brothers: Wonky Inn Book 16 (Release date TBC)

Spellbound Hound

Ain't Nothing but a Pound Dog: Spellbound Hound Magic and Mystery Book 1
A Curse, a Coven and a Canine: Spellbound Hound Magic and Mystery Book 2
Bark Side of the Moon: Spellbound Hound Magic and Mystery Book 3
Master of Puppies: Spellbound Hound Magic and Mystery Book 4
Up, Pup and Away: Spellbound Hound Magic and Mystery Book 5 (Release date TBC)

Wonderland Detective Agency

Dead as a Dodo: Wonderland Detective Agency Book 1

The Rabbit Hole Murders: Wonderland Detective Agency Book 2

Tweedledumb and Tweedledie: Wonderland Detective Agency Book 3

The Curious Incident at the Pig and Pepper: Wonderland Detective Agency Book 4

A Tragic Tea Party: Wonderland Detective Agency Book 5

The Pool of Tears: Wonderland Detective Agency Book 6

ALSO BY

The Complete Wonky Inn Series

(in chronological reading order)

The Wonkiest Witch: Wonky Inn Book 1

The Ghosts of Wonky Inn: Wonky Inn Book 2

Weird Wedding at Wonky Inn: Wonky Inn Book 3

The Witch Who Killed Christmas: Wonky Inn Christmas Special

Fearful Fortunes and Terrible Tarot: Wonky Inn Book 4

The Mystery of the Marsh Malaise: Wonky Inn Book 5

The Mysterious Mr Wylie: Wonky Inn Book 6

The Great Witchy Cake Off: Wonky Inn Book 7

Vengeful Vampire at Wonky Inn: Wonky Inn Book 8

Witching in a Winter Wonkyland: A Wonky Inn Christmas Cozy Special

A Gaggle of Ghastly Grandmamas: Wonky Inn Book 9

Magic, Murder and a Movie Star: Wonky Inn Book 10

O' Witchy Town of Whittlecombe: A Wonky Inn Christmas Cozy Special

Judge, Jury and Jailhouse Rockcakes: Wonky Inn Book 11

A Midsummer Night's Wonky: Wonky Inn Book 12

Halloween Heebie-Geebies: Wonky Inn Book 13

Owl I want for Witchmas is Hoo: A Wonky Inn Christmas Cozy Mystery

Oh Mummy!: Wonky Inn Book 14

Pieces of Hate: Wonky Inn Book 15

A Barbarous Band of Blood Brothers: Wonky Inn Book 16 (Release date TBC)

Spellbound Hound

Ain't Nothing but a Pound Dog: Spellbound Hound Magic and Mystery Book 1

A Curse, a Coven and a Canine: Spellbound Hound Magic and Mystery Book 2

Bark Side of the Moon: Spellbound Hound Magic and Mystery Book 3

Master of Puppies: Spellbound Hound Magic and Mystery Book 4 (May 29th 2022)

Wonderland Detective Agency

Dead as a Dodo: Wonderland Detective Agency Book 1

The Rabbit Hole Murders: Wonderland Detective Agency Book 2

Tweedledumb and Tweedledie: Wonderland Detective Agency Book 3

The Curious Incident at the Pig and Pepper: Wonderland Detective Agency Book 4

A Tragic Tea Party: Wonderland Detective Agency Book 5 (July 29th 2022)

The Municipality of Lost Souls

Midnight Garden: The Extra Ordinary World Novella Series Book 1

Beyond the Veil

Crone

A Concerto for the Dead and Dying

Deadly Encounters: A collection of short stories

Keepers of the Flame: A love story

Non-Fiction

Losing my best Friend

Thoughtful support for those affected by dog bereavement or pet loss

Follow Jeannie Wycherley

Find out more at on the website www.jeanniewycherley.

co.uk

You can tweet Jeannie

twitter.com/Thecushionlady

Or visit her on Facebook for her fiction

www.facebook.com/jeanniewycherley

Follow Jeannie on Instagram (for bears and books)

www.instagram.com/jeanniewycherley

Sign up for Jeannie's newsletter on her website

Printed in Great Britain
by Amazon

15671039R00192